A western and a love story. Enjoy!

THIS NEW DAY

A NOVEL

HARLAN HAGUE

Graycatbird Books

ISBN: 9781693949968

Cover image by Brett Whaley. Donna Yee designed the cover.

Love is composed of a single soul inhabiting two bodies.

—Aristotle

Love is a serious mental illness.

—Plato

Chapter 1

Molly stepped away from the wagon and watched the day come. The orange globe rose slowly as the lacy layer of pink cloud at the horizon thinned and disappeared. It was the best part of the day. Every sunrise promised a beginning, a promise that faded as duty and memory intruded. She sighed, looked down and walked to the fire circle.

She knelt at the small cooking fire. The buffalo chips burned with a low blue flame, emitting a subtle fragrance that had repelled her when she was first introduced to the prairie fuel, but which now had become familiar and evocative. She stirred the glowing chips with a dry stick, then dropped the stick into the flames.

Molly looked older this morning than her thirty years. She had neglected to comb her hair or cover her head. Worry lines between her eyebrows and tiny crow's feet marked her pretty face. She wiped tears with a sleeve, looked up. The sky was crystal clear cobalt, empty but for a single yellow-breasted bird that flew over the stationary wagons.

Wagons were circled or double-lined in groups, describing separate companies in the migration. The groupings stretched westward on the trail along the Platte River and down the back trail until they disappeared from view a mile away over a rising. There was no other sign of habitation or humanity on the rolling prairie.

She sat on the ground, collected her long skirts and tucked them around her ankles. The material was soiled gray with dirt and ashes and almost black at the hem where it usually trailed in the dust and mud.

Molly had declined to follow the lead of a few women in the caravan in abandoning long skirts in favor of bloomers, which had appeared only the previous year and grew steadily in popularity. The garment was named after Amelia Bloomer, the women's rights activist and most notorious promoter. Inspired by Turkish pantaloons, bloomers were trousers-like and billowy, secured at the ankles. The early styles featured a short skirt over the trousers, but the skirt was soon rejected by most. Worn in private at first for comfort and practicality, bloomers were soon worn in public.

The first in the train to don the costume had been looked at with disdain by some of the women and humor by the men. But many women decided eventually that bloomers were more practical than long skirts for prairie travel. Some women, including Molly, had brought them in their baggage, just in case they should dare wearing them. As the days passed and the heavy skirts became dirtier and heavier, the bloomers were pulled from bags. Not Molly. Not yet.

The campground was still, quiet. The prairie stretched to horizons north and south from the wagons. The trail was deep dust, but just off the beaten road were patches of green grass where loose stock grazed as they were pushed alongside the moving wagons and where unyoked oxen and mules grazed at noon and evening.

Scattered remnants of spring wildflowers and early summer blossoms colored the flats, the yellow petals of mule's ears, clusters of small white flowers of the Western turkey beard, the fragrant pink flowers of the wild rose just beginning to appear.

The trail generally lay on flats on the south bank of the Platte. People called it a river, but it was like no river Molly had ever seen. It was a mile wide in most places and mostly too shallow to float a boat. It could be five feet deep in holes along the bank, but generally it was two to twelve inches. The water was silty and foul-tasting, but most emigrants used it if nothing else was available. Those not in a hurry often let it set in a bucket for an hour or more so silt could settle to the bottom. They soon learned that water fouled by excrement or dead animals could cause illness, especially cholera, and avoided any such water.

A couple of days ago, a rising in the bank along the river forced the trail away from the stream. A mile or so south of the trail, a line of cottonwoods suggested a small watercourse, though the stream could not be seen.

A few Osage orange trees grew among the cottonwoods. Early on, an unwary easterner had gathered some of the yellow-green pebbly fruits the size of a large orange, figuring they might be edible and surely would be fodder for the stock. Much to the amusement of watchers, he scrunched his face at the first taste and spat it out. His stock would not go so far as a taste.

Now subdued sounds rose from among the stationary wagons. Soft voices, laughter, a father's sharp admonition, the clatter of tin plates and cups, the everyday sounds of awakening. A woman crawled over a wagon's tailgate, rummaged in the goods at the back. A man, scratching his head with both hands, walked around his wagon and checked the water barrel attached to the side. Others began to appear, stretch and yawn, walk away from the wagons to relieve themselves. If they could find a bush, they disappeared behind it. If not, they faced away from the train and pretended they were invisible.

A few scattered shrubs on the plain provided some privacy. The buffalo berry was a thorny bush that produced an edible orange-red fruit in late summer. The arrowwood viburnum was short and compact in dry places but grew higher than a tall man in wetter areas along streams. The western sandcherry, no more than five feet high, was more common on the dry prairie.

Molly looked up and saw a man standing at the

wagon behind hers, stretching and yawning, pulling at his suspenders and tucking in his shirt. He saw her, waved. She nodded, smiled thinly. An oldster, Walter, walked by, touched his hat to her in a salute and smiled.

Walter had farmed a small piece just down the road from her farm outside Franklin, Missouri. When he heard Johnny and Molly talking about the Oregon trek, he pondered and hinted and wondered whether he could join them as a companion and helper. And maybe he could work for them on the new place in Oregon until he decided whether he wanted his own place. He came from a long line of people who had moved westward regularly, always on the edge of the frontier, and he was ready to move again. He had no family, just a few good friends, like Molly and Johnny.

Johnny thought bringing Walter in made good sense, and they worked out an arrangement. His small store of clothing, blankets and tent would be carried in the wagon, and he would help with the stock and driving. At night, he would pitch his tent near the wagon.

Walter was a likable fellow. He was easy-going, smiled often, talked little, content with enough and didn't need much, a good man. Molly liked him. Walter was a little apprehensive that Molly should go on after the trouble in Independence, and said so, but he accepted her decision and hoped for the best. "You're strong, and you can do it," he told her at the start. She wasn't sure he believed it.

Rob appeared from the back of the wagon, hair awry and rubbing sleep from his eyes. He waved to Molly, then turned back and looked inside the wagon. He walked to Molly, bent and hugged her. Molly kissed his cheek.

"Mama," he said. "Kath's crying." Molly stood, laid a hand on the top of Rob's head. "Son, go help Walter with the stock. He's just over there," pointing. She walked to the back of the wagon. Kath sat on her blankets, sobbing, tears streaming down her cheeks. Molly held out her arms, and Kath crawled to her, choking back a sob. Molly encircled her shoulders and held her, and she was still.

"Mama, I . . . I can't . . ." She erupted into sobbing, rocking back and forth.

"I know, honey. I know. It's hard." Molly held her, stroked her hair. She leaned back, pushed Kath's chin up. "Take your time. I'm just now getting breakfast. I'll call you. Lie down a few more minutes." Molly kissed her forehead, touched her cheek. Kath lay down, pulled the blanket over her head.

Molly opened a box beside Kath's pallet and took out breakfast makings. Walking slowly back to the fire, she squatted, laid out pieces of bacon in a skillet, set a cup of last evening's beans on the ground. She half-filled a coffee pot with water from the barrel attached to the side of the wagon. Returning to the fire, she spooned crushed coffee beans into the pot, placed it on the embers. She rubbed her cheeks hard with both hands, looked up, closed her eyes.

If I am about to break down and give up, how can I

expect a five-year-old boy and his eight-year-old sister to carry on?

Molly opened her eyes, shook her head and worked on breakfast. The caravan now was awake, and all around her, emigrants began the morning ritual. Women lit cooking fires and laid out breakfast as their men walked out to the fringes to collect oxen and mules and begin the yoking process. Other men and boys close herded the loose stock, ready to begin the drive once given the word. Everybody wanted to be on the trail immediately after breakfast was finished.

THE ROUTINE WAS SO PRACTICED NOW that no one was surprised when almost all wagons were ready to set out at the same moment. Wagons simply rolled around the odd wagon that was not ready, due either to indolence or some unexpected problem like a lame ox that had to be unyoked and replaced by a spare.

Once underway, the caravan was a solid line of wagons, beasts and humans. On occasion the column bunched up and became congested as some wagons moved slower than others. The column then split and became two parallel lines. This often meant that one line of wagons was moving across grass, which was more difficult for the teams than the bare earth of the trail. As soon as the interval between wagons lengthened, the two lines converged back on the earthen trail.

The usual routine had long since been established. Walter walked beside Molly's lead yoke, occasionally tapping the near ox with his switch, more from habit than necessity. Often he spoke softly to the oxen, pausing as if to wait for a reply, then continued with his end of the conversation. Molly walked in the shade of the wagon top. Rob and Kath walked alongside or behind, usually quietly, sometimes chattering.

If Molly intended to ride that day, her mare was tethered to the back of the wagon, but it usually was with the herd of loose oxen and horses and mules that were driven by a few riders and walkers. She always fretted when the mare was with the herd for she feared losing the horse. She had heard the stories of Indians stealing animals at night. Even in daylight, Indians had been known to lie in ambush in the tall grasses, then jump up and wave blankets, scattering the herd, enabling mounted Indians to make off with choice animals.

Concern about Indians they would meet on their journey was a constant source of conversation in Independence. A tale that had particularly impressed Molly was the one that involved a party from New Jersey. Hardly had they arrived at the gathering place at Independence last year when a young man full of himself declared that he would kill the first Indian he saw.

And he did.

He shot a woman walking alone on the first day the party set out. When the Indian band she was a part of found out about it, they rode to the New Jersey party's camp and surrounded it. The leader of the band demanded that the shooter be handed over to them. The New Jersey party huffed and puffed and wasn't about to turn over one of their own to the savages, as they called them. The Indian leader said if they didn't turn him over, they would kill them all.

Now, this led to some soul-searching among the New Jersey party. The Indians outnumbered the New Jersey people considerably. The Indians were well-armed and well-mounted and angry. Considering their own fortunes, the New Jersey members decided that the young man, after all, had committed a cold-blooded murder. So they gave him up to the Indians.

A couple of the New Jersey members followed the Indians to see what they had in mind. They watched the Indians literally skin the young man alive and apply torches to the quivering body.

This story was repeated up and down the caravan and made its way back to Independence. That was last year, 1849. The story still circulated in 1850 at Independence and on the trail. One who heard the story opined that savagery begets savagery.

Following the recommendation of a couple of old Santa Fe traders who lived near Molly and Johnny's place in Franklin, Missouri—that is, they lived there when they were not in Santa Fe or en route to or from Santa Fe—they had bought two yoke of four-year-old steers and a spare yoke of two-year olds. The traders and others with experience in prairie travel advised oxen over mules or horses. Eastern horses, accustomed to corn and lush green grass, they said, could not forage on the scanty dry summer grasses. You'd have to carry feed for horses. Mules could graze the dry grass, but they were harder to handle than the docile oxen. Oxen were cheaper than horses or mules, easier to handle, and Indians were less likely to steal them. You need to go with oxen, everybody told them.

They also took a milk cow from the farm, usually tied at the back of the wagon. Molly milked the cow each morning, though she was pleased to pass the chore to Kath when she said that she wanted to do it.

The wagon was medium size, larger than the light wagon preferred by many emigrants, especially those that planned to use horses or mules or just one yoke of oxen. Sides and ends were slightly sloped. A seat was built just inside the front of the wagon, though they expected to do more walking then riding.

The traders strongly advised them to choose carefully what was going in the wagon. Don't take heavy stuff that you don't need on the trail, they said, like chifferobes or tables or cast iron stoves. You carry all that stuff, and you'll need four yoke. Johnny and Molly followed their advice though there were some wagons in their caravan that indeed required four yoke. It was these families that early on began discarding property along the trail as their oxen began wearing out.

The traders taught Molly and Johnny another lesson they learned on the Santa Fe Trail. Most in your train, they told them, will want to leave the oxen yoked during the nooning so they can get underway quickly after the stop. That makes for an unhappy animal, they said.

Unyoke the beasts, and let 'em rest and graze. Some of the others in the train had grumbled about time lost when Walter and Molly began unyoking their animals at noon, but most drivers soon decided that it was a good idea and followed suit.

Back in Missouri, Johnny and Molly had listened intently to the advice of anyone with experience in prairie travel. They had treated the wagon cover with linseed oil to shed rain. In addition to the ten-gallon water barrel, Molly's wagon carried a water can large enough for a day's supply for their four and a few swallows for stock. A smaller can filled with milk produced a lump of butter by evening from movement of the wagon. Beside the water barrel, a small tub hung. This would do for washing clothes and the infrequent bath. A bucket of tar swung underneath the wagon. The tar would be used to grease the wheels. When Johnny wondered whether the supply would suffice for the entire journey, he learned that buffalo fat would serve as a handy substitute. Assuming he or somebody else killed a buffalo.

Eggs were packed in corn meal and flour, and as long as the eggs held out, Molly could produce rice pudding and cook yeast cakes in a reflector oven. They packed a small supply of lightly salted jerked beef, expecting to supplement it with game. A good supply of vegetables and fruits, both fresh and dried, sparingly portioned out was expected to produce more nourishing meals than the usual salty saleratus biscuit, bacon and beans, common staples for most overlanders. Bowing to the advice of an old timer who had some experience in the Santa Fe trade, Molly included jars of sour pickles to ward off scurvy.

The grocer who sold Johnny and Molly most of the provisions estimated they would begin the journey with almost a thousand pounds of food. An impressive load, but Molly knew that the fresh provisions would not last the entire trip and worried.

Food, clothing and necessities, such as cloth and needles for patching, were packed in purpose-built boxes of uniform size to fit in the wagon bed and provide a flat surface for the children to spread their thin mattress and blankets on top.

They had bought all their goods and loaded the wagon in Missouri. It was not until they arrived in Independence that they topped off their baggage with a commodity that they didn't even know they needed. Other emigrants in the setting-out camp encouraged them to take goods for trading with Indians. So they bought a small store of beads, mirrors, fishhooks, a few butcher knives, two men's shirts, a small quantity of powder and lead and hoped they would arrive in Oregon with the lot.

One of the last chores before leaving the farm was to dig out and pot a couple of two-foot tall silver maple saplings that had come up volunteer in their backyard. They would carry the pots in the wagon and plant them at their new Oregon place. The saplings would grow to trees and remind them of their Missouri home. They could only hope that the climate and soil of Oregon would be suitable for the Missouri natives. Johnny assigned the care of the saplings to Kath and Rob, a task that delighted them.

Repair materials were slung under the wagon bed: a spare tongue and axle, a wheel and extra spokes, a short length of chain and a hundred-foot coil of heavy rope.

Like many of the emigrants' wagons, Molly's was caulked in case they should need to float the wagon across a stream where they did not find a ferry. She abandoned this plan early. Hardly out of Independence, the train had crossed a shallow stream at a ford that suddenly dropped off, just enough to float the bed. Molly's wagon had leaked in a number of places, and the contents at the bottom were soaked. She resolved that she would not risk that again. She decided that she had a wagon, not a boat.

In motion, the almost continuous serpentine line of wagons stretched from horizon to horizon. Though the caravan numbered hundreds, perhaps thousands, of wagons, it was usual for a few groups of kindred spirits to form into a tight bond based on friendship and common interest. They would help each other when hard times hit.

Molly's company was formed while still in the Independence encampment. Wilfred Bonney, a prominent member of a dozen related Illinois families traveling together, scouted around and enlisted an additional dozen families to form a company that would travel as a unit. Not surprisingly, Bonney was elected captain. It was largely through Walter's conversations with other drivers that Molly's wagon joined Bonney's group. Within a week after departing Independence, their numbers would be increased to thirty wagons. Some companies were larger, as many as fifty, but Bonney's group decided that more than thirty would be too cumbersome.

Some companies, notably those formed locally months before members left home, had a detailed written constitution or by-laws that described acceptable conduct and penalties for misconduct. Molly's company, like most formed at the Independence staging area, had a less formal code of conduct, written or understood, that outlined regulations for camping, rolling and drinking and gambling. There were also provisions for caring for those afflicted with illness. Regulations generally were followed as long as it was practical to follow them. The farther the company moved westward, circumstances and relationships changed, and it became more difficult to enforce the rules.

Bonney was one of few emigrants who had already traveled the overland trail. The captain held the members of the group spellbound around the campfire on many evenings with tales of working in freezing streams, fighting enraged grizzly bears and narrow escapes from murderous Indians. Mostly lies, he confided to Molly at an evening campfire after consuming a large whiskey.

A number of emigrants had guidebooks, written and published by overlanders who had crossed the plains in the 1840s. Most often seen was John C. Fremont's report of his expedition in 1843-1844, published in 1845. A few copies of Joel Palmer's account of his journey in 1845-1846 and published in 1847 circulated. There also were copies of a few brief journals published by earlier emigrants. Most overlanders in the 1850 migration concluded early that most guides were of questionable value since they often disagreed on facts and were not helpful for this particular journey. Emigrants generally agreed that the most reliable guide was a Mormon publication, *The Latter-Day Saints Emigrants' Guide.*

Members of Bonney's company often circled their wagons at night, sometimes herding their stock inside the circle to avoid losing them to Indians or during a storm. The circle also enabled a coming together in the evening, socializing, exchanging plans and concerns.

The emigrants often sat around campfires, staring into the flames, sharing dreams and regrets, telling about what they had left behind, but mostly talking about what they expected to find at the end of this journey. Many, perhaps most, of the emigrants didn't know enough about Oregon to know where exactly they were going. They just knew they were going to this wonderful place, the end of the rainbow, named Oregon.

Molly and Johnny had known from the start where they were going. They had heard about a fertile land called Willamette Valley near the coast. This was their destination.

Most evenings, a violin or accordion or banjo in their own circle or somewhere nearby would attract weary travelers to stroll over and listen. They leaned against wagon wheels, smoking pipes or hand-rolled cigarettes, chatting softly. Sometimes a lively tune could not be ignored, and three or four listeners had to dance.

Molly was usually content to sit at her campfire with Walter after putting Kath and Rob to bed, but occasionally she walked over to listen to the music. She responded to greetings by others, but rarely joined in conversation, nor did she stay long.

On more than one occasion at the gatherings, she had been aware of the stare of Jeb, a middle-aged Tennessean traveling with his twelve-year-old son. Each time she looked his way, his gaze had not wavered. She stared blankly, then looked away.

One evening when she walked toward the music, Jeb stepped from the shadow of a wagon to stand in front of her. She tried to walk around him, but he moved in front of her again. She turned aside at the alcoholic stench on his breath.

"Pretty lady, why don't we move over yonder and talk some? I've got some refreshment I'll share with you. And we can talk." He grinned.

"Out of my way." She tried to step around him again.

He gripped her arm. "Little lady, I know you're just as anxious as me for some conversation and—"

"Let me go, you stupid drunk!" she shouted, jerked her arm back, but he held her tightly.

"What's going on here?" Jimmy and another man stood in the shadow of a wagon, outlined by the campfire behind them where a small circle of people listened to a banjo player.

Jeb looked back, still holding Molly's arm. "Nothin's goin' on, boys, just a little conversation between two people that ain't none of your business."

"We'll make it our business if you don't let her go, Jeb," Jimmy said.

Jeb released Molly's arm, leaned toward her. "I 'spect you'll decide before long that you need some, uh, conversation bad as I do." He grinned, turned and walked away.

Molly rubbed her arm. "Thanks, Jimmy."

"Come on over here, Molly, this banjo guy's good." Molly walked with Jimmy toward the circle of light from the campfire.

The man who had stood with Jimmy at the confrontation stepped aside as they passed. He nodded to her. "Thank you," Molly said to him. He touched his hat, walked into the shadows.

Molly and Jimmy leaned against a wagon. He took out a pouch of cigarette papers and rolled a smoke. Lighting it, he took a long drag.

"Who was that with you?" Molly said. "I've seen him a few times, but never heard him talk, haven't heard any talk about him either."

"Who? Oh, him. I dunno. Think his name is Micah. He keeps pretty much to hisself. Seems his stuff—there's not much of that—is carried on his packhorse. He rides alone and usually camps away from the train. Doesn't even put up a tent unless it rains. Even when it rains, he usually sleeps under somebody's wagon. Disappears for most of the day, sometimes more'n a day. He's sorta strange, don't talk much. I've never seen him smile.

"His packhorse runs with the caravan stock. Except sometimes he takes it with him and comes back at the end of the day with a dressed deer or antelope. He drops it amongst the wagons and invites anyone to take a chunk. Seems like a nice fella, seems withdrawn, like he has something on his mind."

THE AFTERNOON SUN in a gunmetal gray clear sky was searing. Walter walked beside the oxen, tapping the lead ox absentmindedly with a short switch. Rob sat on the wagon seat. Molly and Kath walked on the grass between the line of wagons and the loose stock.

Kath looked up at Molly. "Will we live close to a school in Oregon?" She looked down. "I miss school."

Molly pushed back her bonnet and wiped her face with a cloth. "I sure hope so," said Molly. "Yes, I think so."

"Will our friends have a farm near ours? I hope we're close to friends."

"I do too, honey. We'll see."

Molly glanced at the wagon, saw Rob nodding as he swayed side to side with the motion of the wagon. She looked down the train and saw Jeb two wagons back. He walked beside his lead yoke, staring at her, grinning. She turned back to the front, rested her hand on top of

Kath's head. She'd have to ask the captain why Jeb's wagon was amongst the company wagons. He was not a member of the company.

"Mama, there's another one." Kath pointed at a grave beside the trail. A crude wooden cross was pushed into the bare soil, still moist. As they walked on, Kath pointed to two more burial mounds, but said nothing. Molly laid a hand on Kath's shoulder.

Since leaving Independence, graves had become increasingly common, so much so that they hardly aroused notice. The first few deaths on the trail were treated like burials in a civilized society. Wagons of the deceased and friends stopped, and a service was held, mourners dressed in the darkest clothes they carried in their wagons. The body was buried with all the usual ceremony, and the party ordinarily laid over a day in mourning. The practice was largely abandoned with the increase in deaths.

Many norms of a civilized society were altered on the trail. Early on, many emigrants wanted to observe the Sabbath, stopping on Sunday for church and rest. Later, it was church on Sunday morning and washing in the afternoon. Still later, few observed the Sabbath. Moving was important; worship could wait for Oregon or California.

As the caravan moved westward, death from disease or exhaustion became increasingly commonplace. Less attention was paid to the normal conventions, and burial became a task that hardly delayed the westward advance. Graves along the track increased in number, one or two every mile at first, then two, then ten fresh graves per mile. On one stretch that Molly guessed was less than a mile, she counted twenty graves. She gradually became numb to the tragedy that was playing out and hardly flinched when one day she saw a virtual cemetery, a compact plot of fifty-seven graves.

Some of the burials here and along the trail were marked with crude wooden crosses, others with an elk or deer horn, castoff iron wheel rims, something, anything that satisfied trail custom. Some markers identified the cause of death. One plaque identified a family of seven persons who died of cholera, buried together in one grave. Another noted that the deceased simply wore out. Early on, overlanders tried to adhere to custom and do what was right. Graves were supposed to be noted, remembered. As time and miles passed, graves were not marked at all, or the markers had disappeared.

Defiled graves were a common sight. It was usually the work of hungry wolves that prowled about the camps at night. A rumor circulated that Indians dug up graves at night to steal clothing. Old timers said that this was not likely, but not impossible.

Some emigrants were so bent on their deceased loved ones resting in peace that they dug the grave in the middle of the trail during the noon stop or at night. They walked animals over the grave to pack the soil and erase any evidence of the burial. Wagons rolling over the grave later further disguised the burial site. Coyotes and wolves usually were not deceived. They howled nightly outside the camps at the smell of death.

*****

On a particularly hot day, emigrants were shocked at seeing eleven wagons coming toward them headed eastward, all driven by women. Children peeked out from some of the wagons. On being questioned, a sallow-faced woman walking beside her team said that all their men were dead from cholera. They were going home, with almost no provisions. The westward-moving emigrants had seen other turnarounds, as they were called, people who had given in to deprivation and loss of loved ones, but this was different.

Molly and Walter walked slowly beside the team, watching the wagons pass. She turned to Walter, her face contorted, pain in her voice. "Can't we do something?"

"Molly," he said, "you cain't spare nothin.' " She choked back a sob, borne of desperation.

Molly dropped behind Walter, her head lowered, eyes misty. *Is suffering normal for us now? The Bible says that life is a vale of tears, but why do we choose to suffer? Oh, Johnny, why did we do this? Why did you leave me?*

Molly tried to insulate Rob and Kath from the daily reality of suffering. And death. She was distraught that she had to try repeatedly to explain death and burial to the children. On one morning, as they ate breakfast beside their campfire, Molly had tried to distract Kath and Rob from the spectacle of a man and woman burying a child beside the trail, not twenty feet from where they sat. The children hardly paused in their repast. They had seen enough to know what was happening.

MOLLY STOOD behind a bush where she had relieved herself. As she adjusted her dress, she looked at the western horizon where a thin magenta line was topped by a golden glow. A hint of a breeze cooled her cheeks.

She turned at a sound and saw Jeb beside a bush, looking at her, smiling, buttoning his pants.

"Well, here we are, doing our business right close, and nobody else is around to bother us doing whatever we want to do." He stepped toward her.

"Jeb, you're crazy! Get away."

He reached for her. "Come 'ere, little purty, I know what you need, and I'm—"

"That'll do, Jeb," softly. Jeb spun around and saw the speaker who had walked up unseen. Molly recognized the man who had stood with Jimmy on Molly's first confrontation with Jeb. Micah, Jimmy had called him.

"This ain't got nothing to do with you," Jeb said, glaring. "Stay out of this if you know what's good for you."

"Jeb, I'll say it one more time," softly. "Get away from her, and stay away. I won't say it again."

Jeb reached for the pistol tucked in his belt. Before he could clear it, Micah had drawn and leveled on him. "Do it, and you're a dead man."

Jeb stared at Micah, open-mouthed and wide-eyed. He removed his hand from the pistol. He stiffened, glanced at Molly, back to Micah. "This ain't over, mister."

"Your choice. If I ever see you within ten feet of this woman again, you're in trouble," Micah said. "Now, git!"

Jeb looked side to side, turned and strode toward the parked wagons, his chin thrust upward.

Micah touched his hat brim, turned and walked toward the line of stationary wagons.

That same evening, Molly looked beyond the loose stock grazing beside the trail. She saw Micah sitting at a small fire, two horses hobbled nearby. He bent toward the fire, reading a book.

Chapter 2

Next morning, Molly watched Walter lead the four oxen to the wagon where he talked with the animals as if they were his children, patting backs and stroking heads. She looked toward the loose animals. Micah and his animals were nowhere in sight.

The drive this day was like most other days. Molly walked with the children in the shade of the wagon. Rob occasionally skipped up beside Walter and talked with him. Walter sometimes touched the top of Rob's head or laid a hand on a shoulder. Rob responded with an arm around Walter's waist. Then Rob would stand aside and wait for Molly and Kath to catch up.

Molly closed her eyes a moment, opened them and looked out past the loose stock, at the empty prairie, shimmering in heat waves rising from the parched land. She wondered, as she had wondered so many times, why she was here.

She lowered her head and stared at the ground as she

walked. Why had she been caught up in Johnny's dream of Oregon? Why did she decide to go on when she lost him? Why did they leave what now seems to have been a paradise? Why give up that reality in favor of a hope? Why, why?

She looked again at the prairie and acknowledged that, in her despair, she had been searching for Micah.

That evening, as women began building fires and men were unyoking the teams, Micah rode into the camp with a dressed antelope. He pulled the carcass off the packhorse and laid it on the ground beside the double line of wagons in Molly's group. He cut off a chunk of meat and carried it toward Molly's camp.

"Mama, here comes that man you showed me," Kath said.

Molly was on her knees before a spot in the grass she had cleared for a fire, her hand on a small stack of buffalo chips. She looked up at Micah.

"Can you use this?" he said.

She smiled. "I can if you'll have supper with us."

"I can do that, and I thank you. I'll just take care of my animals, and I'll be right back." He handed her the meat, touched his hat and walked away.

Kath had watched all this and beamed at Molly when he left. Rob walked up and dumped his load of buffalo chips. Kath told him excitedly about their supper guest. Rob dusted off his clothes, clearly unimpressed.

Micah returned, carrying a couple of forked sticks and a wooden rod. He dropped the pieces beside the fire when he saw that Molly had already pushed a metal forked piece on each side of the fire pit. A metal rod lay beside the fire. He smiled, pulled a small knife from a boot scabbard. Cutting the chunk of meat into half a dozen pieces, he put them on the plate Molly offered. She skewered the pieces on the rod and laid the rod into the upright forks.

During the preparations for supper, grilling the meat, cooking the beans and biscuit, Micah talked easily with Rob and Kath. Rob was standoffish at first, but eventually was drawn into a lively, warm conversation. Micah talked more with the kids than Molly.

"I suppose we should know names. I'm Molly Holmes, and this is Kath and Rob." The children smiled at this unusual formality.

"Micah McQueen," he said.

Introductions over, they fell back into an easy conversation. She was surprised, and pleased. She had not felt so content in weeks, not since leaving Independence. The contentment was clouded by feelings of guilt and shame. After supper when he had left and the children were in bed, she cried softly at her place beside the fire.

MOLLY SEARCHED on both sides of the moving caravan the next morning and saw no sign of Micah. Kath and Rob looked as well and asked Molly whether they would see him again.

The children were delighted when he rode into camp that evening. He plunked down a couple of prairie chickens, sat down and began working on them without a word. They bombarded him with questions, and he seemed happy to talk. He looked up at Molly and smiled. She returned the smile.

After supper, after she had coaxed a reluctant Kath and Rob to their beds in the wagon, Molly and Micah sat on the ground at the fire circle. He held a coffee cup, his empty plate at his feet, watching the buffalo chip embers glow and flicker, as fires do when they are almost finished.

"Nice couple of kids you've got there," he said, gesturing toward the wagon. "Figures, since they have such a nice mama. Must have had a nice daddy, too."

She looked up at him over her arm that was crossed over her raised knees. She looked back at the fire. He watched her. "Yes, they had a nice daddy . . . he was a good man. A good husband and a good daddy."

She rocked back and forth, holding her knees, staring into the fire.

"Tell me if you don't want to talk about it."

She glanced quickly at him, back to the fire.

Both silently studied the embers for minutes. The violin and banjo music a few wagons down the line ended, and people strolled back to their wagons, stood at fire circles, watching fires burn out, talking softly among themselves.

Micah picked up a couple of buffalo chips and some sprigs of dry sage and dropped them on the embers. They ignited in a burst of yellow that changed to a blue glow. He spoke softly, hesitantly, to the fire. "Fellow told me you lost your husband in Independence. . . . Mighty sorry about that."

She lowered her chin on raised knees, stared at the embers. "Yes."

"Fella said he died in a hotel fire."

She looked up at him, then back to the low flames. "We were in the café when we heard people yelling. Johnny told me to watch the children, and he ran down the street to help. People who told me about it later said a man in the street was looking for his family and said they were inside the hotel. Johnny wouldn't have thought twice. He tried to go in the front door, but it was afire. He broke a window and crawled through. He never came out." She closed her eyes and turned aside.

"Sorry, ma'am. Didn't mean to cause you any more pain than you already got. Sorry." He reached a hand toward her, pulled it back.

She inhaled deeply. "It's okay. I've got to learn to live with it. With the memory. I haven't talked about it with anyone. It's been too painful."

"I'll walk away if you want me to."

"It's okay. Maybe I need to talk about it. I can't talk about it with anybody else in this caravan." She picked up a couple of patties and dropped them on the fire. "When I pulled the wagon to the setting out place, people looked at me like I was crazy. They had heard about Johnny back in the camp. They gave me their condolences and assumed I would turn back.

"Turn back? There was no place to turn back to. We had sold the farm—we lived in Missouri—and everything we owned that we couldn't load in the wagon. Johnny had no family but an old uncle in eastern Tennessee that he didn't get on with. I have no family. We had friends, but I wouldn't impose on them."

She rocked, looked up at the dark sky, back to the embers. "And I decided that we would do what we set out to do. We'll go to Oregon. Me and Rob and Kath. We'll go to Oregon and start a new life, just what Johnny and I planned to do. We'll . . ." She clenched her eyes shut, leaned forward until it seemed she would lean into the fire pit. Micah moved beside her and put an arm around her shoulders, pulled her gently, hesitantly, to him. She leaned her head on his chest, sobbed.

She pulled back, wiped her face with a sleeve, sat up. "Sorry. It's all pent up inside. I haven't cried since that night when I heard about it. It's hard, Micah. Sorry, didn't mean to talk so much, but I appreciate you listening."

"It's me who's sorry, ma'am. I don't—"

She looked at him, frowning. "And that's another thing, Micah. Would you stop calling me 'ma'am.' I'm not your Mama or your schoolteacher." She tried to smile. "Just Molly."

He smiled, embarrassed. "Yes, ma'am, uh, Molly."

"And you?"

"Me? Nothing to tell really. Cowboyin' mostly. Here and there, Texas some and Kentucky." He picked up his hat from the ground, stood. "Nothin' really to tell about me." He put on his hat. "I'll be getting to my bed." He touched his hat. "Night." He walked from the fire circle into the dark.

IN THE DAYS THAT FOLLOWED, Micah customarily rode beside Molly's wagon, sometimes close and sometimes at a distance. He glanced often at her on the wagon seat or walking beside the wagon. They said little, an occasional comment about the trail, the weather, speculation on what lay ahead, passing the time. When she rode the mare beside the loose stock, he rode with her, watching her as much as the stock.

With Molly's permission, Micah put one of the children behind his saddle, and they rode beside the wagon. When Molly rode, sometimes each had a kid behind. The children had never ridden alone and were delighted when, again with Molly's permission, he put Kath on his saddle and led the horse beside the wagon. Rob took his turn, and both declared that they wanted their own horse when they settled in Oregon.

During the evening after the children had ridden solo, they talked excitedly about the experience at the campfire. They asked him about his riding, what he used to do, before he decided to go to Oregon. He said simply that he was a cowboy and had worked on ranches, and that's about it. He glanced soberly at Molly.

He stood, said his goodbyes, walked to the back of the wagon where his horse was tied, Kath and Rob each hanging onto an arm. He mounted, and they stood back, then watched as he rode from the campfire's circle of light.

Rob and Kath walked back, hand in hand, and sat at the fire. Kath leaned against Molly, and she put an arm around Kath's shoulders. The three stared silently at the glowing embers.

"Mama," said Rob, "is it okay for us to like Micah? Is it wrong?"

Molly turned t him. "No, honey. It's not wrong. . . . Daddy would want you to have friends, and Micah is a good friend."

"Do you like him, Mama?" said Kath.

She stroked Kath's hair. "Yes, honey, I like him. He's a good man."

Molly stood. "Now off to bed, you two. It's late." Kath and Rob stood, each took their mother's hand, and they walked to the back of the wagon. Molly boosted them up over the tailgate, and they crawled inside. She kissed them and walked back to the fire.

She sat down, put her arms around her upraised knees, rested her head on her knees and sobbed silently.

THE PRAIRIE that stretched in all directions from the wagon train was not without form. Far from being flat as a griddle, as most expected from the outset, it mostly rolled in a succession of gentle swells. Covered with a carpet of lush green grass until late spring, by mid-summer, it had turned dry and brown. Green patches were still found occasionally at springs and on stream banks and briefly beside the trail after the infrequent showers.

Wildlife was not common along the trail since the hundreds of wagons ahead had scared the animals away. But occasionally a single antelope or a small band might be seen in the distance, running away or standing rigid, watching the caravan. Prairie dogs were not at all frightened as they stood upright at their holes, alert and watching. An entire family might be lined up before their mound, curious at the spectacle of the strange critters watching them. Molly had to call Rob and Kath more than once, as they stood spellbound, staring at a dog village.

Cottonwoods and willows along watercourses were green and inviting in the heat. A stop at a stream to fill barrels or a short detour at noon stop could be rewarded with a cloud of colorful butterflies, lizards darting about the bank, frogs singing to the unexpected audience.

Wolves were the exception. They approached campgrounds furtively at night, pacing at the edge of firelight, their eyes gleaming, attracted by the smells of cooking and death.

On most days, temperatures climbed rapidly after a refreshing dawn. Sometimes the air was absolutely still, and deep dust in the trail rose in clouds from the hooves of stock, stinging eyes and clinging to moist shirts and neckerchiefs. At other times, a light breeze lifted the fine grit like a dry fog until a driver walking beside the wagon couldn't see the lead ox. When the breeze quickened, it blew grit into faces, stinging cheeks and blurring vision.

Plagued by heat and dust, drivers and other walkers breathed easier at the sound of a soft rumbling. They looked at the northern horizon where black clouds were forming. The rumbling became a rolling peal of thunder, and lightning flashed from the boiling black mass.

Emigrants, now experienced, knew what was coming. They pulled up, set brakes and tied lines to brake handles, jumped down and joined others on the ground who were battening down. If high winds were expected, stakes were driven into the ground on each side of wheels, and ox chains wrapped around stakes and wheels to secure wagons.

Under a darkening sky, the welcome cool breeze, smelling of rain, quickly increased in velocity, and the heavens opened. The stiff wind, often carrying rain blowing horizontally, flapped covers and blew away anything not lashed down, including tents not securely staked.

People huddled on the lee side of wagons or crawled under wagons as yoked oxen drooped where they stood. Loose stock customarily turned tail to the storm, heads hanging, though they might bolt at a sudden crack of thunder.

Often the fury of a storm ended as quickly as it had appeared. The wind dropped, and golden rays pierced the thinning cloud. People walked about, shaking water from clothing, assessing the damage. They collected bits and pieces that had been blown off wagons and rounded up loose animals that had scattered, stopping to listen to birdsong and marvel at the rainbow, a brilliant half-circle, convinced that there was a God in heaven after all.

Other days, a storm might abate but linger and continue as a light, constant, annoying rain the rest of the day and night. Depending on the intensity, the wagons might remain stationary to wait it out, or drivers might decide to tough it out and commence if the rain had not converted the trail into a muddy quagmire.

If the trail lay near a watercourse, the overlanders' problems might not be over, even after the rain ended. Flash flooding could be serious, especially if the squall had dropped torrents that washed rather than soaked into the ground.

So far, Molly had suffered no serious losses from storms, rather relief from the searing heat. Her only water problem had stemmed on one occasion from a lack rather than an abundance.

Drivers customarily filled water barrels at small watercourses that crossed or ran alongside the trail. Approaching one such stream, only about six inches deep and four feet across, the first pair of oxen stepped into the stream, but the ox on the left in the second pair decided that he didn't want to get his feet wet. He balked at the stream bank and refused to step into the flow, stopping the wagon.

Walter was on foot beside the team and tapped the ox with his whip handle. When that didn't work, he prodded the ox with a punch in the ribs with the whip butt. When that didn't work, he cussed the ox and his mother. Walter jerked around to look at Molly.

"Go on! Jab him and cuss him again," she said.

By this time, angry drivers behind Molly's wagon were complaining loudly. The wagon immediately behind her pulled out of line and passed, the driver glowering at Molly. She glowered right back at him. The next wagon followed suit, and the train was in motion again. After ten minutes of whipping and prodding and cussing, Walter succeeded in moving the reluctant ox and wagon across the stream and back into line.

After crossing the stream, each driver pulled aside and stopped long enough to hurriedly fill his water barrel and then move back in line. Both Walter and Molly were so upset by their difficulty in crossing the watercourse and embarrassed at holding up the train that they forgot to fill their barrel.

It was not until Molly went to the barrel at the evening camp to draw water that she remembered. She muttered some choice profanity under her breath, newly acquired from Walter. Now what?

Drivers didn't always fill water barrels to the top. They tried to carry as little weight as possible in the wagon, making it easier on the team. If the wagons were in a stretch where water was generally available, they carried only enough water for two or three days. They filled the ten-gallon barrels only when they needed it for a long waterless stretch. Such a stretch lay ahead, according to the word being passed around.

Molly looked across the flat south of the trail and noticed the line of willows and cottonwoods that traced the course of the stream they had crossed. At this point, it ran parallel to the trail about a mile away.

"Walter, leave 'em yoked." He looked over at her. "We need water," she said. "I'll drive down to the stream. Won't take long. I'll be back well before dark."

"You sure? I can do it."

"Take the kids out to collect chips and sagebrush, and get a fire started. I'll fill the barrel and water the cow."

She took the short whip from Walter and walked to the lead yoke. "Get up!' she called, and the team pulled away.

"Haw!" she called. The team wheeled left slowly and moved off the trail into dry grass, the cow following on her lead tied to the back of the wagon.

The team lumbered across the grassy flat toward the line of willows. Molly shook her head at her forgetfulness, no, her stupidity. She stared at the team, pulling steadily, doing what they had been doing all day.

These poor beasts should be unyoked and grazing right now, and here I am still driving them. Should have let Walter do this, but what I really wanted was to get away from the camp, from people. I can't think, or I think too much. This morning, my mind was racing at the thought of what I'm trying to do here. This afternoon, my mind is empty at the enormity of what I'm trying to do here. Right now, I just want to let it all go, just say to hell with it and let it go. If it was just me, I could do that. But there's Kath and Rob. Oh, Johnny, why did you leave me?

She closed her eyes, wiped them with a hand, felt the cooling breeze of dusk on her cheeks. Opening her eyes, she saw an opening in the willow thicket ahead. When the oxen had almost come up to the willows, she called out: "Gee!" The team turned to the right to put the water barrel at streamside. "Whoa." The team stopped.

Then she saw the three horses, partially hidden by the thicket. Three Indians stepped from the thicket and stared at her.

She was stunned. She had been exhausted from the day's exertions, but suddenly she was alert, tense. She had never seen Indians in their own land. She had seen none at all since leaving the settlements where Indians were pitiable creatures.

These Indians were different. They were young and robust, their cheeks painted vermilion, shell pendants hanging from ears and strings of beads around their necks. One sported the tail of a prairie cock tied into his long tresses. They were dressed in painted, fringed buckskins.

One of the Indians walked to the lead ox, touched its head as Molly watched. The one wearing the prairie cock ornament walked around the team opposite Molly, his eyes fixed on her.

Molly was shaken. She looked at prairie cock. "Hello," she said, hands shaking.

He frowned, looked at his companion at the front

who smiled. Prairie cock took a few steps toward the front of the lead yoke, admiring the oxen, walking around toward Molly. When he looked at her again, he was looking into the receiving end of Molly's pistol. She had slipped it from her pocket and cocked it.

He stepped backward, tensed, his eyes fixed on her. He backed up till he was standing beside his companion at the front. Molly followed his movement with the pistol.

She heard hoof beats at a slow lope coming across the flat behind the wagon. She started to look back but thought better of it and kept the pistol trained on the two.

Micah pulled up behind the wagon. "It's okay, Molly, it's me.

"What have we here?" Unseen by Molly, who had been distracted by prairie cock, the third Indian had walked around the wagon to the back, saw the cow and took its lead. Micah had ridden up before he could cut the cow's rope with the knife that he now pointed at Micah. Micah slowly drew his pistol from the holster and pointed it at him, then motioned him to move away.

The Indian released the rope, lowered the knife and backed away. He turned and walked to the front of the team where his two companions stood. Micah walked his horse, stopped beside Molly. His pistol still pointed in the general direction of the Indians.

"Out for a nice drive, Molly?" He saw her pistol, smiled. "I see you have everything under control."

She was rigid. She was not amused. "Now what do

we do? I don't want to shoot anybody. Was that all for a cow? I forgot she was tied at the back."

Micah sobered, turned to the Indians who stood silently, staring at him. "Tell you what, fellas."

He pushed his pistol into its holster, dug into a leather bag behind the saddle and pulled out a cloth pouch the size of a large fist. He tossed it to the Indian who had been thwarted from stealing Molly's cow. The Indian jumped back, and the pouch fell to the ground at his feet. Prairie cock said something and picked up the pouch. He grinned, said something to the others. They chattered among themselves, backed up, turned and untied their horses. They mounted and rode off, still chattering.

Molly relaxed, uncocked the pistol and returned it to her pocket. "Whooo. What was that all about?"

"Tobacco. Don't smoke myself, but Indians do. I keep some handy, just in case. White man's tobacco is better than the stuff they usually smoke. They can get four-legged meat any time they want, but it's not every day they can get white man's tobacco."

"I don't think the one who looked at me had tobacco on his mind," Molly said. "Or four-legged meat."

Micah raised an eyebrow.

Her eyes opened wide, and she covered her mouth. "I didn't mean . . ."

"I know what you meant." He smiled. "You're probably right."

*****

Molly and Micah sat at the campfire. She poured coffee from the pot into two cups. They sipped, enjoying the fresh breeze, watching the sun drop slowly behind the western horizon, painting the sky from pink to gray to purple.

He took a swallow, looked over at Molly. "Didn't know you had a pistol. Big gun for a little lady. Colt Dragoon, just like what I carry."

"Well, it wasn't bought for me. It was Johnny's. He said we wouldn't likely ever have to use it, but he taught me to shoot, just in case. He said I was good, a natural."

"I believe you, but I hope you never have to prove it." He looked over, saw her long face, her lips pursed. "Sorry, Molly, sorry."

She looked at him, tried to smile, determined not to cry. She sipped her coffee, stared at the fire.

"How did you get your name?" she said to the flames. "Micah is from the Bible, isn't it?" She looked at him. "Is that where you got it?"

"No, I got it from my little brother. He couldn't say 'Michael.'"

"I didn't know you had a brother. How old is he? Where is he?"

"He would be . . . twenty-five." He stared at the horizon. "But he never saw twenty-five. He was carried away by the sickness when he was just ten years old. He was a terror as a little brother, but he was a sweet boy. The same sickness that took Billy took my daddy and mama. All three died within two weeks time." He stared into the glowing fire.

"I'm sorry, Micah."

He looked up at Molly. "That was fifteen years ago. I lost everybody and everything I cared about, and it just about finished me off. I sold everything I could and gave away the rest. I been runnin' ever since. Couldn't get outta Tennessee fast enough. Been cowboying mostly, mostly in Texas. I was working for an outfit driving cows from north Texas to Missouri when I heard about Oregon and decided to think on it." He smiled. "And here I am."

She touched his arm. "And I'm glad you're here, Micah."

He took her hand in his. "I never told a single soul what I just told you. It was too hard talking about it, all these years. Seems like I needed to tell you."

They stared into each other's eyes until she looked over his shoulder at the horizon.

He stood. "I guess I better get off to my bed now and let you get to yours."

She stood, put her hand on his cheek, and he covered it with his.

The moment passed. She withdrew her hand. He ducked his head, absentmindedly touched his forehead and stepped into the darkness.

Standing at the dying fire, she hugged herself, watched him go. Her face clouded, and she wiped her eyes.

Chapter 3

THE NEXT DAY AT MID-MORNING, Molly walked with Rob in the wagon shade, and Kath sat on the wagon seat. All watched Walter who walked beside the lead ox, absentmindedly, gently tapping the ox's back with a switch.

Molly looked north and saw Micah riding abreast of the train, but at a good distance. She caught him looking her way more than once. She turned and watched Walter, smiled when he spoke softly to the ox. Wiping the perspiration from her cheek with a sleeve, she looked aside for Micah, but he had disappeared.

She felt a cool breeze on her cheek, closed her eyes. The breeze quickened, tousling loose strands of hair and billowing the wagon top as it blew through the canvas tunnel. She looked to the north. As she watched, the gray sky gathered and thickened to a dark cloud. Lightning flashed at the edges of the churning mass, and a low rumbling increased in volume.

"Gonna be a blow," Walter shouted over his shoulder. "Maybe we ought to think about stopping."

"Let's wait for the captain," she said.

The black mass expanded and lowered, and rain began to fall, a soft pattering at first, then a heavy downpour, obscuring the horizon. A blast of wind hit the wagon, and the rain became sheets of large hailstones.

"Stop! We're stopping! Tie down!" The rider galloped down the caravan. An explosion of thunder sent his horse shying and set the caravan in motion. Terrified oxen and mules surged forward.

"Get down!" Molly shouted at Kath at the first burst of thunder. Kath jumped down from the wagon, tumbled when she hit the ground. She scrambled up to stand beside Rob. "Get away!" said Molly, swinging an arm, and they ran aside, away from the line of jolting wagons. Molly pulled up to the wagon seat as the team surged ahead. Walter was left standing beside the trail.

Molly gripped the seat. "Haw!" She slid sideways on the seat, regained her balance. "Haw!" She recoiled at the sight of the wagon ahead lurching to the right when the bouncing rear wheel broke into pieces that sprayed outward. The wagon leaned gradually to the right until it slid on its side, crushing the near oxen under the sliding wagon.

"Haw! Dammit, haw!" she shouted.

Suddenly Micah was there. He rode up beside the lead yoke, lashing the ox with a quirt. He reined his horse hard against the ox, bumping it leftward.

"Micah! Be careful!" Molly gripped the seat,

leaning forward. Gradually, the team veered leftward, out of the path of the stampeding teams behind.

"Stop! Whoa! Stop!" Micah and Molly shouted in unison. The oxen slowed, trotted, stopped, heaving.

Micah reined in beside the lead yoke. He looked up at Molly, still gripping the seat, rigid, eyes bulging.

"You all right?" he said.

She hunched her shoulders to control the trembling. "Yeah." After a moment, "find the children."

He wheeled the horse and galloped down the back trail. Molly set the brake, climbed down and walked to the lead yoke. She stood there, watching Micah gallop along the line of wagons.

In ten minutes, he rode up and reined in. "They're fine. They're walking with Walter. You're okay here. I need to see if I can help." He whirled his horse and set out on the back trail at a lope.

Molly walked about, picking up pails and tools and other debris that had bounced off her wagon, or other wagons. She replaced her things on their pegs or hooks. Things she didn't identify as hers she piled beside the trail, hopefully to be recovered by their owners.

She walked around her team, talking with them, rubbing their backs. Though the sun, showing dimly through a thin gray overcast, was directly overhead, which usually signaled nooning, she would leave them yoked until receiving word from the captain.

Molly saw the children and Walter coming from the back trail, Walter in the middle, hands on Kath's shoulder and Rob's head. Molly bent and hugged them, then hugged Walter, to his wide-eyed surprise.

"We'll wait for the word from the captain," she said to Walter, "but surely we'll stop for noon and repairs, maybe for the day. I'll get something to eat."

Molly went to the back of the wagon and rummaged in the food boxes. She looked up when Micah pulled up and dismounted, tying the reins to the back of the wagon. All sat in the wagon shade, and Molly dished out cold beans and venison from yesterday's dinner.

"I'm glad nobody was hurt in the wagon ahead, the one that lost the wheel," said Micah. "I'm told they lost a couple of oxen, and they have only one spare. Hope they can make it on three."

"Maybe we could"

"No. You need to keep your two-year-olds. Same thing could happen to you."

She stared at her hands in her lap, looked up at the grazing loose stock, now close herded since the stampede. "You're right, of course, but it's hard not to help people when they need it."

"You're not in Missouri, Molly. Things are a bit different out here on the prairie."

"Yeah, sure is." She looked at him. "What did you see on your ride?"

"Some wagons got pretty beat up and lost a lot of stuff. Some beasts fell and were injured. Some will be okay, but some were hurt so bad they had to be killed. One driver shot a lead ox during the run to try to stop the team. That didn't turn out as expected. It caused a crash that killed another ox. So they lost two oxen and are down to just two now. They're gonna have a hard time."

Molly's company laid over the rest of the day for repairs and collecting goods that had been bounced off during the melee. Most members emerged intact, but some who lost stock had some serious adjustments to make, including trying to buy or barter with others for a spare ox or two. Few were willing to part with an animal at any price.

Next morning, the train passed a melancholy sight. The back half of a wagon, not of their company, lay on the bank of a flooded draw. The front of the wagon was submerged, the front yoke was completely under the surface of the stagnant water, and the tips of the horns and spines of the rear yoke were barely visible above the surface.

NOONING. Most drivers had unyoked oxen and driven them to a patch of grass nearby where the loose stock grazed. Some diehards who wanted to get back in motion quickly after the stop left their oxen or mules in harness.

Molly watched Micah and Walter who stood by a pair of oxen they had just unyoked. The pair had walked unsteadily to the grass.

Walter rested his hand on the back of an ox. "This

one limped just a little yesterday, but I figured it was nuthin.' Then he was worse this morning." He pointed to the other ox. "That one just started limping couple of hours ago. I'll yoke the two-year-olds with the other pair, but we gotta do something about these two. We'll be needin' 'em again for sure. I'll ask around to see what can be done."

Walter walked back down the line, stopped and talked with three men who stood beside a wagon, smoking. Molly went to her wagon, rummaged in a box in the back for dinner goods, greeted Kath and Rob who had walked up from visiting with friends.

"Where's Micah," Rob said.

"Just up there," motioning toward the loose stock. She looked and didn't see him. "Maybe he's with Walter." She looked back and saw Walter with the three men. Micah was nowhere in sight. She shook her head, dug into the food box.

NOONING WAS FINISHED, and the wagons were back on the trail. Walter had yoked the untested two-year-olds behind the two old hands, and all appeared in order. The two lame oxen limped along on the dry buffalo grass just off the trail, but kept up with the slow-moving loose animals. Molly and Walter walked beside the team, particularly watching the two-year-olds. Rob and Kath walked in the shade of the wagon. Molly said they could ride in the wagon in a couple of hours.

Molly was annoyed that Micah had disappeared without a word. Again. *Why does he do that? He just goes off. Where is he going? Wait a minute, Molly. You have no right to be annoyed at anything he does. Snap out of it! You have no claim on him. Still . . .*

The drive today was particularly uncomfortable. And vexing. The air was still, not a whisper of a breeze. The ox team plodded, heads down. Walter rested a hand on the back of the lead ox. He turned often to check on the two-year-olds. Looking over at Molly, Walter nodded, wasting no words in the heat.

She looked ahead, leftward over the flat, then over the oxen's backs to the right. She turned and looked at the back trail. *Why does he do this to me!*

She signaled to Kath and Rob to get in the wagon. They climbed into the back, pushed the prickly blankets aside and lay on the thin mattress.

When the sun hovered just above the horizon, the caravan slowed and stopped. A few wagons pulled out of line, moved up beside compatriots and stopped. Teams were unyoked or unharnessed and let to graze.

Bone tired, Molly drooped. She could hardly think of making supper but knew she must. She walked to the back of the wagon and opened food boxes. Her head came up at Micah's voice. He was talking with Walter.

She hurried around the wagon and, in spite of her intense fatigue, strode toward Walter and Micah who stood beside the loose stock. She stopped. *Hold on! You're about to make a fool of yourself. You're going to chastise him? Watch out.*

Micah and Walter turned and saw her. "Look at this, Molly," Walter said. He held a handful of leather pieces. "Micah made these. Look." He showed her a round piece of hide, about eight or ten inches wide, with a circle of holes punched into it around the perimeter.

Molly was puzzled. "What is it?"

"This is an ox moccasin," said Micah. "We put this around the hoof, flesh side out, thread this thong through the holes, and it's a drawstring. Pull it taut, tie it, and the ox can walk in hot sand without feeling the heat."

"Look," said Walter. "We got eight of these critters." He showed her a handful of cutouts and thongs.

"Where did you get these?" Molly said.

"Well, there's a good supply of hide on dead animals that we pass every day along the trail. I figured there would be plenty up ahead, so I rode that way this morning. I figured I could be finished with these by the time the train caught up with me."

"And so you did," said Walter. "Let's get these on the beasts right now. That okay, Molly?" Walter and Micah waited.

"Of course, sounds good."

Walter strode toward the oxen, energized at this solution to the problem that had worried him all day.

Molly caught Micah by the back of his shirt. He turned around. "Thank you," she said. He smiled. "But you big galoot, tell me something before you take off like that again. I've been afraid you were carved up by

Indians or eaten by a grizzly or . . ." She choked back a sob, lowered her head.

"Molly. I'm sorry. . . . I'm not used to anyone taking notice of what I do. I'm sure not used to anyone caring about what I do."

"Well, I do. Now go on and help Walter."

"Yes, ma'am." He smiled.

She cuffed him on his arm. "Go on!" He turned to go.

"Ooooooh."

She whipped around and saw Rob and Kath, grinning. Rob, shoulders hunched, held his hand at his mouth.

"You two! Get to the wagon! You're helping with supper tonight." She stomped to them, grabbed each by a handful of shirt and walked them toward the wagon. They could not see her smile.

THE SUN HAD JUST DIPPED below the western horizon and left a hint of pink there. The air was cool, bracing. Supper was finished, dishes collected and stacked. Kath and Rob, seated on each side of Micah, each hung onto an arm and listened to his retelling, at their insistence, the story of how he made the ox moccasins.

Now Walter and the children had withdrawn, Walter to his tent and the children to their wagon pallet. Molly and Micah sat at the fire, holding coffee cups.

"Will the ox mocs work?" Molly said. "Have you seen them work before?"

"Never used them. Never even seen them. Just learned about 'em before the caravan left Independence. I overheard a couple of Santa Fe traders at a saloon back there talking about 'em. They were giving advice to a man who was about to leave for Oregon. They had used the moccasins on the Santa Fe Trail and said they worked. If they weren't just telling stories, your animals should be okay in a couple of days. I'll make more so we can shoe all the beasts."

"Could you put the mocs on the milk cow? She walks like her feet are sore?"

"Sure. I'll do that."

"Have you seen the man the Santa Fe traders were talking with in our caravan? You said he was going to Oregon."

"Haven't seen him. Might be ahead or behind. I'll keep my eyes open when I ride out."

"Micah, when you ride out, could you . . . would you mind telling me? You know, just so I'll know where you're going and when you'll be coming back. If you don't mind. Course, if you mind, it's okay. I just thought that . . ."

He smiled. "I don't mind. I'll tell you. At least, I'll tell you when I'm leaving. I don't always know where I'm going or when I'll be back. Depends on what I see and what I'm thinking."

She hesitated, wondered what was going on inside that head, this man who appeared from nowhere and was beginning to fill an empty place. Every time she thought of him, she was torn between elation and guilt.

"I understand," she said, "and it's okay. Just, when you can, if you don't mind."

He tipped his cup, emptied it, handed it to her. He stood, looked down at her, smiled and walked past the wagon toward the tent he had set up before the meal.

She watched him until he was just a shadow. Lowering her head, she closed her eyes. *What am I doing here, Johnny? Why did we leave Missouri? We were happy. We had good friends. The children liked their school. They had good friends. That's all gone. I can't bear what's happening. Sometimes when I close my eyes, I can't see you anymore. I'm losing you, Johnny.*

She put both hands to her cheeks and rocked back and forth, back and forth.

MOLLY SAT WITH WALTER, Kath and Rob in the shade of the wagon at noon stop. They had finished a cold lunch and now silently watched the oxen grazing just off the trail.

A low rumble of excited conversation down the line of parked wagons interrupted their reverie. They looked and saw a crowd huddled between two wagons.

"What's going on?" said Molly.

"Probably th' court trying that murderer," Walter said.

Molly frowned. "What murderer?"

"Happened when you were out gettin' water yesterday."

"You kids help Walter get the oxen yoked," Molly said. "I won't be long." She stood and walked toward the commotion.

Before she had passed three wagons, Micah intercepted her. "Molly."

"What's going on down there?" She started to walk around him, but he caught her arm.

"You don't want to go there." He turned her to face away from the crowd. "I'll tell you what's going on. When we were out last evening, there was a row at a card game down the way. A man who was losing got all hot under the collar and called another man a cheat, said he was dealing marked cards. The man dealing said he was doing no such thing and said that the other guy was losing everything because he was a poor card player and ugly at that. They were both pretty drunk. I think it was being called ugly that sent him over. He pulled his pistol. The dealer went white, jumped up and threw out his arms. Ugly shot him."

"That was last night? What's going on now?"

"The court tried the shooter for murder."

"The *court*. What court?

"I asked the same question. I'm told that just before this caravan left Independence, the company that these people are part of elected a captain and a sheriff since they were going to be outside the law until Oregon."

"I don't remember. Johnny would have been part of all this. I know our group has a captain, but I don't recall hearing about a sheriff."

"Well, anyway, it was these officers that selected a judge and a jury of twelve men that tried the case."

"Tried it?"

"Yes. They tried it and found him guilty of murder. Seems he was shocked. He had told the judge and jury that he didn't intend to shoot him. Said he was drunk and when the dealer jumped up and threw his arms in the air, he thought he was going for a gun. Turns out the dealer didn't have a gun. Didn't matter. They found him guilty anyway."

"What's going to happen?"

Micah turned to look down the back trail, and Molly followed his gaze. Two wagons had been rolled head to head, and their tongues raised, forming an upside-down letter V. The tongues leaned together at the top and were lashed securely. The convicted murderer stood under the upside-down V, a stool on the ground at his feet. A rope that ended in a noose hung from the lashed tongues. The other end of the rope was tied to a wagon wheel. Two dozen or more people stood silently, watching.

Molly and Micah were too far away to hear what was being said, but it was clear that the murderer was pleading for his life while a man stood beside him with bowed head.

The person praying stepped back, and a man placed the noose over the convicted man's head. He tightened the noose and helped the bound man, now shaking convulsively, step up on the stool. Then he kicked the stool away, and the condemned man dropped. The rope jerked taut, and he swung, struggling, kicking, spinning back and forth, winding this way, unwinding that way.

When the convicted man dropped, bystanders had gasped in unison. Now they watched silently as the dying man struggled for minutes, his bound feet kicking wildly. Then the struggling and swaying stopped, and he was still.

When the man dropped, Molly had grabbed Micah's shirt in two fistfuls and buried her face on his chest. She looked up to see the people walking away from the carnage, silently, some looking back to verify that they had actually seen a man officially executed, or murdered, by a mob.

Molly pulled back, embarrassed, her hands crossed before her chest. "Did he have a family?"

"Wife and four children. During the trial, well, what passed for a trial, he pled with the jurors: what's to become of my family? Nobody had an answer. I don't suppose that question is answered yet."

Molly's face hardened. "Why couldn't they have waited till Oregon! There must be courts there. He could have seen his family through this nightmare. Now they're on their own."

"They'll make it. You're making it, and she'll make it."

She looked up at him. "Will you ask around, Micah? Find out whether people in the company they are traveling with have offered to help them. Will you do that?"

"I will."

******

"SHE DIDN'T WANT HELP?" Molly frowned, incredulous.

She walked with Micah beside the moving wagon. He held the reins of his horse. Walter walked alongside the lead yoke, alternately dragging his stick on the ground and tapping an ox lightly on the back. He carried on a low one-way banter with the team.

"When people in her company offered help," Micah said, "she told the lot of them that they could all go straight to hell. When the train got in motion this morning, she pulled her wagon out of line and let wagons pass. She was still there when I left to come back here. Seems she plans to let a bunch of wagons pass, and then she'll pull back in line. Seems she wants to be among strangers."

"Poor woman. She's going to have a hard time of it. I hope she makes it."

"She'll be all right. Her twelve-year-old boy is almost big as me and can do a man's work. A woman in her company said she was the strong one in her family anyway. 'She don't need no drunk for a husband,' one woman said. I got the impression she won't spend much time grieving."

"Well. I still feel sorry for her. I wish she hadn't dropped behind." She walked with her head down, troubled. She looked up at Micah. "What about the family of the other man, the one he killed?"

"I wondered the same thing. He left a wife and two kids. Seems she has kinfolk in the company. It won't be easy for her, losing her husband like that, but the kin will help her over the hard spots."

"Why do good people have to suffer like this? It makes me so angry! I feel so helpless. I don't know what to do. Why can't people help other people? Why can't we help?"

"People who are having a hard time in this godawful trek get edgy," said Micah, "but they haven't taken complete leave of their senses, at least, not most of the time, but the right-thinking people are not always in control. When I was asking around about all this, I heard about stuff we haven't had to deal with in your company. Thieves and people getting violently out of line are whipped with an ox whip. Hurts something awful and brings blood.

"Heard about another killing. It was a couple of weeks ago in the caravan a day or two ahead. A jury of twelve men found the killer guilty, but a lot of people who knew the family said if they executed the man, his wife and four children would be in real trouble. They said they should wait till they arrive in Oregon, then either carry out the sentence or turn him over to the authorities. That way, the wife and children would be safe.

"The jury wouldn't have it, and they hanged him anyway. But there was so much sympathy for the family, they found a driver for the wagon and said they would be sure the family would have enough provisions to finish the trip. They said the wife just about collapsed when her husband was hanged. Seems she and the kids couldn't stop crying."

Molly fumed. "Oh! That makes me so mad, I can't talk! What is the world coming to? It's as if we have left what's real, and now we're living in some other place. Why do people do this? How can they live with themselves?"

"Doesn't always end up like this. Fella told me a story he heard back in Independence. Seems an emigrant last year killed a man in a drunken brawl on the trail. Some in his company wanted to hang him, but others said he was a good fellow and a good husband when he wasn't drunk. This didn't set with others who said they couldn't let a man get away with murder. Anyway, they couldn't decide what to do, so they left him with the authorities at Fort Laramie to let them deal with him. Well, the murderer, if that's what he was, rejoined the train a month later. The authorities at Fort Laramie didn't know what to do with him and let him go."

"I don't know how I feel about that," said Molly. "I hope he was a good man, after all."

"People who haven't had to deal with enforcing the law can come up with different ways to deal with breaking the law. Remember the rider that I pointed out last week, the one who always seemed to be about a half mile away riding parallel with the train?"

"I remember. I wondered about him."

"I wondered as well, and I asked around. Seems that he was from a company behind ours. People in the company knew this man beat his wife regularly, but she didn't complain, so nobody interfered.

"Then he knocked her senseless one time, and the company finally stepped in. Some wanted to beat hell out of him, but they decided to whip him good and send him packing. They told him he had to leave the train, have no contact with his wife or anybody else until they reach the Oregon settlements. Then he can come back and join his wife, if she'll have him."

"Well, that's better than hanging him, but I feel for that poor wife, having to do all the work herself." She stopped, stamped her foot hard. "Why can't people be civil, live with each other in peace!"

Micah shook his head. "Molly, Molly, Molly. As if you didn't have enough to worry about, taking care of your own family, without adding other people's problems to your own."

She sighed, looked aside. "Yeah."

"Sorry. I didn't mean to get personal. None of my affair."

"Oh, stop it!" she said. "My problems are manageable. I hope they're manageable. On that subject, we're running low on food stocks. Either we cut our rations, or we run out of food before we reach Oregon. Can we buy supplies at Fort Laramie?"

"I wouldn't count on it. Did you hear what the commander of the government wagons we passed a couple of weeks ago said? He had twenty-five heavily loaded wagons of provisions. All for the fort and none for emigrants, he said. Emigrants all up and down the line had asked him whether they would be able to buy at the fort. He said he was so tired of having to answer that question that he might make a sign to put on the side of the lead wagon.

"Maybe you could cut portions to stretch them out. I'll see if I can bring in more meat to make up the difference. We're coming in to buffalo country, and I should be able to down a fat cow every now and then.

"Some of the boys in the caravan, old and young, are getting pretty excited about the prospect of shooting buffalo. Always happens early on. Three men up ahead went out couple of days ago, I heard, came back in at the end of the day with no meat and sick from heat and exhaustion. Most greenhorns are disappointed. They think that since there are so many buffalo they can just pick the animal they want. They don't understand that buffalo are wild, powerful animals."

"You be careful. I've heard stories too, about greenhorns who act crazy and take chances and get into trouble. You wouldn't do that, would you?"

"I'm interested in getting meat, not having a good time. I'll be careful.

"On that point, Molly. Until I can bring in some buffalo meat, what about that old milk cow? She's pretty lame. The mocs didn't help much, and you said she's just about stopped giving milk. What do you say we butcher her before she dies on us?"

Molly frowned, looked down. "She's like one of the family."

"Well, she was used to living on good grass and not

walking fifteen or twenty miles a day. She's not long for this world."

Molly looked up at the sky, glanced back at the cow, walking so gingerly that the lead was stretched taut. "Okay. Do it well away from camp. I don't want to see it or hear it. We can share the meat with the company."

Chapter 4

THE SUN at high noon was scorching. The caravan was dead still. There was no movement but the flapping of canvas wagon covers in the light breeze. Molly, Micah and Walter stood beside the oxen while Rob and Kath huddled in the shade of the wagon cover.

The three adults looked ahead at the caravan that stretched for a couple of miles toward a line of cottonwoods and willows that suggested a stream.

"Wonder what's going on," said Molly. "We've not moved in an hour."

"Couldn't say," said Micah. "I'll have a look." He walked to the back of the wagon, untied the reins of his horse, and mounted. "I won't be long." He set out at a lope and joined two other riders from Molly's group heading in the same direction.

Since they couldn't move, the captain decided to make this the noon stop. Walter unyoked the oxen while

Molly worked on a meal of coffee and cold beans and bacon cooked that morning.

She called the children and Walter after she had finished preparing lunch. They sat in the shade of the wagon and ate as Molly watched the trail for any sign of Micah. After three hours, she began to worry.

Then she saw him coming at a slow lope. He pulled up, dismounted and tied his horse at the back of the wagon. He hunkered down with the others in the shade. Molly handed him a plate.

"There's a stream up ahead. Seems there's been some heavy rains upcountry, and the water's too deep to take the teams across. The current has slackened, but the stream is still wider than usual. There's a ferry, but it can take only two wagons at a time. It's slow going. It's gonna take a long time, days, before they get to us."

"So we wait," said Molly.

"Maybe not too long. We rode along the bank to see whether we could find a ford. Didn't find a ford, but we did find a boat. It was sunk near the bank, only the top rails showing. We talked it over and decided that we could save a lot of time if we could turn this wreck into a barge and haul our wagons across. So we dug it out and pulled it up on the bank. I left the two boys working on it. Shouldn't be too hard if they can find materials to do some repair. Looks like it might have been used as a ferry before. If we can get if fixed up, we should be able to get our wagons across without waiting for the regular ferry."

He stood and stretched. "I'm off." He walked to the back of the wagon where his horse was tied, mounted and rode up the line of wagons toward the stream.

OXEN WERE YOKED after the nooning, but the caravan was still stalled. Some drivers fidgeted and pulled out of line, but they were subjected to such a barrage of angry shouts and threats that they returned to their place in the stationary line.

All eyes were on Micah when he galloped up and reined in at Molly's wagon. He told Molly and Walter that the dredge had been repaired and was ready to begin ferrying the wagons in Molly's group.

Following Micah's instruction, Walter pulled the wagon out of the stationary line and into the parallel track. Walter walked beside the lead yoke, urging the oxen ahead with a gentle tap of his stick and soft conversation. Molly and the children walked in the wagon shade. Micah rode down the line to pass the word to the other wagons in Molly's company.

When drivers in the stalled train saw Molly and the others in her group pull out of line and move ahead in the parallel track, they shouted angrily: What are you doing! Get back in line! The shouts turned to obscenities that made Molly wince and try to cover the children's ears.

She frowned and turned aside for she knew she would react the same way if she were in the stalled caravan. There was an unwritten law, an understanding, at least, that no wagon passed another unless the wagon was stopped for a reason, like repairs or taking care of a sick person. Molly wished she could explain to the angry drivers what was happening, but Micah had warned her that any mention of the makeshift ferry would send hundreds of other wagons rushing for it. So she ducked her head and tried to ignore the shouts.

In three hours time, they pulled up at the ferry. The craft touched the shore at a cut in the bank. A man from Molly's company standing on the boat called Walter to move the wagon on board. While Micah, Molly and the children stood on the bank watching anxiously, Walter moved the oxen to the ramp. The oxen balked at the bare planks that lay from shore to deck. They did not respond to pats, shouts, pokes with whip handles or soft pleas. They shook their heads and stood firm. Walter then showered the beasts with choice oaths without success.

Micah and the two other men, standing on the bank, had watched all this. Now they pondered, frowning, hands on hips.

"What if you threw some dirt and leaves on the planks?" said Molly. "They're not used to walking on wood."

Micah looked back at her, grim, then smiled. He turned to the other men. "Let's give it a try." They scooped up loose soil from the bank with their hands and spread it on the planks. Then they collected dry leaves from the ground under trees, stripped leaves from low-hanging branches and distributed them over the planks.

Walter spoke to the oxen softly, then tapped the lead ox with his stick. The team leaned into the yokes, and the wagon rolled slowly over the planks to the deck, Walter walking just ahead of the lead yoke, grinning ear to ear.

This first crossing of Molly's wagon was without incident, and all breathed easier. The boat was pulled back to the near landing, and the next wagon rolled on board.

At that moment, a man came running down the bank toward the ferry. He shouted: "Hey, what th' hell's goin' on here! That's my boat!" Micah stepped in front of him. The man pulled up, bent over, panting. He looked up at Micah. "That's my ferry, by god, and you owe me $5 for every wagon that crosses."

Micah frowned. "Maybe that's your ferry, and maybe it isn't. Where did you last see your ferry?"

The man blinked, looked side to side. "Well, it wasn't a ferry, but it's my boat."

"What was the condition of your boat when you last saw it?"

"All right, all right. It sunk, two months ago, but it's still mine, and I can prove it, and you gotta pay for using it."

Micah frowned, jaw clenched, staring at the man, which caused no end of squirming and glancing side to side. "Tell you what," said Micah. "We'll return your boat to you, which is now a pretty good ferry, thanks to our repairs, after we get the rest of our wagons across. We'll consider the repairs we made as payment for our using it.

"If you'll turn around, you'll see a line of wagons that stretches just about to the Atlantic Ocean. Soon as we give you possession of your new ferry, you tell those folks that you'll carry them across for a fee, and see how fast they line up. How's that?"

The man looked at the line of wagons that stretched eastward to the horizon. "All right, let's get to the boat . . . ferry. I'll help. How many wagons you got yet to cross?" He and Micah strode toward the landing.

Molly laughed. She turned to Rob and Kath. "Come on. Looks safe enough. We'll cross with this wagon." They walked down the bank to the landing.

A heavy rope coiled around a thick stake secured the ferry. The end of the rope was tied to a tree on the bank. A wagon and two yoke of oxen almost filled the deck space. A man stood at the bow, his hand on an ox. His wife and three children stood at the back of the wagon, all four looking anxiously over the gunwale at the water.

"Got room for three more?" called Molly.

"Climb aboard," said Micah. He extended a hand and helped Molly down the cut in the bank to the boat. She stepped up to the deck, faltered with the motion of the boat, and grabbed the wagon tailgate. Rob and Kath scrambled up beside her, both looking a bit apprehensive. Both peered over the gunwale at the water that pushed gently against the side of the boat and flowed around the stern.

"Here's the way it works, folks," said Micah. "Three stout fellows on the other bank are going to pull on that rope tied to the bow. I'll lift this coil off the stake, and you'll move across the stream. There's just a light current, so you'll move right across. Hold on."

He lifted the coil of rope from the stake and stepped aside, shouted to the far bank: "Okay, pull!"

The men on the other bank began to pull on the rope. The ferry lurched gently, causing all aboard to start. Rob had not been holding, and he jerked toward the stern. Molly grabbed him, and his expression of open-mouthed terror turned to an embarrassed grin. She smiled, turned to Kath.

But Kath was not there. Molly looked at the stern and forward decks around the side of the wagon. She was not there. *Kath! Where are you!*

Molly looked at the water just as Kath's head and shoulders rose to the surface beside the boat, her arms flailing.

"Kath!" Molly stepped up on the gunwale and jumped toward the struggling child. She splashed in beside Kath, her long skirts billowing about her shoulders, and grabbed her under the arms, lifted her, both gasping. Molly stood on the bottom, the water level just below her shoulders.

Kath threw her arms around Molly's neck. "Mama! Mama!"

"Easy, honey," she said, softly, "you're okay. Ease

up, Kath, you're choking me." Only then did Molly see Micah. He stood in the shallows beside her.

"Look, honey, Micah's here, too." Kath leaned back, reached for Micah. With an arm around each of her saviors, she pulled them to her, and they were almost nose-to-nose.

Micah smiled at Molly's bewildered look. He pulled back, turned to Kath. "Okay, little water baby, let's get you back on board."

The men on the opposite bank had stopped pulling when they saw the commotion, and the boat drifted slowly with the current. Micah waded toward the floating rope, caught it and pulled it to take up the slack. He wrapped the rope around his chest, bracing himself to stop the boat's drifting.

"C'mon, you two. I'll hoist you up at the stern where the gunwale's the lowest." Holding Kath on her arm, Molly waded to where Micah stood. Molly laid Kath on the gunwale, and Micah helped her climb over. The other woman who, with her children, had watched all this, wide-eyed, helped Kath stand.

"Now, you," Micah said to Molly. She looked at him, as if to say: how're we going to do this? He smiled, bent and picked her up, as one picks up a child, and lifted her to the gunwale. She crawled over and stood, pushing her soaked long skirts down. She looked down at Micah.

"Thank you," she said.

He smiled. Stepping around the stern, he shouted at the far bank. "Okay! Haul away!" He waded toward the shore, paying out the rope as the men on the far side pulled.

When the ferry nudged the far bank, the women and children at the stern edged around the wagon and oxen and stepped over the gunwale to the shore. Molly breathed a heavy sigh of relief, waved at Walter who stood beside their wagon in the shade of a stand of cottonwoods. The women and children jumped aside when the oxen lurched off the ferry and struggled up the cut to solid ground.

Molly looked back at Micah who now stood on the far bank. He and two other men had already begun to pull on the rope to retrieve the empty barge. Molly took the children's hands and walked up the grassy bank.

MOLLY STOOD with Micah beside her wagon. Walter leaned against the wagon, pulling on a pipe. Rob and Kath squatted nearby in a circle with the three children they had met on the ferry. They leaned in, heads almost touching, talking softly, concocting secrets.

A dozen wagons were arrayed on the flat in no particular order. Families stood idly or dug into sacks and boxes in the backs of wagons. These wagons were the first of Molly's company that crossed on the ferry. They now awaited the rest of the wagons that must cross one at a time, a slow process.

"Molly, there's something you should know," said Micah. "You too, Walter." Walter walked over, shaking out his pipe. "We've tried to get word to every wagon in our company, and we've sent word to the main caravan. If you see anybody who looks like they're going to drink from the stream or fill barrels, tell them not to do it. We're downstream from the main crossing where they're swimming loose stock across. The water is fouled at that crossing and flows down here. Drinking this water can cause all kinds of ailments. Illness, especially cholera, gets real bad past this crossing. The water may have something to do with that."

Molly had listened quietly. "What about Kath? She swallowed a lot of water before we got to her."

Micah frowned. "She's probably all right. She's a strong little girl. Everybody that drinks bad water doesn't get sick. She'll be okay."

"Hell, I had a drink myself!" Walter said. Molly and Micah turned to him. "I was pretty dry on that last stretch. Got a couple uh handfuls over the side when we was crossing." He knocked out his pipe on the side of the wagon. "But I'll hold off on the next drink till we can fill our barrel."

"The ferry operator up the way said there's a good spring about five miles ahead," Micah said, "just off the trail. We'll fill the barrels and water the stock there. We'll be okay."

Molly nodded, walked to the circle of children, stopped beside Kath and touched the top of her head. Kath looked up at her, smiled, and turned back to the chatter of the others. Molly watched them a moment, turned and walked toward the wagon, pulling at her skirts, still wet from her plunge.

*****

MOLLY POKED her head from the back of the wagon and peered around the canvas cover. The children were still there in their circle, chatting and laughing softly. She saw Micah and Walter standing beside a wagon nearby, talking with two other men. She recognized the men as members of her company. She withdrew abruptly inside the wagon, then came out slowly and climbed down, looking around furtively. She wore bloomers.

As if on signal, Micah and the others turned her way. Micah and Walter stared for a moment, then walked slowly to her. Micah looked her up and down. His face was blank.

Walter grinned from ear to ear. "Well, missy, you're all dressed up to do a day's work, and that's a fact."

"Thank you, Walter." She turned to Micah who still stared, his forehead wrinkled. "Well, say it."

A hint of a smile played about his lips. "Wondered when you were going to get to the bloomers. You're almost the last holdout. Real practical. Now you can ride with the best of 'em."

"Well, it's done, and no need to talk any more about it." She turned to walk toward the children, stopped and turned back. "On the point of riding, I want to go with you when you go out for buffalo. Can I do that?"

He frowned. "Are you sure? It's hard riding in rough country, Indian country at that. And buffalo can be ornery. They're not cows. Might not be a good idea."

"You just said I can ride with the best of 'em."

He grimaced, smiled. "So I did."

THE CARAVAN MOVED AT A SLOW, lumbering, steady pace. A walker with an ounce of energy, staying in the shade of the wagon, could easily keep up, even outpace the wagons. Caravans had been known to make as much as forty miles on an exceptionally good road and a cool day, but that was not usual. The average was more like fifteen to twenty miles.

The sun was scorching, and there was not a hint of a breeze. Oxen and people alike plodded along, heads down, panting. Walter walked beside the lead yoke; Molly and Rob walked in the wagon shade. Kath lay on the pallet in the wagon. Every few miles, the children would switch places.

Molly walked up beside Walter. She wiped her face with a sleeve. "Hotter today. We won't make fifteen miles today, same as yesterday."

"Made eighteen and a half miles yesterday," he said.

"Eighteen and a half? I don't think so. I'm guessing fifteen."

"No guess. The roadometer thing said eighteen and a half."

Molly looked at him, frowned. "Roadometer. What's that?"

Walter smiled, pleased with himself. "It's a round brass thingamajig attached to a wheel that rolls around and counts up the number of miles the wagon has traveled. I hear the Mormons invented it." He looked sideways at her, smiled.

"I'd like to see this."

"It's a few companies back. Cap'n Bonney told me about it."

"I still want to see it."

Molly looked ahead, frowned. A dozen or so wagons up the line, some people stood at the side of the trail, facing the oncoming caravan. As Molly's wagon moved closer toward them, she saw that it was a woman and three children, the kids probably under ten years old. One of the children clutched her mother's dress. Another held his sister's hand, and the third sat on the ground, leaning against her mother's legs.

Increasing her pace, Molly moved ahead of her wagon and came up to the family. "What's going on? Where is your wagon?"

"Back yonder," said the woman, pointing down the back trail. "A few days back. Our oxen died, and we had to leave it."

"How did you get here?"

"A wagon in our company took us in, but they said they were going to run out of food, and they made us get out."

Molly frowned. "They just left you? With nothing? When?"

"Yes, ma'am. That was yesterday."

"You were out here all night, like this? With nothing to eat?"

"Yes, ma'am," said the woman. Her eyes brimmed.

"What are we going to do?" She burst into tears, shaking.

"Were you traveling alone, I mean, you and the children?"

"My husband died of the cholera. I've been driving the team for two weeks now. I mean, before all this happened."

"Molly." It was Walter who had pulled the wagon up beside her. She looked down the line of wagons and saw Micah riding up from the back trail, approaching at a lope.

She pondered. "Walter, pull the wagon out of line, stop up here."

Walter frowned. "Molly, you shouldn't—"

"Do it, Walter! Do it!"

Walter frowned, nodded. "Giddyup! Haw!" he called to the oxen, and tapped the lead ox on the back with his stick. The team veered left off the trail. "Whoa!" he called, and the team stopped.

The wagon behind moved ahead. "You okay?" the man walking beside his team shouted.

"Okay," said Walter. "Move on."

Micah pulled up beside Molly, dismounted. "Molly, I know what you—"

"Micah, go find our captain. Tell him to tell every wagon in our company to pull out of line. We're going to help these people."

Micah spoke to Molly, ignoring the family. "Molly, I understand how you feel, but you must think of your family. You shouldn't—"

Molly glared. "Dammit, I'm not asking! Can you do this? If you can't, tell me, and I'll do it myself." She leaned into his face. "Tell me!"

"Okay, Molly," he said softly. He mounted and rode off at a lope.

Molly turned back to the family. "Hang on," she said softly. "We have a good bunch of people. We'll sort this out."

The wife reached for Molly's hand and held it in both of hers. "Thank you, you are a saint. The Good Lord will reward you for your kindness."

Squeezing the woman's hand, Molly released it and walked toward her wagon. She mumbled to herself, "I wonder where the Good Lord was when these people saw their oxen die one by one, and when they were left on the trail to die." She shook her head.

THE CARAVAN MOVED at its usual snail-like pace. After a stop of less than an hour, the wagons in Molly's company were back in line. The captain sympathized with the abandoned family, but he had been reluctant to jeopardize the survival of the company's members by taking in four people who had no resources to contribute. Other members of the company agreed.

Molly would listen to no argument. We are caring human beings, she had said, not animals or devils. We are not leaving here until we decide how to take care of these people.

Molly persevered, and the captain and company

finally agreed, but not without considerable grumbling and long faces. Beth and two of her three children, Olin, ten, and eight-year-old Jessie, were taken in by Rebecca and Jacob Manly, both of whom had been poorly for a week or so. Perhaps the destitute wife could help. The Manlys agreed to include the children as long as they weren't too loud and didn't eat too much. Molly took the youngest girl who was six, two years younger than Kath.

Rob, Kath and Mary, their new cousin, as Kath described her, walked in the shade of the wagon. Kath told her all about their routine, their sleeping arrangements, chores, fears, real and imagined. Mary listened, said little. She looked back often to the wagon behind where her mother, walking alongside, waved. Molly had already told Mary that she could walk with her mother whenever she wished, but to remember that she was taking meals here and sleeping with Kath.

Molly and Micah walked on the other side of Molly's wagon, heads down. Micah looked aside at the prairie, looked back at Molly, started to speak, thought better and said nothing.

She looked at him. "Well?"

He looked abruptly at her, then back to the ground. "Well, seems like it worked out fine." He looked at her. "Molly, I'm real sorry. I—"

"No, I'm sorry. I shouldn't have spoken to you like that. I was just so . . . so angry and so distressed that something like this happens."

"It's going to be fine. Because of you. You said she

called you a saint. Well, you are a saint. You probably saved their lives. That family will never forget what you did.

"Now, your saintly qualities are going to be put to a test. You said you wanted to go on a buffalo hunt. So we're going. Tomorrow. I've got a couple of boys to go with us. We need to get some meat for the company, convince them that the new additions are not going to be a drag on resources. A buffalo or two should be welcome. How about it?"

Her face had brightened as he spoke. "I'll be ready. Sounds wonderful!"

"Wear the bloomers."

She swatted him on his arm as he jumped aside. She had a sudden impulse to hug him. But she did not.

MICAH, MOLLY AND TWO OTHERS rode through parched, rolling country, broken by depressions and outcroppings, making a new trail through scattered sage and cacti. Micah held the lead of the packhorse. The two youngsters, nineteen and twenty years old, had listened wide-eyed the previous night as Micah told them about the buffalo hunt. Their nervous conversation this morning revealed no loss of that excitement.

"Are we gonna run 'em?" said Jimmy.

"You weren't listening," Micah said. "You're not an Indian or a mountain man. Neither am I. The best way for greenhorns to take buffalo is for the shooters to hide in a safe place downwind from a herd while riders move around the herd upwind. Then they move the herd toward the shooters. Slowly, slowly, don't get 'em excited. A walking buffalo is easier to hit than a running buffalo. Molly and I are the shooters; you two are the drovers."

"Drovers? Ain't we gonna shoot?" said Andy.

"Not this time. Next time we go out, you can be the shooters, and I'll drive. Okay?"

Jimmy pouted. "Okay," he said, obviously not pleased with the arrangement. "Hell, I thought huntin' buffalo meant shootin' buffalo."

"You'll have your chance," said Micah. "Next time. If that's not okay, you two can go off on your own, or you can head back to the wagons. What do you say?"

Andy nodded, grim.

Topping a barren rising, they looked down into a narrow valley. A creek of clear water flowed through a green meadow. Scattered cottonwoods grew on banks that were lush with tall grass and ferns. Faint bird song came from the trees. Beyond the stream, a line of tall white cliffs loomed over the valley, with dense copses at the base.

They came down the slope, horses sliding on flint and agate chips. Riding through the ferns, they flushed a large rabbit that burst from its cover and scampered up the slope disappearing over the crest. The four riders dismounted and led their horses to the bank, knelt and cupped hands to sip the cold, clear water while the animals drank beside them.

Molly stood, wiping her mouth with a sleeve. She

straightened. "Look," she said softly, almost a whisper. She pointed toward the woods at the base of the cliffs. A dozen elk had stepped from the dark stand of willow. More animals emerged, alert, intent on watching these intruders.

"First elk I've seen on this crossing," Micah said softly to Molly. "I wonder . . ." He walked slowly to his horse, gripped the stock of his rifle and began to pull it gently from its scabbard.

"Man, that water's cold!" said Jimmy, still on his knees at the bank. The elk wheeled and bolted into the forest as Jimmy stood abruptly, jaw hanging, as the elk crashed into the woods. He shot a glance at Micah.

Micah dropped his head, staring at the saddle, slid the rifle back into the scabbard. He turned to Jimmy, his face hard, hand resting on the rifle stock. "Jimmy, if you expect to turn into a hunter, you gotta act like a hunter. Keep your eyes open and your mouth shut. If you don't need to say anything, then don't say it. If you need to say something, you whisper, or you do hand signals. You just cost us some elk meat."

"Yeah, sorry," said Jimmy, ducking his head. He shot a glance at Andy, a nervous smile playing about his lips.

Micah looked around at the valley. "This is Laramie Creek. We're not too far from the fort. We'll reach it in a week or so." He gathered his reins. "Let's go find us some buffalo."

Molly frowned. "Laramie Creek? The fort? How do you know—"

"We need to go." He mounted, held the packhorse's lead behind him, and set off on a game trail that ran up the slope. The others mounted hurriedly and followed.

After riding an hour through a parched rolling landscape of sand, sagebrush and cacti, Micah signaled a halt and, leaving them, rode up the side of a gentle slope. Nearing the top, he peered over the peak, turned and held out a hand to stop the others from advancing. He reined down the slope beside them.

"There's a herd in the swale couple miles away, could be five hundred or so." Andy's eyes popped open, and Jimmy's jaw dropped. "Now listen, here's what we're doing. Molly and I will ride along this bench, then over the top where there's enough cover to stay out of sight of the herd. We'll move down the slope above the swale till we can find a spot where we can hide. We're downwind of the herd.

"Jimmy and Andy, you ride along this bench a couple of miles till you're upwind. Stay out of sight of the herd. At some point, you're going to have to dismount and crawl to the top of the bench to be sure you are past the herd and upwind. Okay so far?"

"Okay," they said in unison.

"Okay. Now you're past the herd and upwind. Mount and ride slow over the top and toward the herd. They will smell you and see you, but if you're real careful, they won't be spooked. Ride real slow, and they will move down the swale toward us. I expect to get side shots at slow-moving buffalo. Okay? Got it? Understand?"

"Yeah," they said in unison.

"Okay, go," Micah said.

Jimmy and Andy set off at a lope. Micah and Molly rode in the opposite direction.

Micah pointed ahead. "We're heading toward that cut in the bench. We'll cross the bench there and should find a place on the opposite slope to hide. And wait."

They rode in silence. Molly watched Micah who rode a few steps ahead. She pulled up beside him. "Micah, how do you know that's Laramie Creek? How do you know we'll reach the fort in a week or so?"

He turned to her, then looked ahead. "Been, uh, talking with the captain. He's been over this trail before."

She started to speak, but remained silent when he raised a hand and pointed ahead. He led off, and she followed.

At the cut in the bench, they rode up the slope and stopped, looking up the swale. "They're still there." The herd of buffalo was a black mass against the gray canyon wall. He pointed his horse down the slope.

"Won't they see us and go the other way?" Molly said.

"Not likely. Buffalo have really poor eyesight, but great hearing and a strong sense of smell. That's why we sent the boys upwind."

He pulled up beside a mass of stunted juniper and dismounted. "We'll tie the horses here. We're going to settle behind that big rock there." He pointed down the slope to a boulder, big enough for cover, but low enough for aiming a rifle over its top. Molly dismounted and handed him her reins. He led the horses behind the juniper and tied the reins. He pulled two rifles, both Hawkens, from the scabbards that hung on each side of the saddle, and they walked sideways down the slope, sliding on pebbles and chips, till they came to the boulder.

He leaned the rifles on the stone face and sat on the gentle slope. "Now we wait. If all goes as I expect, the buffalo will be moving slow in the bottom of the swale down there, and I should be able to get off a couple of good shots. About fifty yards away, I think." He motioned her to sit down, and she sat beside him. "We need to stay out of sight much as we can." He looked up the swale. The herd had not moved.

She frowned. "How do you know so much about buffalo hunting?"

He smiled. "I ask a lot of questions."

He set a small bag on the ground. He busied himself with loading the two muzzle-loaders while she watched. That done, he rested the rifles against the boulder and lay back on the slope, his hands behind his head.

"Why do you have two rifles?"

"Well, I want to get two shots off, and I won't have time to reload. That's where the Indians have it all over us with their bows and arrows. A skilled warrior can get off about two dozen arrows while I'm reloading for a single shot." He closed his eyes.

Molly studied him. *Who is this man? I don't know*

him. She heard lilting bird song and looked around for the source. Suddenly her head came up. "Micah!"

"I heard it." He had sat up abruptly at the sound, a soft rumbling, like rolling thunder. They both saw the billowing dust cloud at the head of the swale.

Chapter 5

"THEY'RE STAMPEDING, COMING OUR WAY." He grabbed a rifle, went to his knees behind the boulder. "Dammit, gonna be a tough shot, running hard like that."

As they watched, the black mass became individual animals, stampeding down the swale, heads down, galloping hard, the leaders distinct, dense billowing dust obscuring the followers.

When the rampaging leaders were almost below their boulder, Micah aimed, fired. One of the leaders stumbled, righted, then collapsed as the followers veered off to avoid the tumbling animal. Micah hurriedly set the rifle aside and grabbed the other one.

Suddenly the remaining leaders swerved from the swale and galloped up the slope directly for the hideout boulder. Molly stood beside Micah, hypnotized by the oncoming horde, deafened by the rumbling of hundreds of hooves.

"Down!" Micah shouted. Molly dropped and rolled

into a ball against the boulder. He aimed, fired. The lead buffalo, no more than twenty yards away, stumbled and rolled, crashing against the front of the boulder as the others flowed around their hideout on both sides.

Then it was over. Molly and Micah turned and watched the last animals in the herd top the crest of the bench behind them and disappear. The rumble of hooves faded and died, and the dust thinned and lifted in the light breeze. The silence was complete. After a minute, the whistling song of a meadowlark broke the spell.

They sat down heavily on the slope behind the boulder. "Whooo," said Molly. She looked at Micah, her lips a twitching smile.

Micah exhaled heavily. "Sure didn't expect that." He stood. "Let's see what we got." He walked around the boulder. A huge bull lay still just before their hiding place, the head resting against the boulder and blood soaking his beard.

In the swale below, a fat cow lay still, black on the parched gray grass. Beside the buffalo, Jimmy and Andy sat their horses quietly, looking down at the carcass. They looked up the slope and saw Micah, glanced at each other nervously, waiting.

Micah offered a hand to Molly and helped her stand. "Okay?" he said.

"Yeah. That was a little more excitement than I wanted."

He led the way to the horses. The animals had been spooked by the stampede, and one of the reins of Micah's horse had snapped, but the other had held. He slid the rifles into their scabbards, untied his and Molly's reins and the packhorse's lead, and they mounted. They rode down the slope to the swale.

Pulling up at the downed cow, he dismounted and handed his reins to Molly. He looked around for something to tie the packhorse's lead to and found nothing suitable. He rummaged in the pack on the horse and pulled out a stake. He pushed it into the ground and jammed it with a boot. Tying the packhorse's lead to the stake, he straightened, flexed his back, and turned to Andy and Jimmy who had watched Micah silently since he rode up.

"Well, boys, if I hadn't shot these two buffalo, I might be aiming at you two 'bout now." Jimmy smiled, but sobered when he saw that Micah wasn't smiling.

"I heard the shots just before we saw the buffalo start running." Micah said. "That wasn't too smart since I told you exactly what you were supposed to do, which didn't mention shooting. Remember that? Shooting at buffalo gets 'em excited, and they start running."

"I told him not to shoot," said Andy, "but—"

"Shut up, Andy," Jimmy said, looking at the ground at his feet.

"Well, I knew—"

Micah cut Andy off. "All right, all right. We don't have time for this now. We'll talk about it later. Right now, we need to butcher these beasts and try to get back to the train before dark. Either of you know anything helpful?"

"I've butchered beeves," said Andy.

"Good. Work on this cow, and load the packhorse. Then come up the hill."

Micah mounted, and he and Molly rode up the slope to the bull. They dismounted, and she tied the reins to a juniper. He pulled a skinning knife from his saddlebags.

Molly watched him butcher the carcass with skillful slicing and trimming. *Pretty good for a greenhorn.*

Micah finished butchering the bull and waited. He was just about to walk down to the swale when Jimmy and Andy mounted and led the loaded packhorse up the slope. They dismounted and watched as Micah adjusted the load and added some cuts from the bull, tying them down securely.

"Not bad for a botched hunt," said Micah. "We'll all carry some cuts tied on our horses." He showed them the chunks. "Let's get these tied on and be on our way. I don't want to be wandering around in the dark. That's not wise in Indian country." Jimmy and Andy looked at each other.

When all was loaded and securely tied, they mounted and set out.

THEY HAD RIDDEN an hour when Micah pulled up, and the others reined in. Micah sat rigid on his horse, staring across a barren rolling plain to an outcropping a mile or so away. The others followed his gaze, looked at each other.

"What is it?" Molly said.

Micah still stared. Finally he turned back and

dismounted. While the others watched, he removed the chunks of meat tied to his and Molly's saddles and tied them on the packhorse. He handed the packhorse lead to Andy.

"You boys take the packhorse and head on back to the train. You've got—"

"You're not leading us?" Jimmy said. "I don't know the way. You—"

Micah sighed. "Jimmy, you've got a loose mouth. You don't know how to listen. Are you ready to listen now? Can you do that?" Jimmy nodded, head down, glanced at Andy.

Micah pointed. "You see that big clump of cactus on the crest of the rising and the little dip in the rising to the left of the cactus? You ride for the dip. Once you're over the rising, you'll see the caravan down the slope couple of miles out. When you get there, ask around till you find someone who can tell you which direction you need to ride to find Captain Bonney's group. That's our group."

"Ain't you coming in?" Andy said.

"We'll be right along. Now, off with you."

Jimmy and Andy pushed their horses to a fast walk, Andy holding the lead of the loaded packhorse. They alternately looked at the sun that hovered above the horizon and the cactus and dip in the rising.

"Would you tell me what's going on?" said Molly.

"I want to show you something." Micah mounted and set out at a lope. Molly kicked her horse into a lope to catch up.

They rode through the parched flat toward the outcropping Micah had been studying. Molly fought to keep her seat, occasionally gripping the horn. She had not ridden much before this Oregon journey, riding customarily at a walk, hardly ever a lope and never a gallop. The mare was better at this than she was.

After a short jolting ride, Micah held up an arm and pulled up. Dismounting, they tied their reins to a stout juniper. They stood before a scaffold built in the bare branches of a dead cedar, a reflection of the melancholy burden borne by the scaffold.

On the platform of poles, about eight or ten feet off the ground, a body lay, wrapped in a red blanket. The cloth had come away on a shoulder, and the decayed flesh and arm bones were exposed, invaded by insects and scavenging birds that had burst into flight when they rode up. A shred of the blanket hung off the scaffold, fluttering in the gentle breeze.

Molly was mesmerized. She stared, mouth open. She turned to Micah who studied the scaffold. "What does it mean?"

Micah spoke softly without looking at her. "The Lakota dress the person who has died in his best clothes and wrap him in a robe or blanket. They also wrap something he cherished, like a pipe or knife or other weapon, and place it on the scaffold with him. They honor him by returning his body to nature, letting his body decay naturally. The scaffold keeps the body from animals. But not from enemies who would desecrate the burial."

"Enemies?"

"Sometimes an enemy will pull the body down from the scaffold and scatter the bones. This is very bad. Sometimes emigrants will pull a body down to see if there is anything useful in the shroud. Sometimes they'll pull it down just out of curiosity or meanness. This is even worse."

He looked at her. "I think you haven't seen the three mounted warriors in the cleft in that outcropping. There." He motioned with a nod of his head.

"I didn't. I see them now."

Micah held up his arm in greeting to the warriors.

The three moved from the cleft and rode at a slow walk to the scaffold. The one who sat his horse at the front had short hair, cut severely with no attempt at order, and his body was smeared with ashes. His face was painted black, and his clothing had been slit in many places.

"Welcome," said Micah in Lakota. "We come in peace." Molly looked abruptly at Micah.

The warriors looked at each other. The warrior with the blackened face answered in Lakota. "How do you know our language?"

"I am Otaktay. I lived in the village of Smoke for two years."

"Otaktay. I know of you," said one of the other warriors. "You had a Lakota woman."

Molly frowned, perplexed, looked from Micah to the warriors.

"Her name was Makawee," said Micah. "She was a

good woman. She was killed by a Crow raiding party. I was very sad."

"I know this. I also know that you and other Lakota found the Crow raiders and killed them all."

"Yes."

"Then you disappeared."

"I returned to my people. But I will always remember Makawee and the Lakota. They are good people."

The warrior pointed at Molly. "This is your woman now?"

"She is . . . with me."

"If you don't want her, I will have her. I will give you five horses."

Micah smiled.

"I will give you a hundred horses." He laughed.

Micah smiled, glanced briefly at Molly, then back to the warrior. "We must go. I am sorry you have lost one you loved. You care well for his spirit." He raised an arm in farewell.

The Lakota raised arms in return. They pointed their horses toward the outcropping where they had kept their vigil.

Micah and Molly walked to their mounts, untied the reins.

"What's this all about?" Molly said. "Micah McQueen, I don't know you."

"We need to get to the train before dark. We'll talk tonight." They mounted, and he kicked his horse into a lope. Molly followed, her mind racing.

*****

By the time Molly and Micah reached the wagons, sun shadows had been replaced by dancing campfire shadows. Before they arrived, Walter had roasted choice cuts of buffalo meat brought by Andy and Jimmy and fed the children. Kath and Rob had wanted to stay up until their mother returned, but Walter assured them that all was well and they should go to bed after they finished their supper, just as their mother would wish. Mary had climbed into the wagon without hesitation or comment.

Molly and Micah hobbled their horses on grass, removed saddles and bridles and gave the mounts a hasty rub. Walter replaced the roasting bar over the fire to warm the cooked meat. He told them what had gone on since they rode away that morning, including a good measure of worry when they did not return with Jimmy and Andy. Molly thanked him for tending to the children, and he withdrew to the tent that he had pitched before supper.

Molly and Micah sat on the ground at the fire, ate in silence, both bone tired from the day's work. When they finished, Molly collected the dishes and set them aside, wiped her hands on a rag, poured coffee into two cups and exhaled.

"Now," she said. "Let's have it."

He sipped the hot coffee, staring into the fire. "I suppose you've guessed I've been in this country before."

"I did suspect that."

"I came out in '46 with a party put together by a man named Parkman. He had some experienced people with him and a bunch of greenhorns. He hired me on since I had lot of experience with animals. We didn't have much trouble since his party was well provisioned, and they had some good hunters. This is when I learned about plains hunting. We always had plenty of meat. There was no cholera that early either."

"You didn't learn the Indian language from that party."

"No, but yes, indirectly. Parkman was fascinated with Indians. Everything about them, culture, dress, language, even warfare. He hoped there would some battles so he could watch.

"I was with him on some of his rides into the countryside around Fort Laramie. That's when we met some Lakota. I was in an unsettled state 'bout that time, and I was taken with the simple, down to earth life of the Lakota. One day after we were in the camp of this band for a few hours, Parkman and the others left, and I stayed. I went with the Lakota to their village. I stayed two years."

Molly had been studying the low flames. She looked up at him a long moment, said nothing. She looked back into the embers, waited.

"I was happy," he said, "happier than I had been since leaving my home many years ago. I was adopted into the tribe. My Lakota name was Otaktay. I had a woman. Her name was Makawee."

"A woman. Was she . . . your wife?"

He looked up. "My wife? I suppose. There was no ceremony. We lived together."

"Did you love her?"

"Yes. I loved her. And I think she loved me, in her way."

"You stayed for two years? Why did you leave?"

He turned aside, stared into the darkness, back to the fire. "A Crow band attacked our village. We drove them off, but not before they killed many people. I ran to our tipi and found her inside. Her throat was cut, and her belly slit open. The baby lay beside her. The cord was still attached."

Molly watched the dancing flames, rocked back and forth as he spoke.

"I ran outside the tipi, crying, yelling that I was going to kill every Crow I could find. I said I would leave none alive. Other warriors said they would go with me. We rode two days and found their village, still celebrating their victory. We killed every Crow man in the village, left the women and children crying. Some of the Lakota wanted to kill them as well, but others said to leave them to grieve their dead. I would have killed them all, but I'm glad that we did not."

Micah slumped, drained. He put both hands to his cheeks and rubbed vigorously. He bent forward, stared at the flames, flickering blue and red.

"I'm so sorry, Micah."

He looked over at her, then back to the fire. "They wanted me to stay, but I said I must go. I said I would always remember the Lakota and Makawee, but I couldn't stay."

"Where did you go? What did you do?"

"I wandered, I hunted for the army, drifted, couldn't stay long in one place. Guess I wasn't very dependable. Finally found myself back at the Mississippi. Did some cowboying in Texas and Missouri, somehow ended up in Independence and heard about this caravan coming together. I didn't actually decide to join it, just thought to ride along a few miles, then a few more and a few more. Then I saw you."

Molly waited, but he said no more. She reached over and put a hand on his. He looked at her, attempted a smile that didn't quite materialize.

He straightened. "Been a long day. Bedtime." He stood. "Night, Molly." He paused, looked down at her upturned face, an awkward moment.

"What did the Indian say when he pointed at me?" she said.

"He said he would give me five horses for you."

"Five horses! That's pretty cheap."

"Not at all. Most women are worth only one or two horses."

"Hmm. I'll have to think on that. What did he say when he laughed?"

"He raised his offer to a hundred horses."

She frowned. "Was he serious?"

"I'm sure he was not. That's why he laughed. No woman is worth a hundred horses."

"Hmm. I'll have to think on that too."

Micah stared silently at her a long moment, and she pondered saying something, or standing. He made a pretend-smile, went to the wagon where he picked up his folded tent and blanket from the ground beneath the wagon and walked into the darkness.

THE NEXT DAY began like every other day. The cool morning quickly gave way to blistering heat and insects and blowing grit. Molly walked in the wagon shade with Rob, Mary and Kath behind. The two girls chatted as happily as if they were playing under the shade tree in the yard back in Franklin, Missouri.

Molly looked at Walter's back as he walked beside the lead yoke, his hand on the rump of the near ox. It was as if he had been there always, and she walking beside the wagon always.

She looked out to the herd of loose animals being driven by two young boys walking and another on horseback. She had searched for Micah behind and ahead and beyond the animals, but he was nowhere in sight. He hadn't told her he was going hunting this morning. That's okay. She had finally acknowledged to herself that he wasn't obliged to tell her his plans. But she still chafed.

She felt a slight freshening breeze on her cheek and looked northward. As she watched, the gray line at the horizon moved upward and darkened. The breeze quickened, and the thin overcast became a dark angry, boiling mass, and the rain came. Sprinkles, then large drops, then a deluge whipped by a fierce wind that blew the torrent horizontally.

Drivers pulled their teams up and frantically drove stakes into the ground beside wheels, wrapping chains and ropes around wheels and stakes. Men and women and children rushed around wagons, leaning into the gale, securing anything that might blow away, running after buckets and pans that had been blown off hooks.

Jagged bolts of lightning pierced the northern sky, and the heavens were rent with explosive thunder, jarring wagons and ears. A low rolling, rumbling grew in intensity until children and their parents, huddled on the lee side of wagons, covered their ears. They looked toward the north and saw a black line enlarging, emerging into shapes that become a huge herd of tightly packed buffalo, shoulder-to-shoulder, galloping from the furious storm directly toward the caravan.

As the line of rampaging buffalo bore down on the line of wagons, the sound of the hooves merged with the thunder and blowing rain to produce a deafening roar that drowned out the shouts of men and women calling their children. Women and children held their ears while men fired rifles and pistols at the lead animals.

Suddenly Molly realized that some nearby emigrants were shouting a warning. Watch out for the rider! Don't shoot at the rider!

It was Micah. He galloped beside the leaders of the rampaging herd. He fired his pistol at the terrified beasts, trying to turn them. A bull swerved toward him, bumping his mount and almost unseating him.

He was having no effect on the stampede and reined aside, passed between two wagons and pulled up on the lee side of Molly's wagon. Sliding off the horse, still holding his reins, he ran to Molly. He grabbed her and pulled her behind the wagon.

Some of the charging buffalo veered away to pass between wagons, but others crashed into wagons, crushing sides and overturning some wagons. Teams still in harness were gored or torn from their yokes and became part of the flood of terrified animals. Beyond the caravan, the stampede bore down on the loose oxen and horses that merged with the rampaging buffalo.

Then it was over. The thunder declined to a low rumbling in the north and ended as the rainfall dwindled to a light sprinkle. The fury of the storm and stampede gave way to a strange quiet broken only by the cries of injured animals, some still in harness.

The light rainfall ended, the overcast lifted, and a weak sun appeared. Emigrants wandered about, still in shock from the melee. Captains spread the word that the caravan would not move until order had been restored and repairs made. Micah and others who had riding horses at hand mounted and rode out to look for stock.

Women and children wandered about the site, searching for anything that had been blown away or dislodged by the stampede. Their men worked on repairing wagons and tending to wounded oxen. Those that were beyond hope were killed and butchered.

Riders searching for loose stock made a melancholy discovery. They found the body of a herder who either had not been able to return to the safety of his wagon, or he had chosen to remain with his charges. His body lay beside three dead oxen, apparently all struck by lightning.

By sundown, riders had recovered some of the stampeded stock. They resolved to resume their search the next day.

Molly's wagon was spared damage, but she had lost two of the yoked oxen, gored by the charging buffalo. Her pair of two-year-olds were among the stock recovered, so she still had a four-ox team.

She also had lost some of her food supplies. The wagon cover had been stripped off during the storm, and food containers were drenched. She salvaged what she could as Micah and Walter worked on stitching up the torn cover.

They took stock of their condition. They still had a wagon and a team, a skillet and coffee pot, a full water barrel, some food supplies that been saved, and the blankets and buffalo chips would dry. Molly and Micah and the children were unscathed and in good health. They would survive.

This segment of the caravan that had been hit by the stampede laid over the rest of the day for repairs and recovery, taking stock of what was left and repacking wagons, washing and drying.

Emigrants slept lightly that night, awakened often by the bellowing of distant buffalo, a sound too akin to rolling thunder.

*****

At first light, Micah joined other men who rode out for a last search for loose stock while their women readied for the departure. A couple of riders said they had seen Indians on horseback in the distance moving some animals, horses most likely. Indians weren't interested in oxen or mules, but they coveted the emigrants' horses. On more than one occasion they had crept up on the loose stock at night, then jumped up and flapped blankets to stampede animals. Hobbled animals couldn't go far, but loose animals scattered. Emigrants recovered some in daylight, but some were lost to the raiders.

By the time Micah returned to the wagon, Molly and the children had finished a cold breakfast, and the children had gone off to visit with Beth.

Micah sat down beside Molly in the shade of the wagon. She handed him a plate of cold rice and beans and a cup of water. He nodded his thanks and ate silently. She took his empty plate and cup and put them in a basket of dishes for washing later.

They looked around the encampment. Some of the people in Molly's company fussed around their wagons, apparently ready to set out. Others were still busy with repairs and repacking. Wagons that were behind in the caravan and not affected by yesterday's stampede rolled around the stationary wagons. Some of the passing drivers spoke to the stalled men and women, but most walked on, with hardly a sideward glance.

"How long before we get moving?" said Molly.

Micah stood, looked around. "Looks like we'll get

underway pretty soon. At least, you will. I'm going to butcher one of the buffalo carcasses we shot yesterday. Some of the boys have already been working on them. I'll catch up soon as I can."

THE SUN at late morning was searing, and dust rose at each step by the team. Walter walked beside the lead ox, tapping it with a switch. He hummed, occasionally singing a line, then looked around sheepishly to see whether anyone heard.

Molly and the children walked in the shade of the wagon. She squinted when she saw a wagon ahead, a turnaround, stopped beside the moving caravan. The wagon had only three oxen, two in the lead yoke and one in the yoke behind. As Molly's wagon moved toward the stationary wagon, she made out a woman leaning against the wagon, and a girl about Kath's age, clutching to her mother's skirts. A man stood on the trail and appealed to the drivers of passing wagons. The man who walked beside the team on the wagon just in front of Molly's wagon shook his head without even a glance at the speaker.

When Molly was almost upon the man, he spoke to her. "Ma'am, can you spare any food of any kind. We're all out, and the child needs something. Anything?"

Walter stopped, turned around and looked sternly at Molly.

Molly ground her teeth, grimaced. She strode to the back of her wagon, reached into a food box and pulled out a small chunk of buffalo meat, the last of Micah's most recent kill. She had intended to cook it while he was away today. She walked to the man and gave it to him.

The man took the meat, nodded to her, almost broke down, struggled to speak. "Thank you, ma'am. You don't know . . ." He nodded again, turned and gave the meat to the woman.

"God bless you, ma'am," said the woman, "God will reward you for your kindness."

The man touched the lead ox with a switch, and the wagon moved off.

Molly watched the wagon moving slowly down the back trail. She lowered her head. *How many times will those poor people have to beg for food, and how many times will they be turned down? Will they make it to Independence, or will their bones be scattered and bleached on the prairie?* She shivered.

Walter had watched all this. He tapped the near ox with his stick, stopped and waited for Molly to catch up. He walked beside her.

"Molly, I know how you feel about this, but you can't afford to give stuff away, especially since you lost so much in the storm."

"But Walter, how can I not when they have nothing? Did you see the child's pinched face? She was hungry."

"Molly, I don't know why they have nothing. You still have food 'cause you planned carefully, and you used carefully. If you give it all away, pretty soon, you'll be just like them, and you'll have nothing. Then you'll be a turnaround, just like them. Do you want to end up in Oregon or Independence? Or somewhere in-between? Sorry, Molly, but If you can't think of yourself, think of the children."

Molly looked up and saw two more turnarounds approaching. When they were abreast, the man on the ground approached Molly. A woman and two small children walked in the shade of the wagon. The children, hand in hand, huddled together, solemn faces looking at Molly. He asked if she could spare some food, anything.

"Molly," said Walter, softly. He looked at her, his face hard.

She dropped her head, said softly. "I'm so sorry." She looked up. "Drive on, Walter," she said, staring at the backs of the oxen. The wagon pulled away. Molly looked back, saw the children still watching her. She faced forward, sure those eyes would haunt her the rest of her life.

They had hardly moved off when they saw another turnaround approaching, a man walking beside the oxen and a woman walking in the wagon shade. The walking driver appealed to Walter who ignored him, then to Molly who did not look at him, instead studied the ground as she walked on, her eyes brimming.

At noon stop, the oxen were left in harness since the stop would be brief. Molly decided that she would talk with Rob and Kath and Mary about the turnarounds. They would have no lunch today to try to understand the suffering of people who had run out of food and hope.

Molly, Kath, Rob and Mary sat on the ground beside the wagon. The children drank water from cups and listened to Molly, glancing occasionally at each other. Walter leaned against the side of the wagon, sipping from his cup, listening. When they were finished, Molly walked with the children, hand in hand, to the sage bushes.

The afternoon seemed to stretch out to eternity. The walkers squinted in the scorching sun that seemed unusually brilliant. No one spoke, heads hanging, feet dragging. Molly stumbled, caught herself as Rob reached for her.

Is this the way it begins? If we had no food, is this when we would begin begging, the way so many others must beg? God, where are you now?

Molly glanced across the prairie and saw what appeared to be a rider. She squinted, her eyes watering, a rider with packhorse trailing.

Micah, I had almost forgotten you. How could I forget you? Micah!

The supper that evening was a deliverance. Micah brought slabs of buffalo and three prairie chickens. All ate their fill. Walter was unusually talkative, and the children chattered and laughed between bites, buffalo fat glistening on their chins.

"That's just about the finest supper I've had in a hundred years," said Walter. He stood, beckoned to Rob. "C'mon, boy. How 'bout helping me water the beasts?" Rob jumped up. They headed toward the animals, Rob alternately skipping ahead and dropping back to hold Walter's hand.

While Kath and Mary crawled under the wagon, Molly and Micah sat at the fire, sipping hot coffee, staring into the embers. She told him about the turnarounds and her grief that she was helpless to do nothing about it.

"I feel less than human when I see suffering like that," she said. "I shudder to think of how those poor people are going to end up."

"Most people in this train are good people and would help if they could," Micah said. "I heard a story about a man who emigrants thought was a turnaround when they saw him coming. He wasn't. He had come from Oregon with a wagonload of food that he gave to anybody who needed it. He wouldn't take any money. He was just a good man. His name was Lot Whitcom, a Good Samaritan, they called him. They won't easily forget him."

"When was this? In this train? Where'd you hear about it?"

"Uh, um, don't remember." He took a couple of buffalo chips from the stack and placed them on the embers.

Molly frowned, collected the plates. She paused, plates in hand, when she heard giggling from under the wagon. Kath and Mary talked softly, played patty-cake with clapping hands, as if they were living one of the happiest days of their lives, unaware they might have been on the edge of oblivion.

Molly watched them, smiling. "Look at them," she said to Micah. "I'm glad to see poor little Mary finally smiling." She silently watched them playing patty-cake. "She could be . . . sorta like Kath's little sister. Mary was born the same year as the baby I lost. Little Annie would be six now, same as Mary."

Molly set the dishes on the ground, and her hands went to her face, and the tears came. "Oh, Micah, why is it all so hard?"

Micah put his arms around her shoulders and held her. "Don't know what to say, Molly. Bad things happen too often. We have to hold onto the good things when we can."

Molly's head came up when she heard Mary shout and laugh, followed by a giggle. Molly smiled and wiped her tears. She poured water into a bucket, put the supper dishes in and picked up a washrag.

Hold onto the good things. What do we do if we run out of good things?

Chapter 6

"MAMA, HERE COMES TWO NEKKID MEN."

Molly looked up from the basin of dirty dishes, saw Kath and Mary standing at the back of the wagon, looking to the north. "Kath. Do you know what 'nekkid' means?"

"It means somebody with no clothes on."

Molly concentrated on washing dishes. "Well, do you see two men with no clothes on?"

"Yes."

Molly looked up, frowned. "Mary, do you see two men with no clothes on?"

"Yes, ma'am."

Molly wiped her hands with a cloth and dropped it beside the washbasin. She stood and walked around the wagon and saw what the girls saw: two barefoot stark naked men walking gingerly on lacerated feet toward the train. Molly turned the girls' heads around and pushed them toward the fire circle. The girls looked back over their shoulders, giggling.

Molly motioned to Micah who was brushing his horse, and they walked to the back of the wagon. They watched three men carrying coats and a long slicker run from the caravan to the naked men. The two men pulled the coats on while walking with their rescuers toward wagons down the line.

Micah walked down the column and stood in the group encircling the men, identified as Josh and Bert, members of Captain Bonney's company.

"You might think we don't look like we were lucky, but I think we was," said Bert. "It was early morning, and we were off our horses gutting this elk when these four bucks rode up. They had their rifles on us before we had any chance to get ours. They had a sprightly conversation, I suppose about what to do with us. Course, I didn't understand a word. Two of the bucks was drunk as a skunk. I guess they had got their whiskey from a trader somewhere."

"Yeah," said Josh. "I think the two sober guys wanted to kill us. They kept poking their rifle barrels at us, and they was mad about something. The two drunks were smiling and laughing and I suppose poking fun at us."

"One of the drunks dismounted and come over to me," said Bert. "He fingered my mackinaw and motioned me to take it off. I did. He looked it over, showed it to the other drunk, and they both laughed. The friend pointed at Josh here and motioned for him to give him his coat. Josh pulled it off and handed it to him. The two sober bucks just watched.

"Then one of the sober bucks pointed at both of us and made motions that we soon realized he was telling us to take off *all* our clothes. We did and dropped 'em on the ground. They was all laughing now. There we was, standing there in our boots and birthday suits until one of the bucks motioned to take off the boots. We did.

"They picked up our clothes and boots, mounted and rode off, laughing their heads off. They slowed just long enough to untie our mounts and lead them away. Didn't even take the elk. Having too much fun, I guess."

The men crowded around Josh and Bert agreed they had a close call and were lucky to escape with their lives. They looked at each other, stifling smiles. Then everybody laughed, including Bert and Josh.

Micah slapped each of the two on the back. "You'll be telling this story for the next fifty years in Oregon." Micah walked back to Molly, still smiling.

MOLLY LOOKED east where the sun disk had just peeked over the horizon, coloring the lacy cloud layer shades of orange and pink. She bent and dropped a handful of buffalo chips on the new fire, stirred the chips with a stick. She looked up to see Kath walking unsteadily from the back of the wagon, her hair wild.

"Good morning, honey," said Molly. "How—"

"Mama, Mary messed herself."

"Uh-oh. Sit down here by the fire. I'll have a look."

Molly rushed to the back of the wagon where she saw Mary, sitting up on the pallet, crying softly. Molly tried not to notice the smell.

"I want my mama," said Mary, sobbing softly.

Molly put her hand to Mary's cheek, wiped her tears. "I'll get her, honey, right now. Just sit there, don't move. Okay?"

Mary nodded, whimpering.

Molly looked back down the line of wagons and saw Mary's mother standing three wagons back at the water barrel. Molly walked briskly to her.

"Beth, Mary is crying and asking for you. She messed her pants pretty bad."

Beth's hand went to her mouth. She strode, then ran, to Molly's wagon. She reached for Mary, and they hugged tightly. Beth pulled Mary's arms from her neck and leaned back.

"Let's get you down from there and get you cleaned up." She helped Mary crawl over the tailgate. Mary stood stiffly, shivering, her arms extended outward away from the mess, her dress soiled from waist to hem.

"Beth, why don't you get some clean things for Mary, and I'll get some water to clean her up. Her things are in this box here." She touched the box under the pallet.

While Beth rummaged in Mary's box, Molly reached in another container and pulled out a cloth. She went to the water barrel and wet the cloth. As she drew the water, she noted the remaining supply, speculating when she would be able to fill the barrel. It was an automatic calculation. She did it consciously or unconsciously every time she drew water. This was different. She shook her head vigorously. *Shame on you, Molly. Use as much water as you need.*

She went back to Mary, pushed the dress from her shoulders and pulled it down, helped her step out of it. Molly wiped her down, wringing out the cloth and drawing more water, until Mary was clean. She stood naked with her hands clenched against her chest, shivering. Beth pulled a dress over her head and helped her push her arms into the sleeves.

"There," said Beth, "that's better." She tried to smile.

"Mama, my stomach hurts." She sobbed, gasping.

Beth darted a look at Molly, her face grim, pinched.

"You go sit by the fire with Kath," said Molly. "We'll get you some breakfast." Mary nodded, her arms against her chest and hands clasped under her chin. She walked slowly to the fire and sat on the ground by Kath.

Beth watched Mary, then looked at Molly. Tears filled Beth's eyes and rolled down her cheeks. "What am I going to do, Molly? I can't lose her. I'll die if I lose her."

"Maybe it's just an upset stomach. We'll see how it goes today."

"A woman and her little boy in the wagon behind us died of the cholera yesterday," said Beth. "They buried them last night. Just left them. They'll never see them again, not even their graves." She bent over, sobbing. "I don't know if I can stand it. I want to die, not Mary." She leaned on the wagon, turned her face away.

Molly laid her hand on Beth's shoulder. "I'll let you know how things go here. Now I need to get breakfast going."

Beth straightened, wiped her tears with a sleeve. "Thanks, Molly. I'll watch you from our wagon." She walked away, rubbing her face with both hands. She looked back to Molly, her face contorted. She quickened her pace.

Molly walked around to the side of the wagon. She glanced at Rob, still sleeping under the wagon on the pallet that he shared with Molly. Kath and Mary sat side by side at the fire, silently watching the low flames. Kath dropped a chip on the fire. Molly walked to the back of the wagon and rummaged in a food box.

"Morning," said Micah. Molly had not heard him walk up.

"Morning, Micah. I hope you slept well."

"Can't complain."

"Mary messed herself last night."

"Umm. Not good. Any other symptom?"

"She said her stomach hurts. Maybe it was just bad water, but none of the others have complained about anything. We'll hope for the best." She gathered breakfast makings and walked to the fire. Micah followed and sat by Kath. He pinched her cheek playfully. She smiled and pinched his cheek as he flinched.

Molly worked on warming cooked buffalo meat, beans and coffee.

She looked up from the fire and saw Walter walking toward the wagon with two oxen in tow. "Walter, breakfast is ready."

He stopped, looked at Molly. His face was drawn. "I'll skip breakfast this morning, missy. Feeling a little outta sorts." He continued to the wagon and moved the oxen to the yoke.

Only then did she realize that Walter had shuffled, dragging his feet. This was not like Walter. She looked at Micah. He frowned, shook his head. She stood, tugged at his sleeve. He stood and walked with her to the back of the wagon.

"Not Walter, too!" she said softly. She slumped.

"It's too soon to know, Molly. We'll just have to watch and see what happens."

Molly looked back at the two girls at the fire. "I feel so sorry for little Mary, but I don't want Kath to sleep beside her. Kath will have to sleep under the wagon with me, or in our tent if we decide to put it up."

"How about putting Rob with me? There's room in my tent."

"Would you do that, Micah? It would really help. He'll love it."

MOLLY AND MICAH walked in the shade of the wagon, and Rob and Kath followed quietly. Mary lay on the pallet in the wagon. Molly clenched her eyes every time she heard Mary whimper.

"Walter!" Molly said when they saw him stumble and almost fall against the near ox. Micah ran to him, steadied him.

"I'm okay, I'm okay," he said, "just a little sun." He grimaced. "Stomach's kinda funny."

"Walter, let's get you up on the wagon seat," Micah said. "You've earned a ride." He took Walter by the shoulders and guided him to the wagon front. "I'm going to help you climb up there. Okay, ready?" Walter nodded, and Micah helped him step up and boosted him to the seat. Walter landed heavily on the seat, inhaled deeply and exhaled. He slouched, stared at the team. Micah stepped back and waited for Molly. They stood while the wagon moved ahead.

"Walter, too," she said softly, almost a whisper. "God in heaven, not Walter, too. What can we do? Is there nothing we can do?"

They walked beside the wagon. Micah glanced at the oxen that continued to pull without supervision. He pursed his lips. "All we can do is wait and hope. Somebody told me there's a doctor about a quarter mile down the line. He said that the doc told him that he had long since used all his medications and that there is nothing he can do now but pray."

"Pray!" she said loudly, looked back to see Kath and Rob walking behind the wagon, apparently not listening. She turned back to Micah. "Who are we going to pray to? I learned in Sunday School that everything that happens is part of God's plan. Where in hell does cholera fit in God's plan? Where's the merciful and loving God my mama and daddy prayed to? Micah, I just don't understand." She wiped her eyes with a hand, shook her head. "I just don't understand," softly.

Micah didn't tell Molly all he knew about cholera. He had talked with a number of people in the caravan about the scourge, people who had dealt with it and others who had investigated it before or during the trek.

Most cases began with diarrhea. If caught at this point, a dose of laudanum, perhaps accompanied by pepper, camphor, ammonia, peppermint or some other stimulant, usually led to a cure in minutes. If pain in the bowels persisted, another dose was called for. If a pain in the legs appeared, a larger dose was given. If vomiting occurred, especially accompanied by cramping in the legs and cold sweats, then treatment usually ended because all was lost. He didn't tell Molly all this. Nor did he tell her that his search for laudanum anywhere in the caravan for miles in each direction proved fruitless.

Micah put an arm lightly around her shoulders. "I don't understand either, Molly. I wish I did. I wish I could do something. We'll just watch and hope."

WHEN THE CARAVAN stopped for the night, Micah helped Walter down from the wagon seat and walked with him to the grassy edge of the trail. He helped him sit and went to the wagon where he collected Walter's tent and blanket. He erected the tent and, against Walter's objection, said he would bring his supper to the tent.

As Molly predicted, Rob was delighted when told he was to sleep in Micah's tent. Micah had become a best friend to the children. He talked with them as equals, though they still looked up to him and respected him.

After supper, after the talk around the campfire, Molly kissed Rob goodnight, he took his blanket and walked with Micah toward his tent. He looked back, grinning, and waved to Molly and Kath.

Molly, grim, looked into the fire. It was the first night that Rob would not be within reach. But he would be with Micah, and that was good. She smiled, looked over at Kath who was stirring the embers with a stick.

Then she heard Mary retching. By the time she reached the back of the wagon, Mary had vomited on the blankets and was bent limply forward, lying on the mess. Molly called Kath, sent her to tell Mary's mother.

Beth came running. While Kath watched, Molly and Beth cleaned Mary as best they could where she lay. She was weak as a kitten, her eyes slits, lazily opening and closing, unfocusing, her limbs limp and unresponsive. Beth rolled her to one side as Molly pulled the soiled blankets from the pallet and dropped them in a tub that she had taken from its hook on the side of the wagon. She pushed the tub under the wagon with a foot. Rummaging in the back of the wagon, she found a clean sheet and blanket. With Beth's help, she put the sheet on the pallet and the blanket over Mary who was now breathing evenly, eyes closed, seemingly sleeping.

Beth leaned over the tailgate, rubbing Mary's leg absentmindedly through the blanket. Molly watched, drained, sure that she could say nothing to ease Beth's suffering, so she said nothing, just laid a hand on Beth's shoulder. Beth glanced at Molly, her eyes glazed. She put a hand on Molly's hand, stood upright.

"Is it okay if I sleep here tonight?" she said, almost whispering. "Here on the ground?"

"Of course, honey. I'll be under the wagon with Kath, and you call me if I can do anything for you, hear?"

Beth nodded. "I'll get my blanket." She turned and walked toward her wagon, as if in a trance, dragging, weaving, head lowered.

Molly watched her go, then turned to see Kath who had watched silently. Molly reached into the wagon and found their blankets. She put an arm around Kath's shoulders, and they walked to the fire. Kath sat on the ground, picked up a buffalo chip from a stack and dropped it on the flames. Molly went to the wagon, dropped a blanket on the ground under the wagon and prepared to spread another blanket.

Kath looked up at Molly. "Is she going to die?"

Molly stopped, the blanket held in suspension. She dropped the blanket, walked to Kath and sat beside her. Encircling her shoulders, she pulled Kath to her. "I don't know, honey. She's real sick. We'll just have to do what we can for her and wait and hope . . . and pray."

*****

Molly stirred, sat up. Was the sound in a dream or . . . She looked down at Kath beside her on the blankets, breathing evenly, sleeping. Molly rubbed her face. There was it again. An animal sound? She rubbed her face again.

She heard the sound again and recognized soft weeping. Pushing the blankets down, she crawled from beneath the wagon. She stood and walked to the back of the wagon where Beth leaned over the tailgate, rubbing Mary's leg. The soft moonlight traced the tear tracks on her face.

"She's gone," Beth whispered, without looking at Molly. "I got up to check her, and she was cold. I pulled the cover up to warm her, but she was cold. She wasn't breathing."

Molly put her arms around her, and Beth was enveloped in her embrace. Her head lay limply on Molly's shoulder.

"What am I going to do?" Beth said. "Why did we come to this godforsaken country?" She shook her head slowly, her hands on her face. "I've watched other people die on this journey, children, and people have said that we must bear it; it's God's will. Why would God do this to me, Molly? How can I bear it? What am I going to do?"

"Beth, you're going to take care of your boy and your girl, and you're going to make it to Oregon and make a new life. You can do it."

Beth pulled back and looked at Molly. She inhaled deeply, exhaled. "Yes." She looked up at the moon, then down the back trail toward her wagon. "I suppose I must—"

"I'll help you do what must be done. Wrap her in the blanket that's on her. Talk with the children. Come back here at daybreak, and I'll help. I'll tell Micah."

Beth nodded, turned and walked toward her wagon, feet dragging and head hanging.

Molly returned to her bed, lay down slowly, hoping Kath would not wake. She lay on her back, pulled the blanket up to her neck, stared in the darkness at the wagon bottom.

AT FIRST LIGHT, Molly pushed the blanket down and crawled from beneath the wagon. She had not slept since talking with Beth, her mind racing until perspiration beaded on her forehead and rolled down her temples. Now, standing beside the wagon, looking around at the shadows and ghostly forms, she felt exhausted.

She walked to the back of the wagon and started when she saw Beth and her two other children standing there. Waiting. The eight-year-old girl and her five-year-old brother clung to their mother's skirts and each other. The girl sobbed softly, a fist at her mouth. Her brother watched her, unaware of what was happening. Molly wondered what Beth had told the children. What could they know of the finality of death?

Molly saw the little burden in the wagon. Beth had wrapped Mary in the blanket that had covered her last night when Molly had last seen her. Now it covered her cold body.

"Beth, you know what must be done," Molly said.

Beth nodded. Molly lowered the tailgate, and they reached in and pulled the little burden from the wagon bed and gently laid it on the ground. Molly walked to the side of the wagon and took a shovel off the hooks and laid it on the ground. She looked toward Micah's and Walter's tents, searching for Micah. He was not there.

She turned back to Beth. "Is that okay?" said Molly, motioning toward a grassy spot off the trail between two large sage bushes.

Beth nodded. Bending, they picked up the body wrapped in its blanket and carried it to the sages, Olin and Jessie following, and gently lowered it to the ground. Molly stepped toward the wagon, intending to retrieve the shovel, and saw Micah coming, carrying the shovel. And there stood Kath beside the wagon, watching all this.

"Why don't you go and work on breakfast," Micah said. "I'll tend to this. I'll let you know when I'm done."

Molly looked at Beth, then at Olin and Jessie.

"They should stay," Beth said.

Molly frowned. "Are you sure?"

"Yes. We're burying their sister. They need to say goodbye." The children looked at each other, then at the little bundle on the ground. Molly went to her wagon.

Micah pushed the shovel into the heavy sod, moist for an inch or two, but hard below from too little rain, as

Beth watched. She sat on the ground beside the body, her hand resting on the blanket over Mary's head. Olin and Jessie came to sit beside her. They watched as Micah dug, grunting, perspiration rolling down his face and dripping on his shirt.

After two hours of this, he straightened, dropped the shovel. They looked into the rectangular hole, about three feet deep. "Sorry, that's the best I can do. Ground is too hard."

Beth stroked Mary's head through the blanket. She collapsed, sobbing, on the little body, her hands on the blanket at Mary's face. The children, bewildered, looked alternately at their mother and Micah, standing beside the grave, still holding the shovel.

Micah looked toward Molly's wagon. Rob and Kath sat at the fire, watching Molly preparing breakfast.

"Beth, we need to finish up here. I'm sorry."

She nodded, stood with some difficulty. Micah stepped down into the hole, turned and lifted the little burden and lowered it gently to the bottom. He stepped out and picked up the shovel. Beth looked up at him, questioning.

"You begin. Take a handful of dirt, and drop it in," said Micah.

Beth bent and took a handful of loose soil. She held it over the body and opened her hand. The soil fell in a trickle to the blanket, making a soft pattering sound like muffled raindrops on a tin roof.

She reached toward the children, and they stood.

"Take a handful of dirt," she said, "and drop it on . . . the blanket. Say goodbye to Mary."

Jessie erupted into sobbing, her hands at her mouth. Olin watched her. Beth, tears streaming down her cheeks, put a hand on Jessie's shoulder. Jessie looked up at her, and Beth tried to smile. Jessie bent and took a handful of soil, reached over the grave and opened her fist. The soil trickled to the blanket.

"Now you, son," said Beth. Olin reached down, took a handful of dirt and tossed it in the hole, spraying some on the blanket and some on the sod beside the blanket. He looked up at Beth, and she nodded.

Beth stood between Olin and Jessie, her hands on their shoulders. "We'll see her again, children. Someday we'll see her again. She'll be wearing a long white gown, and she'll be smiling and laughing." Beth collapsed to her knees and sobbed, rocking back and forth. Olin and Jessie leaned on her, their arms around her neck.

Micah bent and took Beth by the shoulders, helped her stand. "It's done here. Take the kids, and go to Molly's fire." She made an imitation of a smile, wiped her face with both hands, nodded, and walked slowly toward Molly's wagon, holding hands with Olin and Jessie on each side of her.

Micah shoveled soil into the grave, mounded it slightly. He found his horse among the loose stock, led it to the grave and walked it back and forth over the site, trying to erase any evidence of the burial. The grass would recover, and perhaps it would escape the attention of animals and Indians.

Micah walked to Molly's wagon, hung the shovel on its hooks on the side. He turned to Molly who sat alone at the fire. "It's done. Sad business. How's Beth?"

She stared into the fire. "She'll be all right. Eventually. She and the children have been walking. They're over there." She pointed.

Beth and the children stood in the sage flat near the loose animals, hand in hand, looking eastward where the sun had just cleared the horizon, coloring the lacy cloud layers twenty shades of yellow, red and pink.

Molly shook her head, turned back to Micah. "I haven't seen Walter this morning."

"I tried to wake him, and he just grumbled, turned over and said he needed to sleep some more. I started to walk away and heard him sort of moaning. I went back to check, and he seemed to be asleep. I'm going to check him now."

Molly stood. "I'll go with you."

They walked to Walter's tent, stopped and looked at each other at the stench. Bending, they looked inside. Walter's trousers and his blankets were soaked by the watery diarrhea, and his shirt was soaked with vomit.

Molly stood abruptly. "I'll get his clothes and some wet rags from the wagon. See if you can undress him." She ran back to the wagon.

During the next hour, Molly and Micah undressed Walter who was limp and unresponsive. His eyes were slits, and he moaned softly. Micah took down the small tent and pitched it again on a dry site near his own tent. They carried Walter to the tent and gently placed him on clean sheets.

Lying on his back, Walter appeared to rally. He drank a few swallows of water that Molly brought and ate a few bites of roast buffalo before waving off the plate.

"Thanks, pards," he said almost inaudibly, "don't think I'm gonna be much help today."

"You take it easy, Walter," said Molly. "We're laying over while you get your strength back."

He rolled his head to face Molly. "No you ain't," he said softly, almost a whisper. "I know what I got, and I know I got it bad. You need to keep movin.' You cain't stop. You need to leave me." He grimaced, eyes clenched.

"Leave you!" said Molly. "We will not! You rest, and then we'll talk about moving. We need you to work the team." Walter rolled onto his side and closed his eyes. Molly and Micah looked at each other, faces grim, and crawled backward from the tent.

They walked toward Molly's wagon. "Walter's right, you know," Micah said. "You need to keep moving. It's already late in the season. You need to get past Fort Laramie and over the mountains before winter sets in. Even now, an early snow could be . . . I don't even want to think about it."

He stopped, took her arm, and she turned back. "Here's what going down, Molly. Walter's not going to make it. I think you know that. I'll stay with him, and you keep moving. I've seen you work, and you should be able to handle the oxen. It'll only be for two or three days. I'll keep my mount and the packhorse. I'll need provisions for a couple of days."

Molly looked down, her face drawn. "Two days. I guess you're right, but I sure don't like it." She looked up at the clear blue sky, eyes closed. Rubbing her face with both hands, she opened her eyes. "What's happening, Micah? It seems so futile sometimes. What's it all for?"

He put his arms around her shoulders and held her. She rested her head on his chest, and the tears came.

"It's about making a new life in a new country," he said. "And you'll make it." He leaned back, and she looked up at him. "We'll make it," he said. She put her arms around him and leaned her head against his chest.

They released and walked to the wagon. Molly held his arm a few steps, then dropped her arm when she saw Rob and Kath, sitting at the fire circle, watching them come.

While Molly collected the dishes, Micah went to the back of the wagon. He pulled out all of Walter's things and packed a few provisions in a cloth bag. He carried these to his tent, slid them inside and walked to the herd of loose animals. With their four oxen in tow, he walked them to the wagon and yoked them.

All around them, forward and behind, wagons were just about ready to move out. Micah went to Molly at the front of the wagon. Rob and Kath stood, waiting, at the back of the wagon, looking toward the gravesite.

"I've told them what we're doing," she said. "They are a little puzzled, but I think they understand."

"Anything we need to talk about?" said Micah. "After . . . things work out here, I'll hunt and catch up with you. I'm afraid it won't be long."

Molly looked silently at Walter's tent, and she wiped a tear. "I've known him forever. I wanted to say goodbye, but how could I do that to his face? I wish I was a believer, without any doubts. Then I could say goodbye in my heart, knowing it wasn't the end. But I . . . I can't."

She grabbed the folds of his shirt, pulled him to her and leaned her head against his chest. "I don't know what would have happened to us without you, Micah," softly.

He leaned back, took her face in his hands, looked long into her eyes, bent and gently kissed her lips. "Watch for me."

"I'll watch for you, but you watch out for bears, coyotes, wolves, buffalo bulls and bad Indians." She reached up and kissed him again. "I'm getting used to having you around." She smiled and touched his cheek.

THE NEXT DAY began as it always began with sleepy men, women and children scattering to the bushes to relieve themselves, drivers yoking oxen while the womenfolk prepared breakfast and helped the children do what they must do to get moving.

Micah and Molly checked Walter while the children

still slept. Micah tried to awaken him to ask if he would eat something. He breathed fitfully, twitching, and did not respond.

They walked to the stock, found their oxen and moved them to the wagon. Working together to yoke the animals, Micah told her what to do next, how to solve a particular problem if it should occur, how to react to peculiarities of the oxen. He asked repeatedly whether she understood. She responded with a nod, or a "yes," or a frown. She finally assured him that she could handle oxen as well as he. She cocked her head, and he smiled thinly, both acknowledging the end of the instruction.

While Molly prepared breakfast and helped the children get moving, Micah rummaged in the provisions boxes for a few items to tide him over after Molly's departure with the wagon. He stuffed the supplies into a canvas bag, took the shovel from the side of the wagon, and pushed everything inside his tent.

He came back to the fire, sat down beside Rob and Kath and took the plate Molly offered him. He chatted with the children while he ate. Molly watched, thinking to herself how this man had become a part of her life, how well he fit. For a moment, she wondered whether she could get on without him, whether she could have gotten this far without him. Then she remembered Johnny and turned away as guilt washed over her.

Breakfast finished, Molly collected dishes and put them away. Micah and the children stood beside the wagon, saying their goodbyes. While Molly watched, Kath stood on her tiptoes and kissed him on a cheek. He patted her head, gave Rob's arm a squeeze. Molly tried to smile, her eyes watering.

Molly looked at the wagons ahead. "They're leaving," she said. "We need to go." She walked with Micah toward his tent. They stopped before they reached the tent, faced each other.

"You will take care," said Micah. "Ask help from the others in the company if you need it. I talked with them, and they know what's going on."

"I'm okay. You take care of Walter. And yourself. You . . . you've filled an empty spot, Micah McQueen. I won't have anything happen to you. Hear?"

He smiled. "Nothing's going to happen to me unless you're part of it. Hear?"

She looked into his eyes, leaned into him and kissed him on his lips, a soft, sweet kiss. She turned abruptly toward the wagon where Kath and Rob huddled together, watching, giggling.

"Go," he said. "I'll catch up."

She walked to the wagon, stopped in front of Kath and Rob, hands on her hips. "So?" she said. They giggled, Kath wriggling, Rob's hand over his mouth. She grabbed both and hugged.

"Now, let's get moving." She picked up Walter's stick and went to the lead yoke. "Get up! Giddyup." She tapped the near ox on his back, and the team leaned into the yoke. "Gee!" Molly said, and the team veered right into the line of the moving caravan. The children, walking beside the wagon, waved to Micah, and he returned the wave. Molly looked straight ahead.

Chapter 7

THE DAY WAS MILD, with a light overcast and cooling breeze. A gray cloud in the north hinted rain.

All things considered, Molly decided that the morning went reasonably well. The oxen had long since learned to follow the wagon ahead without much help from a driver. The children had not had much to say, and they had kept up the pace with no complaint or urging from Molly.

The noon stop was uneventful. Molly didn't like to see oxen kept in harness during the nooning, but she decided that on this first day on her own, she would not risk a problem in getting them yoked again in time for the leaving. When the caravan stopped later for the night camp, the oxen were unyoked, and Rob and Kath helped her move them to grass beside the trail among the other loose animals.

Molly pointed to her mare in the herd and asked Rob and Kath to give her a rub while she fixed supper.

Sitting around the fire later, they ate with little comment. Molly realized how much she and the children had come to rely on Micah for conversation. He usually had something to break the monotony of the usual routine, even if it were only telling what he had done that day.

After collecting the supper dishes and laying them aside in a pan, Molly walked with the children to the back of the wagon. She kissed each and boosted them up over the tailgate. They sat on their bed and pulled the blanket over their legs.

"Will Micah be here when we wake up?" said Kath.

"Maybe not when we wake up, but maybe some time tomorrow. You know why he stayed behind, don't you?"

"Yes. Walter."

"I miss Walter," said Rob.

"I do too, honey," Molly said. "He was a good man." She turned aside, realizing that she had declared him gone. Turning back, she touched their legs through the blanket. "Lie down now. Goodnight." She took her blankets from a box.

Walking toward the fire, she dropped the blankets under the wagon. She went to the front of the wagon beside the empty yoke, stopped and looked up. The overcast had dissipated, and now the sky was crowded with brilliant stars, twinkling and pulsing. She hugged herself and shivered. *Funny how being alone makes you aware that there is a world beyond this campground and this caravan. How small and unimportant we are. Just passing through.*

She walked back to the fire, arms still crossed, her head down. She confirmed that the fire was only glowing embers, knelt, crawled under the wagon and made her bed. She lay on the blanket and pulled the top cover to her chest. She knew she would not sleep.

But she did. She woke abruptly when she felt something on her blanket.

"Mama, my stomach hurts." It was Rob.

Molly reached for him and pulled him to her. "Lie down here, sweetheart." He lay beside her, and she pulled the blanket over his shoulders. She touched his cheek, rubbed the top of his head.

No, no, no, not my boy, my little boy.

She slept no more this night, dreading the dawn, knowing she had no answer for the sickness that surely was coming.

Morning was a trial. After Kath crawled down from the back of the wagon, Molly put Rob inside on the pallet and brought a bowl of broth, coaxing him to try to eat. He took a few tiny bites and some sips of water and held both down. Molly was cheered even by this small success.

Worrying about Rob, Molly yoked the oxen, but she had lost all her confidence. She asked Jonathan, the driver of the wagon behind her, to check her work. He pushed and pulled the yoke and assured her that she had done a good job. He smiled and returned to his wagon.

She took a deep breath. *Okay, if you say so,*

Jonathan, but I'll never be sure of anything again. Molly was ready when the train lurched into motion, and the day began. Kath walked beside Molly for the first mile, then dropped back to walk in the wagon's shade.

At the noon stop, again against her instincts, she left the oxen yoked. By chance or somebody's plan, the camp lay near a shallow creek. She carried buckets of water to each ox, then poured two buckets into the barrel attached to the side of the wagon.

Rob took a few bites of rice and some sips of water. He did not appear to have improved, but he had no other symptoms. He seemed to be sleeping when Molly checked him during the morning drive.

When the caravan made evening camp, Molly looked in on Rob and found him breathing evenly, apparently sleeping. She unyoked the oxen and moved them to the herd.

Returning to the wagon, she forced herself to make supper. Her mind was elsewhere, and she spilled beans on the wagon sideboard. She cleaned the spill and spooned rice and beans on two plates. Handing a plate to Kath, she sat beside her at the fire.

Kath nibbled at her food.

"You need to eat, honey," said Molly. "Sorry it's cold. We'll have a hot breakfast."

Kath pushed the beans around the plate with her spoon, looked up. "Is Rob going to . . . going to . . .?"

Molly put an arm around Kath's shoulders. "He's going to be fine, honey."

Molly set her plate on the ground, stood and walked to the back of the wagon, touched Rob's foot. "Can you eat something, honey?"

Rob stirred, rose on an elbow and sat up. "What's the matter with me, Mama? Am I going to die?"

Molly recoiled. "No, honey, no. You've got an uneasy stomach. You'll be fine. Do you think you can eat something?"

He shook his head, leaned back on an elbow and lay down heavily on his back. Molly pushed the blanket to his shoulder, rubbed his leg.

She stood there, rubbing absentmindedly, her head bowed. *Please, God, let him live, and I will be a good churchgoer again. I will believe again.*

She pulled her blankets from the box beside Rob's pallet. Walking around the wagon, carrying Rob's plate, she saw Kath still sitting at the fire, bent forward, vomit soiling her lap and dripping from her chin.

Molly dropped the plate and blankets and ran to Kath, knelt beside her and laid a hand on her shoulder to steady her. With the other hand, she wiped Kath's chin, wiped the hand on her own sleeve.

"Here, honey, let me help you." She set Kath's plate aside, went to the water barrel and drew a cup of water. She knelt beside Kath and put it to her mouth. "Don't swallow it. Just swish it around in your mouth, and spit it on the fire." Kath rinsed her mouth, leaned forward and spat, water dripping from her chin.

"Stay right there while I get some clean clothes and get our blankets set out. Okay?"

Kath nodded, bending forward, open mouth dripping. Molly ran to the back of the wagon, pulled a dress from a clothes box and a couple of washrags from another. She hurried back to Kath and helped her stand. Only then did she notice that Kath's dress was soiled. Nor in her anxiety had she noticed the smell.

"Mama, I messed myself," Kath mumbled.

"It's okay, honey, we'll get you cleaned up and get you into bed." Molly trembled as she pulled Kath's dress over her head and tossed it aside. She drew water on a cloth and rubbed Kath, her arms held away from her body, shivering.

"Mama, it hurts," her teeth chattering.

Molly gritted her teeth, tense, rubbed Kath with the dry cloth, tossed it away. She pulled the clean dress over her, helped her push her arms into sleeves. "Now, into bed with you." She quickly spread the blankets and walked Kath to the wagon, helped her kneel and crawl underneath to the blankets. Molly threw the top cover over Kath and straightened it over her. She laid a hand on Kath's cheek.

"Now you sleep, honey. You'll feel better after you sleep." Kath looked up at Molly, her eyes wide open, then narrowed to slits. Kath closed her eyes, and Molly pulled the cover to her chin.

Molly crawled from under the wagon to the fire circle. She turned and sat down heavily, her legs splayed. She took a deep breath, head raised to the heavens, exhaled, eyes closed. She opened her eyes, stared at the cold fire and sobbed, rocking forward and backward.

She remembered the words from the Bible that had always frightened her: Curse God and die.

She stood, looked around, her mind blank. *What can I do?* She looked about the camp, as if searching for something. *What can I do?*

At that moment, she saw Jeb. He stood at a fire circle, two wagons back. She had forgotten about Jeb. He grinned. He had not forgotten her.

She stomped to her wagon, reached under the seat at the front, pulled the Colt from the bag. She held the pistol at her side and stared at Jeb. *C'mon, you son of a bitch. I'm ready for you. I'll shoot you and feel good about it. C'mon!*

Jeb grinned and walked slowly behind his wagon.

THE NEXT MORNING, Molly went to each of the children and found both breathing steadily. She built a fire and made breakfast as she had done every morning. She fixed a plate for Kath and crawled under the wagon. Raising Kath's head, Molly tried to awaken her. Her eyes blinked open, and she licked her lips, but she would eat nothing. Molly held the cup while Kath took a few sips of water, then closed her eyes and lay her head down.

"It's okay, honey, you rest."

Molly took a plate to Rob who sat up and took some

sips of water, but refused the food. He lay back, seemingly exhausted.

Molly went back to the fire, sat and slumped. She was drained. Her mind was blank as she stared at the loose animals beside the trail. She looked around at the bustle of breaking camp and yoking and harnessing animals.

She would not move today; how could she move? She would layover as long as it took to nurse her children back to health. She shook her head at the thought.

"Yes! To health," she said aloud.

She went to the loose animals and found her mare and the four oxen. She brought the animals to camp and tied them with loose leads to the wagon.

The caravan and loose stock moved out, and wagons rolled around Molly's stationary wagon. Some drivers frowned while others waved, knowing too well the circumstances that led to a party laying over.

Molly checked the children often, finding that they were breathing evenly with no difficulty and no new signs of distress.

Most of the morning, she spent sitting at the cold fire, watching the passing wagons and staring at the empty prairie or into space.

Is this what so many others have gone through? I'm not the first to have to deal with cholera. Is this the way it ends? You do what you can, and it's not enough. They slip away, and there's nothing you can do. Pray? What to pray for? God, how about sending me some laudanum? Wait, you don't even need laudanum. You can just say, you are healed. Throw off your blanket, rise and be well again. She rubbed her face vigorously with both hands, her face raised to the heavens and eyes closed.

She opened her eyes abruptly. Hoof beats? She looked at the back trail and saw a rider coming at a gallop. Was it Micah? Her mind heavy with pain and foreboding, she had forgotten Walter and Micah.

Micah pulled up, his horse sliding to a stop. Dismounting, he tied the reins at the back of the wagon and went to Molly. He bent and kissed her upturned face. "Where are the kids?" he said. She motioned to the wagon. He saw Kath on the pallet under the wagon, then hurried to the back of the wagon where Rob lay. He went back to the cold fire and sat by Molly.

"They're both sick," she said, staring into the fire pit. "They won't eat. I don't know what to do." She turned to him. "Walter?"

"He died last night. I buried him where you last saw him. I got here as quickly as I could. I need to hunt, but we need to talk first. There's something new. During nooning yesterday, I talked with some people. They told me things about cholera I didn't know. They said it was most likely caused by bad water. I've suspected that, but they said they are sure. For a fact, the streams where we get water are likely all fouled by dead animals and buffalo carcasses.

"They said the most important treatment is to get the sick person to drink lots of good water to replace all the fluids lost by diarrhea and vomiting. They also said that they had dosed sick people with a solution of sugar and salt with lots of good water. In early cases, the solution seemed to work as well as laudanum. Do you have sugar and salt?"

Molly had listened to every word intently, eyes widening, and had grasped his arm before he finished. "Yes. Johnny liked lots of sugar with his coffee, so we have a good supply. I've hardly touched it. And we still have salt."

"Good. The people I talked with said that they have a man out searching for springs every day so they'll have good water. They told me about a spring just a few miles off the trail back there. I'm riding to that spring right now. I'll take both my canteens and your two buckets. I'll need some cloths or skins to cover the buckets. I'll be back by the time the train stops this evening. Be ready with sugar and salt."

Molly grabbed his shirt and pulled him to her. She hugged him, tried to speak, but could not. She inhaled deeply. "I'll be ready." She kissed him, and both stood.

He took the buckets from hooks on the wagon side while Molly searched in the wagon and found cloths wide enough for tying over the tops of the buckets. He stuffed the cloths and cords into a saddlebag and strapped the buckets on the packhorse. Without another word, he mounted and galloped away, packhorse on its lead following, buckets clattering.

Molly stood beside the wagon and watched him

until he rode over a rising a mile away. *Hope is a man called Micah.*

MICAH PULLED up at Molly's wagon just after the caravan stopped for the night. Drivers unyoked oxen, and women worked on supper while children wandered outside camp collecting buffalo chips.

He dismounted and tied his horse to the back of the wagon. Molly helped him unlash the buckets. Water dripped from the buckets, but the covers had saved most of it.

"Is this from the spring?" Molly said.

"Yes, there were four others there. The word is getting around."

"I have the sugar and salt ready. Let's try it now. It's going to be dark before long. We need to do this now."

Micah pulled back covers from the buckets, poured some of the water from one bucket into the other, filling it to the brim. He replaced the cloth over the full bucket and handed the partially filled bucket to Molly.

"Mix in this bucket. People who use the sugar and salt treatment couldn't agree on the dosage. They just said to experiment." He pondered. "This bucket is about half full. Let's start off with a cup of sugar and about a tablespoon of salt. If they can hold it down, we'll make it stronger."

Molly's hands trembled as she measured out the sugar, poured it in the bucket. She dipped a spoon into the saltcellar, spilling part of the salt.

She gasped. Micah steadied her hand as she reached again for the cellar. Her hand shook. She choked back a sob.

"Easy, Molly. We'll get this done."

She handed the spoon to him, still trembling, and her hands went to her face. "Hurry, Micah," hardly more than a whisper.

He took the spoon, dipped into the cellar, and emptied the salt into the bucket. She stirred the water with a long spoon. "Now? Can we do it now?"

"Keep stirring till the sugar has dissolved. It's almost ready."

She stirred round and round, then reversed direction. "Now?"

"Get a small cup. Who first?"

"Kath, Kath."

They bent and crawled in beside Kath. Micah lifted Kath's head while Molly dipped the cup into the bucket. Molly had calmed, and her hand was steady. She held the cup to Kath's mouth.

"Honey, wake up. I have something good for you. Drink a little of this." Molly touched the cup to her lips. Kath's eyes fluttered open, and she looked up at Molly. She opened her mouth slightly, took a sip and turned away. "A little more, honey?" Kath closed her eyes and moved her face away from the cup.

Molly lowered the cup, dropped her hands to her lap. "Oh, Micah."

"This will take time. Rob now?"

They backed out from under the wagon, stood and

walked to the back. Micah helped Molly climb up into the wagon beside Rob's pallet. He set the bucket beside the bed. Molly dipped the cup in the bucket and raised Rob's head with her other hand. His eyes opened to slits, and he looked at her.

"Rob, honey, I have a nice drink for you. Take a sip."

At the touch of the cup to his lips, he opened his mouth and took a swallow. Then another and another. Then he turned away. Molly lowered his head. Micah took her hand and helped her climb down.

She seemed to wilt, and he caught her in his arms. She leaned on him, her arms dangling and her head pressed against his chest.

She pulled back. "Let's try Kath again."

They went to Kath and repeated the process. She took two small sips before turning away.

They hurried to Rob and this time, he took a few small swallows before pushing the cup away.

Walking back to the side of the wagon, Molly stopped and took Micah's hand. She reached up and kissed him. "It's going to work," she said. "They both took some, and that's a beginning. It's going to work. We'll make it work."

He smiled. "Yes, we will." Taking the cup from her, he attached it to the bucket, pulled the cloth over the bucket top and tied it. "I'll take care of my animals, and I'll tend to yours. We'll keep them on leads so they won't follow the loose stock. I'll water them and find them some grass.

"After I finish with the animals, I'll work on the fire while you work on a fat prairie chicken I'm about to give you. That bird ran right alongside me on the way here, just asking me to shoot it. Maybe our luck is turning good, Molly." He walked toward his horse, his face grim.

After caring for the animals, Micah worked on building a fire pit while Molly went back to Kath with a filled cup of sugar and salt solution. The chicken Micah gave her lay on the ground beside the pile of buffalo chips he had collected. He stood, dusted off his hands and crawled under the wagon to help Molly.

Micah gently raised Kath's head. "Sweetheart, please take a sip," said Molly. She touched the cup to Kath's lips, but her mouth remained closed. "Just a sip, honey. Please try." Kath's eyes opened, seeming to stare at the wagon bottom. Her lips parted a slit, and Molly poured a few drops into her mouth. She closed her mouth and turned her head aside. Micah lowered her shoulders slowly to the pallet. They watched a moment as she breathed evenly, then both crawled outside.

They stood, and Molly brushed her bloomers with both hands. "She took a bit, and she's resting nicely. We'll let her sleep and get back to her later. Let's see to Rob." She pushed back the cover from the bucket, dipped the cup in the water, replaced the cover. She walked toward the back of the wagon. Micah stood a moment, watched her disappear around the wagon side, then followed.

Molly climbed up into the wagon beside Rob's

pallet. Holding the cup with one hand, she raised his head and shoulders with the other. He opened his eyes lazily and looked at her. "Sip this, honey. It's good sweet water." His mouth opened, and she pressed the cup to his lips. He took a swallow, made a face, then leaned forward as if to ask for more. She tilted the cup, and he took more swallows. "That's wonderful, honey. Can you drink some more?" He nodded. She kissed his forehead, handed the cup to Micah.

Micah ran around to the bucket and filled the cup, came back and handed it to Molly. She raised it to Rob's mouth, and he drank, finishing the cup.

"More," he said, a weak whisper. Molly gave the cup to Micah, held Rob in her arms, tears rolling down her cheeks. Micah reappeared with the full cup, and she held it to his mouth. He emptied the cup, then leaned back. Molly lowered him to the pallet.

"Sleep now, honey. I'll be back." She watched his steady breathing a while, then climbed down. On the ground, she grabbed handfuls of Micah's shirt and sobbed against his chest. He encircled her shoulders and held her. They walked to the side of the wagon.

"We'll lay over in this camp till they are up to moving," she said.

"Rob is doing pretty good," Micah said. "How about putting him in my tent? I'll set up Walter's tent right alongside, and I'll sleep there. We can put Kath in the wagon, and you'll be close by. Will that work?"

She put her arms around his waist and rested her head on his chest. "Yes, that will work. Thank you,

Micah McQueen. Thank you for everything. Thank you for being here."

"You're a strong woman. You'll make it through all this."

She squeezed him hard and released. "Now let's get some supper. Can you build up the fire so we can have some light?"

"Good idea. I'll try to find some wood to put on the chips." He raised her chin and kissed her lips. "I'm sorta getting used to you fixing supper."

She smiled in spite of recently thinking that she may never smile again. That thought was quickly replaced by her conviction that the children were going to survive this ordeal, and she would laugh every day the rest of her life.

Molly plucked the chicken while Micah built up the fire with dry sticks collected under the nearby cottonwoods. That finished, he took the two small tents from the wagon and walked to the grassy edge of the trail where he pitched them side-by-side.

Micah returned, sat down, and they ate without comment, spooning cold rice from plates and pulling strips from the roasted bird. Molly wiped her hands with a cloth and stood. "I'm going to check Kath." She filled a cup with sugar water and stooped to crawl under the wagon.

"Mama." It was Rob. Molly straightened and ran to the back of the wagon, still holding the cup. The wagon interior was almost dark, but there he was, sitting, wide-eyed. "I'm hungry."

Molly squeezed her eyes shut, opened them, determined not to cry. "I'll get something right now, honey." She reached over the tailgate, took his hand and kissed it. "Be right back." She ran to the fire.

"Micah, Rob said he's hungry! Fix him a plate, please, while I check Kath." She crawled under the wagon to Kath, still carrying the filled cup.

Molly slid a hand under Kath's head and lifted it to the cup. She stopped, leaned back so the firelight would illuminate Kath's face. Her eyes were open, seeming to stare, unblinking. Molly lowered Kath's head and set the cup down. She touched Kath's cheek. It was cool, showing a light blue pallor. She put her hand lightly on Kath's chest and knew it was finished. She held her own cheeks in her hands, rocking back and forth. Gently closing Kath's eyes, she leaned over, encircled her shoulders and lifted her, hugging her sweet daughter as the tears came.

She lowered her to the pallet, pulled the blanket to her chin and caressed her cheek. Crawling from under the wagon, she stood and went to the fire. She sat down heavily beside Micah, rocked back and forth. He put an arm around her shoulders, and she rested her head on his shoulder.

"She's gone," Molly said softly. "What am I going to do? Why couldn't I help her?" She leaned forward, sobbing into her hands.

"You did everything we knew to do. There's nothing else you could have done."

She sat upright suddenly. "Rob! I told him I would bring him some supper. I must do that."

"You asked me to do that. Got it right here." He showed her the filled plate of rice and small strips of chicken. "I'll take it to him."

"No, I want to do it. I need to take care of Rob." She took the plate and leaned into him, sobbing, gasping.

"Let's both do it. C'mon."

They stood, walked to the back of the wagon, Molly carrying the plate and the cup of sugar water. With Micah's help, Molly climbed over the tailgate and sat beside the pallet. In the near darkness, she touched Rob's cheek, and he stirred. "I have some supper for you, honey," she said. He sat up, rubbed his eyes, and she set the plate in his lap. She fed him small pieces of the hen and spoons of rice. "Slowly, honey. You haven't eaten in a while, and you need to get used to eating again, so a little at a time."

After cleaning his plate, he took the cup from Molly and emptied it without lowering it.

"That's my boy." She took the cup and plate, kissed his cheek. He lay down, snuggling as she pulled the cover to his chin. Climbing from the dark interior to the ground, she turned and looked at Rob a long moment.

She took Micah's arm, and they walked to the fire and sat down. He picked up a couple of chips, dropped them on the embers. The chips ignited, and the low flames glowed blue and yellow.

"I want to bury her in Oregon," she said, staring into the fire.

"You know that's not possible, don't you?"

She stared into the flames. "Yes. . . . I don't think I'll ever get over just leaving her here on this prairie."

They sat silent, alternately watching the dancing flames and studying the starry heavens.

Micah looked over at her. "Why don't we plant one of the saplings you brought from your farm? I'll put it in the green grass in that swale over there." He pointed at dark shapes dimly outlined by firelight. "There's a little stand of pines in a low spot. Looks like it holds moisture pretty good. You might want to come back and visit this spot someday. I'll draw a map, and we'll estimate how far east it is from Fort Laramie, and I bet we, uh, you, could find this place again."

She studied his face, looked back at the fire. "I would like that."

Chapter 8

AT FIRST LIGHT, before sunrise and before other emigrants stirred, Micah began digging the grave beside the wagon, right where the fire circle had been. He had explained to Molly that teams and wagons would pass over the site, and all traces of the burial would be erased. The ground would be packed, and animals and Indians would see no evidence of a grave.

Molly and Rob, a blanket wrapped around his shoulders, watched Micah shovel loose soil from the trench. Rob held Molly's hand, alternately watching Micah and looking up at Molly.

She had a hard time talking with Rob that morning and was not sure that he grasped the full meaning of death, that he would never again see his sister in this life. Molly had never broached the subject of an afterlife with the children since her doubts had just about been replaced by disbelief. She wished now she believed. She will always be with us in our hearts, she had told him.

She was not sure he understood; she was not sure she understood.

Micah stopped digging when the sides of the hole were level with his waist and the hard sod would yield no more. He wiped perspiration from his face with a hand, wiped the hand on his trousers. Climbing out, he dropped the shovel and walked to the wagon.

He crawled under the wagon and tightened the blanket around the little burden that had been Kath. He picked her up, scooted out, then stood and walked to the grave. He knelt and laid the body gently beside the excavation.

"Molly?"

She nodded. Micah slid down into the hole, picked up the blanket-shrouded body and laid it gently in the bottom. He climbed out and, standing beside the grave, scooped up a handful of soil from the mound. Molly took Rob's hand, and they walked to the grave. She picked up a handful of loose soil, reached over the yawning pit, opened her hand, and the soil trickled down to the blanket. Micah dropped his soil over the body.

"Rob, would you like to do this?' said Molly. "It's our way of saying goodbye. And . . . and we'll see you again in a better place." She looked at Micah.

Rob looked up at Molly, frowning.

"Would you do it, honey? For me? And Kath. You'll be glad you did."

Rob bent down, took a handful of soil and tossed it into the pit. He looked at Micah, then Molly. "I'm going to the wagon." Head hanging, he turned and walked away slowly.

Molly reached for Micah, hung on his arm and sobbed. Micah put his arms around her shoulders and held her.

"We're going to see her in a better place?" she said. "Why did I say that? I still hope . . . I still wish . . ." She choked back a sob.

"Don't think about it. Not now. You're going to make it, Molly. You've got a fine little boy, and he's going to grow up to be a fine young man. And you're going to have a good farm in Oregon."

She squeezed his arm, inhaled deeply, exhaled, looked up at him. She wiped her face with a hand. "Why do we always want better when we have good? I wonder whether I will ever look back on all this and see any good in it."

He frowned and looked down.

She looked up at him, squeezed his arm, looked down. "I don't mean you, Micah. You know that. You're the only good thing that has happened to us since we left Independence."

He smiled, ducked his head. "Why don't you see if you can come up with some breakfast while I finish up here. Then I'll plant that tree, if that's okay."

"Yes, please."

They looked at the line of wagons, now in motion. "The train is moving," said Micah, "and that's okay. We'll leave when we're ready."

As the caravan rolled around Molly's wagon, some

drivers nodded or waved. Most moved ahead, ignoring the wagon at the side of the trail, knowing why it was stationary, hoping that the next wagon pulled off the trail would not be theirs.

Micah finished filling the grave and tamped it down with the shovel. He brought their four oxen from the herd and walked them over the grave, back and forth, back and forth, until all traces of a burial were obliterated.

He yoked the oxen and ate a cold breakfast of beans and hard biscuit with Molly, standing beside the wagon. She had fed Rob at his pallet in the wagon. He was hungry and thirsty, which lifted Molly's spirits, but he was quiet and asked if he could stay in the wagon for a while. Stay as long as you want, she told him.

When Micah finished planting the tree, he called Molly. She went to Rob and asked him if he felt good enough to come as well. He climbed down and followed her to the copse where Micah stood.

"I think it will do fine here. It will get morning sun and shade in the hot afternoon. Judging from the healthy green grass in this low spot, it will get the moisture it needs. When you see it again, it's going to be big and strong."

"Thank you, Micah." She took Rob's hand, squeezed it. "This is from the farm, honey. When we see it again, it will be as big as the big tree in the front yard. Do you remember that one, the one with the swing?"

"Yeah, I remember. I like that swing." He looked up at Molly. "Can I have a swing at our house in Oregon?"

"You will have a swing. Promise."

"Speaking of Oregon . . ." said Micah.

"Yes." She turned to Rob. "Do you want to ride or walk this morning, sweetheart?"

"Can I ride a while? Can I ride in the front?"

"Yes, as long as you like, anywhere you like. Go on and climb up. We'll be right along."

They watched him go. Molly took Micah's hand and looked down at the sapling. "I will come back someday." Her eyes glistened. "Did you draw the map? I want to know how to find where she is buried."

"I have, a pretty good map, if I say so myself. I made two copies. You should put them in different places."

"You keep one, will you, in case . . . in case . . . in case I lose mine."

She put her arms around his waist, leaned her head against his chest. He encircled her shoulders and held her.

"Micah, Micah. What are we going to do? I'm so torn."

"We don't need to make plans, Molly. We'll just go along like we've been going along and see what happens. Right now, we need to get moving. Oregon and the snows are not going to hold still while we're holding still."

She didn't move.

"Time to go," he said.

She hesitated. "I need to show you something." Taking his hand, she walked to the back of the wagon.

She pushed blankets aside to reveal the purpose-built boxes underneath that held everything from clothing and needles and thread to food supplies and utensils. In the center of the bed, two boxes from the tailgate, she carefully lifted a box and set it aside.

"Now that's interesting. I thought all the boxes were the same size."

The box she put aside was half-height. She reached into the space, took out another half-height box and laid it beside the first one. She released the latch on the box and opened the lid. Setting aside a piece of folded burlap, she untied the leather laces on a heavy canvas bag, reached inside and pushed the top open.

"There," she said, stepping back.

Micah leaned over the bag. His eyes opened wide. "Whoa. Did you rob a bank or somethin'?" He looked at a sack of gold coins. He turned to Molly, frowning.

"We got a good price for the farm, really more than we expected. That's our farm in that sack. Our old farm in Missouri and the new farm in Oregon."

Reaching into the sack, he picked up a handful of coins. Mostly ten-dollar gold eagles, with a few five-dollar half-eagles and some of the new twenty-dollar double eagles. He turned them over and over, as if examining, pondering.

"I'm . . . sorry I haven't told you about the money," she said. "I just . . . I just needed, uh—"

He turned to her, smiled. "You don't need to apologize to me, Molly. You needed to know that I was going to be around for a while. You needed to know that

I wouldn't decide that I needed that sack of gold more than I needed a sweet woman."

She wrapped her arms around his waist and squeezed. "Well? How did I know you weren't just some ol' lonesome cowboy who drifted into my life and was just as likely to drift out of it the same way?"

"Well, now I know what you think of me. A drifter." He frowned, then a hint of a smile.

She leaned back. "No, Micah, no, you know that's not what I think. Not now."

He turned away, and she released him. He put the coins he had been examining back into the sack and tightened the drawstrings. "Now let's put this stash away before some lonesome cowboy drifter sees it."

She hit him on the arm and pushed him away. "I'll do that. You go on about your business."

"Okay." He watched while she replaced the folded burlap and closed and latched the box. "Now that I know where it's hid." He smiled and jumped back as she took another swing at him that found only air.

She mumbled aloud as she pulled the blankets over the boxes. "Now I gotta find someplace else to hide the bag." He laughed.

"You okay up there, Rob?" Micah called. Rob waved. Micah turned to Molly. "Does Rob know about that stash?"

"No."

"You need to tell him. That belongs to him, too."

*****

MOLLY'S WAGON was back in line. She and Micah walked beside the lead ox. Molly looked back occasionally to check on Rob. He sat on the wagon floor at the front, partially shaded by the seat and the sloping top.

They had been on the road less than an hour when they saw a small cast iron cook stove at the side of the trail.

"If we were five miles from the Willamette Valley, I would want that stove," said Molly. It wasn't the first castoff they had seen. They saw the first only a week from Independence, a large chifferobe. Since then, abandoned goods had become commonplace. A stove, table, bedsprings, heavy tools, even bedding, anything that was not essential at the moment, anything that was beginning to make the haul harder on the draft animals.

"Leeverites," the emigrants called the abandoned goods: "leave 'er right here."

Some of the early castoffs had notes attached, inviting any following to claim the piece for their own. There were few takers. As days and miles passed, emigrants became increasingly aware that their teams were wearing down. They decided that abandoning anything in their wagon clearly not essential could only give relief to the animals.

"Mama." Molly looked back to see Rob standing in the wagon bed at the front. "I want to walk." She hurried to the wagon, reached up and helped him climb down. He smiled.

"You're looking like the old Rob. How do you feel?"

"I feel pretty good. Let's walk!"

She bent and kissed the top of his head. Taking his hand, they walked in the shade of the wagon.

"Micah!" he shouted. Micah turned and waved, and Rob returned the wave. Molly laid a hand on his head, looked up into the cloudless, blue sky. *Thank you, Lord, if you had a hand in this.*

"Look, Mama, Indians." A dozen mounted Indians about a hundred yards ahead reined in and stopped beside the train. Three dismounted, and one spoke to a driver who pulled his wagon out of the moving caravan. When Molly's wagon caught up, Micah pulled the wagon out and stopped behind the stationary wagon. He walked toward the Indians.

"What's going on?" said Molly.

He stopped, held up a hand to Molly, turned and walked ahead.

What does that mean?

"I want to go see the Indians," said Rob.

She smiled, cocked her head, took his hand and walked to Micah who by this time had come up to the Indians and driver. An Indian was speaking to the driver in his own language, leaving the driver mute and confused.

"You are Cheyenne, I think," said Micah in Lakota.

The Indian looked at Micah, frowning. He replied in Lakota. "We are Cheyenne. How do you speak Lakota?"

"I lived with the Lakota. I am Otaktay. How do you speak the Lakota language?"

"My woman is Lakota. She said she would not stay unless I learned her language. She is a good cook and warms my bed. I learned Lakota."

"You are a wise man. What do you say to the emigrant drivers?"

"The whites cross our land. Your animals trample our grass and eat our grass, and your hunters kill our game. Each wagon must pay trade goods or fifty cents to cross our land."

"Fifty cents? Where did you learn of our money?"

"Traders at Fort Laramie say fifty cents. They say we can buy things at the fort with the money."

Molly had listened to the conversation, knowing it was friendly, but nothing more. "What's going on, Micah?"

"They are Cheyenne, friends to the Lakota. They want fifty cents a wagon to cross their lands. Seems a reasonable request. I'll pay it."

"Their lands? Indians own land? I thought the plains Indians weren't settled down. I thought they moved around."

He looked at the Indian, who had listened intently to this conversation, looking back and forth between Micah and Molly as they talked, likely understanding nothing. The other Indians watched and listened as well.

Micah turned back to Molly. "We need to talk tonight at supper."

Micah pulled a small leather pouch from a pocket,

extracted a fifty-cent piece and handed it to the Cheyenne. "I will pass the word to the other drivers," he said in Lakota. "Some will pay, and some will not. Take what you are given, and be content. Look at this caravan." He pointed to the line ahead that stretched to the horizon and to the line behind that disappeared around a distant outcropping. "Every wagon has three guns. We come in peace and will continue to pass through your country. Soon cold and snows will come, and we will be gone. There will be only the Cheyenne and the Lakota and the buffalo and antelope and wolf."

The Cheyenne looked hard at Micah. "You speak wisely. Maybe you should come to our village and learn our language. We will give you a Cheyenne name, and you will take a Cheyenne woman."

Micah smiled, and the warriors laughed. He took Molly's arm and Rob's hand, and they walked toward their wagon.

Molly frowned at him. "What was that all about? What were they laughing at?"

"We'll talk. I'll tell you." He smiled.

"Michael McQueen. You . . ." She punched him on his arm.

Rob looked from Molly to Micah, frowning. Micah looked down at him. Rob smiled, gripped Micah's hand tighter.

MOLLY STACKED the clean supper dishes in a box at the back of the wagon. She walked to the fire, wiping her hands with a towel. She sat at the fire circle beside Micah.

"Okay," she said. "The Indians."

"Right," he said. He told her about the conversation with the Cheyenne warriors, their respect for him, the invitation to come with them, the assurance that he could take a Cheyenne woman.

"Were they serious?"

"Oh, yes. It was light-hearted banter, but they were serious. They might have been surprised if I joined them, but they would have accepted me as one of their band without thinking about it."

She stared into the fire. "Did you think about it? About going with them?"

He did not look at her, watching the flames. "No. It's over. It's behind me. I am done with it, but not with the memory. It's possible to hold to a beloved memory without being consumed by it, without letting it fill the empty places and prevent something new." He looked at her. "Does that make sense?"

She took his arm and leaned her head on it. "Yes, Michael Micah McQueen. It makes a lot of sense." She leaned back, pursed her lips. "What doesn't make sense was the Indian that wanted payment for crossing their land. I thought Indians didn't own land?"

"That's complicated. They don't own it in the sense that we understand land ownership. A tribe believes that it has claim to certain territory for the use of the whole tribe. They will fight anyone who disputes this claim on their ancestral lands. No individual, even a chief, can sell the land. There is confusion sometimes when a chief or headmen accept money from somebody, say, the U.S. government. The government thinks it has bought the land; the Indians believe they have given the government permission to use the land in some way, but they don't believe they have sold the land. I suppose they believe they have accepted a fee for joint use of the land. The problem comes when the government, believing they have bought the land, tries to make the Indians obey certain rules or when the government tries to move them off the land.

"Sorry if this isn't clear. I'm not sure I understand it myself."

"I understand. I think."

MICAH RODE out at first light. He had taken nothing on his last hunt, and they had been without meat for four days. He said he would be back by sundown. She had watched him until he disappeared over a rising. She stared now at the spot where she last saw him. Shaking her head, she turned and walked around the wagon. *Stop it. You are not dependent. You are independent. . . . But I love that man.*

Molly sat at the fire, took a pan from the embers and poured hot water into a bucket. She began washing soiled breakfast dishes and some others left over from yesterday's supper. She watched Rob strolling in the short wet grass beside the trail, bending to pick the small pink flowers an emigrant called Lady's Thumb because, she said, they looked like a lady's thumb. A light rain in the afternoon had settled the dust on the trail and left the grass sparkling in the slanting sun's rays. The rain cloud had moved westward, and on the horizon, miles ahead of the caravan, rain fell silently in a silver curtain.

Rob handed the flowers to Molly. "Thank you, honey," she said. "They're sweet." She put the bouquet in a cup she filled from the water bucket.

"Mama, can I go see Olin? They're right there." He pointed.

Molly looked down the line to see Beth and Olin standing three wagons back, waving.

"Yes, honey. Stay in sight so I can see you."

"If they ask me to stay for supper, can I?"

"You can, but wave to me, and get my attention so I'll know. I want you back here well before dark. Hear me?"

"Yes, Mama." She watched him walk away and stop at Beth's wagon. Beth waved again, and Molly returned the wave.

Molly and Beth had walked together and visited each other as often as their chores and proximity permitted. Beth and Olin and Jessie were happy with their situation and in as good health as might be expected on this grueling journey. The two mothers avoided any comment about cholera, which had altered their lives for all time and still hung like a specter over the caravan. Both hoped that some old timers in the caravan who had been on the trail before were right when they repeatedly urged anyone who would listen to hang on till they reach the mountains. That's when the cholera tapers off, they said.

Molly stood and put the clean dishes in the back of the wagon. She leaned against the sideboards, pushed her hair back and rubbed her face. She looked across the prairie in all directions for any sign of Micah.

The dark cloud in the west had thinned, and the orange sun disc hovered just above the horizon. Rob had returned after having a cold supper with Beth and the children, and Molly had helped him climb into the wagon to his bed. Now shadows of sagebrush and wagons lengthened, and the land turned gray. Molly strained, searching the prairie, but he was not there.

What if he doesn't come back? What if he remembered his life with the Indians and decided to go back? To escape the turmoil of this godawful journey. Maybe he will decide that he doesn't want to even think about a settled life on a farm in Oregon where he would be planted as sure as the wheat and tomatoes are planted?

She leaned against the wagon side. A light breeze tousled loose strands of hair and cooled her cheeks. She closed her eyes, lowered her head.

What am I doing, Johnny? I miss you so much, sometimes I want to search for you wherever you are. Then I remember Rob. And Micah, and I don't know what to do. I can't let you go, Johnny. People here tell me to get on with my life. They say you're gone, and I'll never have you again. Make a new life, they say. What should I do? Oh, Johnny, if only you could tell me what to do.

She opened her eyes and looked westward over the line of wagons. Only the top of the orange globe showed above the line of the horizon. Gradually, the lacy cloud layer above the setting sun turned a dazzling array of pastel colors that gathered, lengthened, arced and touched the ground at each end to form a perfect rainbow. She leaned forward and stared, her eyes wide, mouth open.

Then she saw the horseman. He was in the center of the arc of the rainbow, riding toward the wagons. As he approached, she made out the loaded packhorse behind.

Her hand went to her mouth, and she sobbed. Then she smiled, laughed out loud, gasped and sobbed again.

Micah reined in, dismounted quickly, let the reins trail and ran to her. "Are you okay? What's wrong?"

She put her arms around his neck. "Just hold me," sobbing, laughing. He put his arms lightly around her waist.

He leaned back. "What's up?"

"We'll talk. I'll tell you."

He smiled, wrinkling his forehead. "We have lots to talk about."

They went to the packhorse where he untied two prairie hens and handed them to her. He untied the dressed antelope carcass, lowered it to the ground and pulled it to grass off the trail. Leaving it, he led the two horses to a patch of grass and hobbled them. He watered them with a bucket of water drawn from the wagon's barrel.

Returning to the antelope, he cut off small chunks and deposited them in a container in the wagon bed. He pulled the carcass to a double line of wagons nearby, told bystanders to help themselves and walked away. They shouted their thanks to his back and immediately began carving the welcome bonanza.

Micah returned to the fire circle where Molly was roasting one of the prairie hens. He sat down, grunting, exhaling heavily.

"Tired?" she said.

"Yep, and hungry." He leaned over and kissed her cheek.

"Micah, where have you been?" It was Rob, walking hand-in-hand with Beth. She smiled and waved.

"Hello, Beth," said Micah. He pretended a punch in Rob's stomach, and Rob recoiled, laughing, and fell into his lap.

"Have you two had supper?" said Molly.

"Yeah, it was good," Rob said.

"I'm on my way," Beth said. "Been a long day, and I'm for my bed. G'night, all." She smiled, raised a hand in farewell.

"Night, Beth," Molly said.

"Bye," said Rob, "thanks for supper." Beth waved over her shoulder.

Molly turned to Rob. "And you're off to bed, too, sweetheart. Head for the bushes, and we'll get you to bed. Rob jumped up, ran behind a sage at the edge of firelight, then returned buttoning his pants.

"Night, little buddy," said Micah. Rob hugged him around his neck while Molly cocked her head. Micah watched them walk to the back of the wagon.

Molly returned after a minute and sat on the ground beside Micah. "I think he likes you." She took the rod from the forked irons and pushed the roasted bird onto a plate on the ground between them. He pulled off a leg, steam rising from the cooked flesh. She cut a slice from the breast, skewered it with a fork and ate slowly, looking up at him occasionally. Waiting.

They ate in silence as campfires up and down the caravan lowered and died one by one. The darkness left them sitting in a small globe of light that was, for this moment, their universe. They looked up at the sky, crowded with brilliant, sparkling stars.

He moved close, put an arm over her shoulders. "Now you tell me why you were giggling and crying at the same time when I rode up."

She smiled and told him. At the very moment when she was looking for some sort of sign that would set the course of her life, to see him riding out from the very heart of the most beautiful rainbow she had ever seen was inspiring. And hilarious. She stifled a sob, gasped and laughed out loud. "Don't you see," she said. "Does that make sense?"

He smiled. "Well, you got me there. That's a question that I can't answer for you. You got to answer that yourself."

The fire hissed as raindrops began falling. Molly scrambled up, pulled her shawl over her head. "Under the wagon. I already put the blankets down."

"Uh, I can get my tent up."

"You'll be soaked before you can get a tent up."

Hunched over, they ran to the wagon and crawled under as the sprinkles turned to large raindrops.

She sat on the pallet, removed her jacket and shoes, wriggled out of her bloomers, lay down and pulled up the cover. She watched Micah.

Micah sat beside her on the blanket. He removed his coat, set it aside and looked down at her. She stared at him, her face blank, both hands holding the cover at her chin. He tugged on the cover, and she released it.

"You'll need to take your boots off," she said.

"Yes, ma'am." He pulled off his boots and slid under the cover.

She moved close, and he unbuttoned her shirt, slid a hand under her camisole and found a breast.

"Ooh, cold!" she said.

"Warm me up." He kissed her as he fumbled with the drawstring on her drawers. She pushed his hand away and pulled the drawstring, opening the waistband. He pulled her to him as she felt for his belt.

Chapter 9

FIRST LIGHT. Molly kneeled at the fire, turning the spit holding a chunk of meat cut from the antelope Micah had bagged the day before. The buck had stood just off the trail at the edge of a pine copse, he had said, still as a statue, watching this strange apparition, the column of wagons snaking across the prairie.

She pulled the steaming coffee pot to the edge of the embers. Moving the biscuits around in the skillet, she lifted one with a fork to see the bottom. She looked up to see Rob walking toward the fire, rubbing his face, hair flying in all directions.

"Honey, come to the fire," she said.

He walked toward Molly, then stopped when he looked under the wagon and saw Micah who had stirred at Molly's voice. Now Micah sat on the blankets, looking at Rob.

Rob turned toward Molly, frowning, puzzled, then back at Micah, back to Molly.

Molly was about to speak when Rob crawled under the wagon and sat on the blanket beside Micah.

"Morning, Rob," said Micah. "Ready for some breakfast?"

Rob looked at Molly, back to Micah. "Are you going to marry my mama?"

Molly snorted, recovered. "Come to breakfast, you two. The meat's ready, and the biscuits are going to burn. Come on over here."

Micah tousled Rob's hair and threw the blanket off. "Go on, buddy, I'll be right there." While Rob crawled outside, Micah struggled into his pants and buttoned them. He pulled his boots on and crawled from underneath the wagon. He stood, stretched, and ran past the fire across the trail and disappeared behind a large sage.

While Rob and Molly watched, Micah reappeared and ambled to the fire circle. "I'm ready for some hot breakfast and hot coffee," he said. "How 'bout you, little buddy?"

"Yeah, I'm hungry," said Rob. Molly handed him a plate holding a fork, a steaming biscuit and small bits of venison she had cut up. He took a bite of the biscuit and forked a piece of meat. He turned to Micah. "Are you?"

Micah took a plate from Molly and concentrated on it. Molly was caught between laughing and blushing. She filled her plate and commented about the sunrise, the temperature, the tasty venison, and did they like the biscuits, the first she had made in weeks.

Micah quickly complimented her on the biscuits,

agreed that the sunrise was beautiful, though he had not seen it, and that the venison was tasty. He stood, said he had to get the stock ready for the leaving.

"You haven't had your coffee," said Molly, stifling a grin.

"Oh, uh, no, I haven't. I'll take it with me. If that's all right."

She poured coffee into a cup and handed it to him. He took the cup, nodded his thanks, tousled Rob's hair and walked toward the loose stock. Molly smiled, pursed her lips, leaned over and kissed Rob's cheek.

Molly pulled the pan of hot water from the fire and commenced washing the breakfast dishes. She smiled to herself, remembering the night, then sobered.

How can I ever feel good about anything again when I have lost my precious Kath?

She shook her head, wiped the dishes vigorously, wincing when her hand remained too long in the hot water.

She looked at Micah's back as he moved through the loose animals, apparently searching for Molly's oxen. He sipped from the cup as he walked.

Molly laid the clean dishes on the board beside the fire circle. They would dry while she helped Micah with the yoking. She stood and looked for him. The herd had moved a good distance from the train during the night, and a number of drivers walked among the animals collecting their beasts.

The herd was too far away to recognize the men walking among the animals, but she surely would recognize Micah. But she could not be sure. Maybe he had walked into the streamside willow copse beyond the animals to relieve himself again.

MICAH STEPPED GINGERLY DOWN the steep bank of the stream. He squatted at the water's edge, dipped the cup in the water and rinsed it, filled it and sipped. It was clear and cool. He would suggest to Molly that they drive down to the stream to fill the water barrel before setting out this morning.

He stood, stretched, and rubbed his hands to dry them. Turning, he looked down to find his path up the steep bank. He took one step and looked up into the barrel of Jeb's pistol.

Jeb grinned. He stood at the top of the bank, looking down. "Now ain't this a predicament? You always seem to git th' drop on me. Now I got the drop on you. You ain't going to get in my way with th' little purty no more. You ain't gonna be around."

Micah looked in both directions in the streambed and on the bank, searching for help or an opportunity. He saw nobody, nothing. He looked up at Jeb.

"Jeb, you better think about this. If you shoot me, the drivers at the stock will hear the shot. They'll come down and find you holding a pistol and standing over a dead man. What do you think's going to happen then?"

Jeb frowned, shifted his feet. He brightened. "I'm gonna git outta here before they git here. There's this bunch of trees there." He motioned with the gun toward the willows.

"There's no place to hide, Jeb. Why don't you just put the pistol away and get back to your wagon and your boy? What's going to happen to your boy after they hang you? I think you saw the hanging a while back."

Jeb shifted his feet nervously. "Yeah, I saw it, but that ain't gonna happen to me. And you ain't gonna get in the way again of me having my way with the little purty."

He raised the pistol, aimed. A shot exploded, Micah jerked back, and Jeb pitched forward. He rolled down the bank, coming to rest at Micah's feet.

Micah looked up and saw Molly walk to the edge, holding the Colt at her side. She was rigid, her face ashen.

He climbed up the embankment, took the Colt from her shaking hand and wrapped his arms around her shoulders. She shuddered, gripped his shirt with both hands and buried her head in the folds.

"You're okay, Molly." He held her tightly. "You saved my life."

"You're shaking," she said softly into his ear.

"I am. I thought I was dead. I've never been that close to being dead." He inhaled heavily, exhaled. He leaned back.

"How did you know I was down there on the creek bank? You couldn't see me."

"I saw Jeb passing through the loose stock. He was looking the way you had gone. I followed and saw him standing on the bank, looking down. I heard him talking. I couldn't understand what he was saying, but I knew he was talking to you. I was quiet, but he wouldn't have heard me if I was yelling my head off. He had you on his mind. Finally, I heard what he was saying."

"Well, I'm sure glad you did. Now, we need to get back." He stopped, held up a hand, climbed down the bank and retrieved his cup. He showed it to her. "Don't want to lose this."

They walked back toward the wagon, meeting half a dozen men who had heard the shot and came running to investigate. "Did you hear the shot?" said one. "Did you see anything?" said another.

"You'll see a dead man down by the creek," Micah said. "I'm reporting to the captain." The men ran toward the creek.

Molly and Micah stopped at their campfire. "Before I see Bonney," Micah said, "how about some more of your good coffee? I need to stop shaking."

While Molly poured coffee, Rob ran up from Beth's wagon where Molly had sent him when she went to look for Micah. Molly set the coffee pot down and grabbed him, hugging tightly.

"Ow, Mama."

She released him, smiled. "Little man, help me collect the oxen and yoke them. Time you started to pull your weight around here."

"Yeah!" said Rob. Micah gave him a playful punch on the arm. Molly took Rob's hand, turned to Micah.

"You gonna be all right?" she said.

He nodded, held up the coffee cup. "Long as you keep making good coffee, I'm okay. I'll check with the captain and be back before you pull out."

Molly and Rob found their four oxen and had just finished yoking when Micah returned.

"What did Captain Bonney have to say?" said Molly.

"He listened without a word. I think he had something on his mind. Anyway, he said he wouldn't be surprised at anything Jeb would do. Jeb was a troublemaker, and he had complaints from other people in the caravan about him. He said he would assign a couple of men to a burial detail, and said the affair was settled as of now. Okay by me. I asked about Jeb's boy. He said he would see he was taken care of. Glad I'm not the captain."

"Now what?" said Molly.

The train moved slowly as wagons a mile or so ahead veered off both sides of the trail and stacked up. A line of scattered cottonwoods and willows suggested a stream causing the congestion.

When Molly's wagon neared the gathering, they saw that wagons were crossing the stream, narrow but with deep holes. Some wagons briefly floated, accompanied by a barrage of shouting and cursing before pulling up the far bank.

One driver was not so fortunate. As onlookers on each bank watched in horror, his wagon floated in midstream, and water washed over the backs of the terrified oxen. The driver, standing knee-deep in the shallows on the far side, watched everything he owned swept away.

Most drivers chose not to risk a water crossing. They stacked up before a crude bridge of logs and rough-hewn planks. Every wagon that reached the bridge was stopped by half a dozen Indians that confronted the driver who generally responded with arm waving and cursing. A few meekly paid the required toll.

"What do you suggest?" said Molly.

"Pull into the line. You don't want to risk the water."

They waited, strolled about, chatted with other drivers, listening to complaints mostly. Every delay, every activity other than driving oxen westward, was interpreted as the loss of California gold or Oregon land.

Molly's wagon finally reached the bridge. The Snake spokesman held up a hand, signaling a stop, and said simply, "twenty-five cents." In the other hand, he held a white feather.

Micah pulled out his small leather pouch, extracted a twenty-five cent piece and handed it to him. The Snake frowned, obviously surprised to be paid without argument. He stepped aside.

"Giddyup," Micah said. With some urging and whip touches, the team pulled across the rough bridge. Molly and Rob followed the wagon. Across the bridge, Micah drove the team to an open spot and stopped, waiting for Molly and Rob.

They were immediately approached by three Indian men, each holding a white feather. Snakes, Micah told Molly.

"Why the feathers?" she said.

"It means they come in peace," he said.

While one of the Indians went to Micah, the other two walked to the wagon and examined the tools and buckets hanging on the side. One went to the back of the wagon and looked inside.

The Snake stopped before Micah. "Trade," he said. "Me good man. See." He pulled some papers from a pouch and handed them to Micah. The Snake nodded.

The papers were handwritten. One read: "Don't have any truck with this Indian. He's a thief and will rob you blind." Another said: "Don't take your eyes off this devil. He will steal anything not nailed down." Micah looked up at the Snake who nodded, smiling, happy to show off the references.

Micah looked to the two Snakes hovering about the wagon. "Hey!" When they looked his way, he motioned them to move away from the wagon. The two stepped away from the wagon and looked grimly at the Indian talking with Micah.

At that moment, Molly walked around the front of the lead yoke. She cradled a rifle in her arms. Micah and the three Indians looked her way.

"You bad man!" the Snake spokesman said. He and the other two turned and walked toward a collection of wagons down the bank.

Micah grinned at Molly, walked to her. "You bad

woman!" He kissed her, took the rifle from her. He checked it, found it was not loaded. "You not very smart bad woman." She smiled.

"LARA-MEE! LARA-MEE! FORT LARA-MEE!" The caravan had just stopped for noon when the rider galloped down the train, shouting to no one in particular. Drivers, some in the process of unyoking oxen, and others stopped what they were doing to watch the agitated rider race past.

The news was most welcome. Fort Laramie was a much-anticipated waypoint in the overland journey. An important fur trade post in the first half of the nineteenth century, the United States Army bought the fort from the American Fur Company just last year, 1849, to serve as a strong point in the Indian wars and to protect emigrants. Three companies of cavalry arrived at the post soon after the purchase.

When it was a fur trading post, the fort was a magnet to Indians who visited often and in great numbers. As a military facility, the post remained more a magnet than a threat. Like the relations between Indians and emigrants, peaceful interaction between Indians and soldiers was more common than hostile contact.

Arriving at the fort, some overlanders hardly paused before pushing on, fearful of an early snow that could make their transit of the mountains impossible. Others camped outside the fort's walls, determined to satisfy their curiosity about this semblance of civilization in the wilderness.

None tarried long. Most emigrants quickly became uneasy if they were not on the trail, moving toward their destinations before the California gold or the Oregon land was spoken for. A week before arriving at the fort, mail carriers from Salt Lake had passed the caravan, heading east. They said they had passed 8,000 wagons between Salt Lake and Fort Laramie. Since leaving the fort, they had stopped counting.

Molly wanted to visit the fort to satisfy curiosity, but she also was drawn to it because of Micah's experience here. As they strolled from the campground toward the fort's entrance, Micah was solemn, responding to Molly's and Rob's questions briefly, then lapsing into silence. They stopped at the entrance to watch a band of two dozen Lakota that held the leads of a dozen packhorses loaded with buffalo hides. One of the Indians talked with a fort employee just inside the gate. The employee motioned the Lakota through the gate. Micah, Molly and Rob stepped aside and watched the Indians file in. Micah noticed that one of the Lakota looked with considerable interest at Molly.

Once the Indians had passed through the entrance, Micah and Molly, holding Rob's hand, walked inside.

Suddenly Rob stopped, stared open-mouthed and wide-eyed at an Indian leaning against a post. Molly and Micah stopped and saw what he saw. An Indian dressed in clean buckskins and new moccasins ignored them and stared fixedly into the fort interior. His face was coal black.

Rob gripped Micah's sleeve, pulled him down and whispered. "Wh . . . what's wrong?"

"Is he sick?" Molly whispered.

Micah smiled. "No, quite the contrary. He's showing off. The black face means he recently took a scalp. A Pawnee, I'm guessing." He took Rob's hand. "C'mon. He'll take no notice of us."

They walked into the open center of the fort, the parade ground, passing Indians with vermillion-colored cheeks, wearing bead necklaces and shell pendants hanging from ears. Rob gawked, holding Micah's hand tightly.

They stopped in the center, glanced around. Molly and Rob listened as Micah told them about the fort. The wall of sun-dried bricks was rectangular with blockhouses at two of the corners. Arrayed around the parade ground, adobe rooms abutted the walls, about fifteen feet high that were topped by wooden palisades. Along the walls, structures included storerooms, offices and living quarters, a blacksmith, public house, a store and, outside the walls, a rudimentary sawmill. At times of Indian threat, horses and mules were brought inside the walls.

"Different since the army took over. Fort looks about the same, but in better shape than it was when I was last here. Indians seem to be as content with the army as with the traders."

"It's so, so peaceful," said Molly. "I had no idea

Indians and soldiers could be so . . . It's almost like they are friends."

"The inside of this fort is another world for local Indians. When they're inside, they consider themselves as guests and enemies of no one."

Indians of different tribes strolled about and lounged, smoking and chatting with each other and occasionally with soldiers, as if there had never been hostility with each other or with the army.

"We need to register," said Micah. They walked down a row of buildings and joined a group of emigrants who waited in line outside an office. Some stood patiently, moving up slowly, while others fidgeted, shifting their weight from foot to foot, grumbling about this latest delay that prevented their moving on.

The registration of emigrants had been haphazard, disorganized and poorly pursued before 1850. But this year, the first overseen by the army, authorities were determined to do it right. So emigrants waited to be signed in. Micah and Molly stood in line, keeping an eye on Rob who walked about, investigating everything in sight.

When it was their turn to enter the office, Molly called Rob, and the three went in together. The sergeant explained the procedure. Molly took the pen he offered and made an entry where he pointed. She wrote: Date: July 21, 1850, #42,251, Molly Holmes, Franklin, Missouri. She made the entry for Rob: July 21, 1850, #42,252, Robert Holmes, Franklin, Missouri. She handed the pen to Micah, and he made his entry: Michael McQueen, July 21, 1850, #42,253, Troy, Tennessee. He handed the pen to the soldier, turned abruptly and walked through the door. Molly hurried to catch up, pulling Rob by an arm.

Outside he strode to the center of the parade, stopped and stood, spraddle-legged, staring up at the ramparts.

Molly took his arm, frowned. "Okay?"

He looked at her, relaxed. "Yeah. I just get . . . sad when I'm reminded of where I came from and who I am. What I've done with my life . . . what I haven't done with my life. Whatever I was doing, I always thought I could do better." He turned to her. "And finally I did better." He smiled, kissed her forehead. She encircled his waist and hugged.

Rob had watched all this, looking back and forth between Micah and Molly. "Are you gonna get married now?" he said, grinning.

Micah smiled, rubbed the top of Rob's head vigorously, laid a hand on Rob's shoulder. "C'mon, boy, we need to get moving!" They stepped off, hand in hand. Molly followed, smiling.

They walked by the Lakota who were unloading their buffalo hides in front of a storeroom. The Indian who had shown interest in Molly at the entrance stopped what he was doing and watched her pass.

"I suppose I should be thinking about my price." Micah cut a glance at Molly.

"What price?" she said.

"The price I'm going to ask. That fella is going to make an offer for you before he leaves."

"He is not!" Micah took her arm, and they strolled. She looked up at him. "Is he?"

"When they leave, he is going to be flush with trade goods, maybe some coin. He will be looking for something to spend his goods on. What better than a new woman?" He smiled.

They walked toward the entrance. At the gate, Micah stopped. "Forgot something. I need to go buy some balls and powder. Just be a few minutes." He strode across the yard toward the fort store.

Molly leaned against the gate stanchion, her hand on Rob's shoulder, looking idly outside at the cluster of tepees and wagons on the flat before the fort. She turned back to see the Lakota who had stared at her earlier staring again. He stood with a grizzled old trader dressed in soiled buckskins, also staring. The trader smiled. She turned away, stepped through the fort entrance with Rob in tow.

Micah walked across the yard, carrying a small cloth bag. When he came up to the Lakota and trader, the Indian held up a hand in greeting. Micah nodded.

"Woman," said the Lakota in English, pointing toward the fort entrance. Micah stopped. The Lakota held out a leather bag. "Five horse, five dollar." He took a $5 gold piece from the bag, showed it to Micah.

Micah smiled. "That's mighty generous of you, but I need the woman to cook my supper."

The trader guffawed. He leaned toward Micah,

grinning. "Tell yuh what. I'll give yuh five horses, five dollars . . . and my old woman! How 'bout that?" He laughed, slapped his knee.

The Lakota had leaned toward the trader, open-mouthed, listening intently. The trader spoke to him in Lakota, telling what he had said to Micah.

The Indian turned to Micah, wide-eyed. "No," he said in English, "woman *old,* she no good cook!" The Lakota and trader laughed, and the trader slapped the Indian on the back.

The trader sobered, turned to Micah. "I don't blame you, not a little bit. You got a real prize, pilgrim. Hang on to her."

Micah smiled, touched his forehead in salute, and walked to the entrance. There stood Molly and Rob.

She looked at the Indian and trader, who still stared at her.

"Do you know those people? They act like they've known you forever. What were you talking about, if you don't mind my asking?"

"You."

"Me. What do you mean?"

"Didn't I tell you the Lakota would make me an offer for you before he left the fort?" He described the conversation in detail, including the trader's advice that he should hang on to her.

"Hang on to me? I'm getting to feel like a sack of potatoes! Someday somebody is going to offer you a price you can't pass up."

He smiled, put his arm around her shoulder and

squeezed. "I think not." He took her arm and pulled her along. "As long as you keep fixing my supper."

She pulled away and smacked his arm as he flinched.

"Mama!" said Rob.

"Just playing, honey," she said, smiling.

They walked in silence along the wall of the fort. Rob ran ahead, trailing his switch along the wall at eye level, making a scratching sound.

Molly turned to Micah. "What did you pay for your Lakota woman? Makawee?"

He looked aside. "Nothing. She chose me. Not common among the Lakota. I wanted to give her father some horses, but she wouldn't let me. She was different."

Molly watched him as he walked, head down. *He's not free of her. He may never be completely free of her. I understand that. What a couple of broken hearts we are. Maybe that's what brought us together.*

At sundown, Molly and Micah walked Rob to the back of the wagon. She said goodnight and kissed him on his cheek. Micah helped him over the tailgate. He leaned back and hugged Micah's neck.

Molly and Micah walked back to the fire circle and sat down. She looked at him, pursing her lips.

"Yeah, I think he likes you," she said. He cut a sideways glance at her, smiled.

Chapter 10

MICAH WOKE at the shout and cussing of an emigrant a few wagons back whose ox didn't want to be yoked this morning. He yawned, pushed the cover back, rolled over and reached for Molly.

She wasn't there. He sat up. She left the bed infrequently during the night to pee, but she was always in bed at dawn. He pulled on his boots, struggled into a jacket. Crawling from under the wagon, he stood and looked around the camp. Nothing was amiss except the five horses tied to a cottonwood sapling just outside camp.

Micah ran to his horse, removed the hobbles and led it to the wagon. Pulling the saddle from the ground underneath the wagon, he saddled the horse and woke Rob. The boy sat up, rubbing his eyes.

"Get your clothes, Rob, your mom is already away, and I need to ride. I'm taking you to Beth. We won't be long."

"Where's Mama. Why—"

"Rob, we don't have time to talk. I need to ride. Now, let's get your clothes, and we'll go to Beth's. You can get dressed there. Quickly."

Rob picked up the pile of clothes and shoes beside his pallet and handed them to Micah. Micah mounted, and Rob stepped over the tailgate into Micah's arms. He kicked the horse into a slow lope, pulled up abruptly three wagons back where Beth and Rebecca were fixing breakfast at the fire circle.

Micah helped Rob down. "Beth, can I leave Rob with you for a bit? I've got to do something."

"Sure," said Beth. "Where's Molly?"

"I'll be back soon as possible." He walked the horse between a couple of wagons and then galloped hard toward the fort.

He pulled up at the hitching rail near the entrance. Dismounting, he tied the reins and strode to the gate.

He questioned a trader who leaned against the gate stanchion, smoking. Inside, he questioned two more men, and one pointed toward the post store. Micah ran to the store and went inside. There he was, the trader who was with the Lakota the day before.

Micah inhaled deeply, catching his breath. "Where is he, the Lakota that made me the offer yesterday?"

The trader smiled. "You going to take him up—"

"I got no time for this. She's gone. The son-of-a bitch took her. He left me five horses." Two soldiers and a storekeeper standing nearby had listened to the exchange and smiled.

"Well, don't that beat all?" said the trader. "That fella's not a bad sort. He's just not the sharpest knife in the drawer." He drew on his pipe, blew smoke upwards.

"Can you help me find him?" Micah had to resist the temptation to take him by the throat to hold his attention.

The trader tapped the pipe on a post. "Sure, I can help you, and I will. That ain't the way to get a woman, even for uh Indian. Let me get my horse. I was at their village just last week. Just a couple hours away. They might still be there."

MICAH and the trader rode into the Lakota encampment. Some of the villagers nodded or waved to the trader. They obviously knew him. He responded with a wave and a smile. Then the villagers noticed Micah. Women stopped what they were doing, leaned toward each other and whispered, staring at Micah. One woman smiled and waved to him, dropped her arm quickly, embarrassed.

"We'll find the head man," the trader said. They dismounted at a tepee where two men stood. The trader and Micah raised hands in greeting.

The trader spoke to Micah in English. "This here is . . . didn't get your name."

"He is Otaktay," the chief responded in Lakota, looking at Micah. "You have been away many years. Now you have returned."

"I'll be dammed," the trader said.

Micah responded in Lakota. "Matoskah, I come to find my woman who was taken from our camp near Fort Laramie by one of your people. If he has harmed her, I will kill him." The trader listened to all this, jaw hanging, looking back and forth between Micah and Matoskah.

Matoskah turned to the trader. "Do you know his name?"

"It was Tashunka."

"Ah, Tashunka." Matoskah frowned. "Tashunka is a free spirit who does not always think about what he does. We will get him." Matoskah nodded to the man beside him, and they started to walk away. Matoskah stopped, turned back and spoke to the trader. "Jules, come with us. You know Tashunka and can help calm him if he becomes excited."

The trader looked at Micah, followed Matoskah.

Micah looked around the village. It was not the same place, but the village was familiar nevertheless. The setting, the people busy but not harried or hurried, speaking softly, laughing easily.

"You have finally returned." Micah turned and saw Makawee's sister. "Makawee told me you would marry me if something happened to her."

"I'm sorry, Wachiwi. I could not stay after she was taken from me. I could not. You would not have been happy with me." He looked past her down the lane where Matoskah and Jules had disappeared. He turned back at her voice.

"I waited for you to come back, almost a year. I have

a husband now and a boy and a girl. I am happy." She smiled broadly. "Maybe I can have two husbands! Some men have two wives. Why can't I have two husbands?" She laughed.

"I don't think you would find many Lakota that would agree with you, men or women." He glanced past her again to the lane, fidgeting. Wachiwi turned and looked.

"I think you know why I am here," Micah said.

"Yes. Takoda was hiding behind the tepee and heard everything. He is only ten, and he likes to tell stories. Now the whole village knows. You must love this woman. What is she called?"

"Molly."

"Molly. A funny name. What does it mean?"

"I don't know. Maybe 'trouble.'"

"I don't—" She looked down the lane. "Here they come."

Matoskah and his companion and Jules, all grim, frowning, strode up the lane. Micah waited.

"They are not there," said Matoskah. "We talked with some women who saw them come in at sunrise. They said Tashunka walked close behind the woman. One woman said the white woman looked scared. Another said Tashunka might have held a knife. The same women said they saw Tashunka and the white woman leave his tepee a short time later and walk to the spring at the bottom of the village beyond the willow trees where the horses are kept. They saw no more since the spring and horses cannot be seen from the village because of the trees."

"I will find them," said Micah. He walked to his horse, checked the cinch and untied the reins from the branch.

"I will go with you," said Matoskah. "I know this country. I think Tashunka does not. Any time the people move, he always follows, usually riding with the women and children."

Micah led the horse back to Matoskah, and they strode down the lane toward the horse herd. People stopped what they were doing and watched the two grim-faced men. Matoskah spoke hurriedly to a woman who stood at a cooking fire. She nodded and rushed into her tepee.

"I will kill him," said Micah. Matoskah glanced at him.

"I think he will not hurt her. He is a simple soul, confused. But the woman said he had a knife. That is not like Tashunka."

"I will kill him and feed his flesh to the dogs," Micah said softly, his eyes downcast.

They reached the herd, and Matoskah found his horse. He spoke to one of the boys who tended the horses. The boy replied and pointed down the swale. At that moment, the woman Matoskah had spoken to on the lane above ran up and handed Matoskah a full bag. He hurriedly tied it around his waist. They mounted and kicked their horses into a gallop along the lush bank of the narrow creek.

*****

Micah and Matoskah sat in darkness under a heavy low cloud cover. Light from their fire illuminated the lower limbs of the spreading cottonwood, suggesting a leafy room. The two men gnawed on hard chunks of dried meat.

"They can't be far away," said Matoskah. "Tashunka will not likely ride at night. Maybe in moonlight, but not when there is no moon. They will be sitting at a fire, just like us." He turned to Micah. "If he can make a fire. I have never seen him make a fire." Matoskah looked into the flames.

Micah stood, wandered about the site, collecting sticks. He gripped a downed dry limb, stepped on it and broke it into pieces. Dropping the armload beside the fire, he sat down, grunting, and stared into the flames.

"We will take up the trail at first light," said Matoskah. "We are riding on wet ground. The trail is clear. We will find them tomorrow."

Micah nodded, stared into the flames. He pulled his pistol slowly from the holster for the third time since they stopped, checked it, verified for the third time that it was loaded.

Micah and Matoskah rode from a dense willow copse into a meadow and saw them. Tashunka and Molly sat at a cold fire circle at the edge of the forest. Tashunka jumped up, grabbed Molly's arm and pulled her up roughly, causing her to step backwards to get her balance. He jerked her in front of him and stretched his other arm up, showing the knife.

Matoskah and Micah rode at a slow walk and reined in at the fire. They dismounted, tied their reins to a low juniper. Micah did not take his eyes from Tashunka. He stepped up beside Matoskah.

Tashunka and Molly had not moved. Micah searched Molly's face and body for any sign of what had happened to her. She appeared to be unharmed. At least, he could see nothing. She looked into his eyes, her face a mask.

"Tashunka," said Matoskah, "you have taken the woman from a friend. This is not our way. You may take a woman from an enemy, but not a friend."

"He is not a friend! He is a white man!"

"He is Otaktay. He is Lakota. We have adopted him into our tribe. You were not with our band when he lived among us."

"No! He is not a Lakota! He is a heyoka, he is a fool, he is not one of us!" Tashunka's words were slurred, erratic. His eyes were slits, then opened wide. Saliva dripped from his chin. He stood behind Molly, gripping her arm tightly, brandishing the knife with the other hand. He waved it in front of her face, then pointed it at Micah.

"She is mine! I paid for her. He cannot take her from me!" He waved the knife high in the air, pointed it again at Micah, then held it before her face. Molly was rigid, frozen, her arms stiff at her sides. Tashunka lowered the knife to her chin level and held it there.

"Put the knife down, Tashunka," said Matoskah, softly. "This is not our way. You shame the Lakota."

"Go away!" Tashunka said. "She is mine, or she is nobody!" He moved the knife horizontally in the air, back and forth, before Molly's throat.

During the exchange between Tashunka and Matoskah, Micah had stepped aside slowly, away from Matoskah, and closed his hand on the grip of his pistol.

Molly saw this. She sighed, relaxed, dropped her chin slightly, almost imperceptibly, then a hint of a nod. Micah replied with the same movement.

Suddenly, Molly jabbed an elbow sharply backward into Tashunka's belly, pulling aside at the same instant. Tashunka bent at the blow, the arm with the knife thrust upward. Micah instantly drew the pistol, brought it up, aimed and fired in a single movement. Tashunka was blown backward, landing heavily on his back.

Micah and Matoskah rushed to the downed Tashunka, Micah pointing the gun at his head. Tashunka was still, his mouth open, staring up into the void. Matoskah bent over him as the ugly red spot on Tashunka's shirt darkened and spread.

Molly rushed to Micah, and they clung to each other. She released, leaned back, took a deep breath and exhaled. "We need to talk," she said, shivering.

"I WISH it had not ended like this," Micah said. He stood

with Matoskah, looking down at the mound of leaves and dry limbs that covered Tashunka's body. Molly stood nearby, holding the reins of Micah's and Matoskah's horses.

"He gave us no choice," said Matoskah. "Tashunka was always a child, sometimes moody, but usually happy, easily led, never disagreeable or angry. I don't know what happened here. Maybe he decided that he was, after all, a man."

They walked to Molly and took their reins. "I will send men to bring his body to the village," Matoskah said. "He has no family to grieve him, but he was one of us and will be treated so."

They mounted, and Micah pulled Molly up behind him. They set out at a slow lope. She held him tightly around his waist, resting her head against his back.

Micah spoke over his shoulder. "Okay?"

She did not answer for a moment, then sighed. "I knew you would come, but I had begun to worry that you would be too late. I realized that he was troubled." Her voice was husky, wavered. "I was afraid he would kill me when he saw you.

"I'm okay now." She snuggled against his back, cleared her throat. "You smell just a little better than he did."

"Hmm. After we get back to the train and get everything in order, we'll find us a stream, and you can wash my back."

She squeezed. "I can do that."

*****

It seemed that everyone in the village was bunched up watching their approach. A boy at the horse herd had shouted to the tepees when he saw them coming. Now the riders pulled up, dismounted, and villagers, men, women and children, and Jules, crowded around Matoskah who told them all that had happened.

When Matoskah finished telling and answering questions, villagers wandered away, chatting, returning to their routine, chores and play. The tumult that had risen on the approach of the riders subsided to the normal soft sounds of the camp. Only Jules stayed.

Micah and Molly had moved aside, watching and listening. Now, as the villagers wandered away, Matoskah, Jules and Wachiwi walked to them.

"Molly," said Micah, "this is Wachiwi, Makawee's sister." Jules watched, a slight grin playing about his face.

Molly looked from Wachiwi to Micah, unsure, puzzled.

Wachiwi spoke to Micah in Lakota. "Otaktay, did you tell her that you were supposed to marry me?"

He responded in Lakota. "Yes. I told her everything. She understands. She lost her husband just before setting out on this journey, and she lost a daughter recently to illness. She understands loss."

Wachiwi took Molly's hand in hers, looked into her eyes, and spoke in Lakota. "This is a good man. I would have loved him and given him many babies. But he is yours now, and I am happy. Be good to him and give him many babies." Jules smiled, looked from Micah to Molly.

Molly smiled, spoke to Micah. "What did she say?"

"Uh, she said she is glad I found you and that you are okay." Matoskah smiled and looked aside. Jules guffawed, stomping, slapped Micah on the back.

Molly frowned at Jules, turned to Micah. "I'll talk to you later."

THE RED SUN ball lay behind lacy pink clouds at the western horizon when Molly and Micah reached the caravan. Wagons of the various companies were arrayed in double lines or encircled. Women busied themselves at cooking fires as men moved unyoked oxen to sparse dry grass off the trail.

"We hit the caravan just about where we left it," Micah said. "That means that your wagon surely is west of here. We'll see." As they rode westward along the line of wagons, they paused often to question emigrants who looked up from their chores. Most shook heads, mumbled a tired "sorry" and went back to work. A few scratched their heads and pointed west.

They rode along the line of wagons another half hour before Molly recognized a woman from her company. She questioned her, and the woman pointed up the line.

"Eight or ten wagons that way, I think," she said.

They rode on until coming up to the Manly wagon.

Molly slid off the horse and surprised Beth at the cook fire.

"Molly! I'm so glad to see you! We were so afraid." She grabbed Molly, and they hugged, both wiping tears.

"Rob is just over there with some kids from the company. I'll get him." She ran between two wagons to the other side. A moment later, Rob came running between the wagons and collided with Molly. He hugged her hard, then turned and hugged Micah.

"You gotta tell me all about it," Rob said, looking rapidly between Micah and Molly. "Were you with some Indians? Did you—"

"We'll tell you all about it, little buddy," said Micah. "Give us a chance to settle in and see if we can help." He turned to Beth. "Beth, that looks like Molly's wagon a couple of wagons ahead."

"It is!" Beth said. "We couldn't leave it behind, and I didn't think I should stay with it by myself. Jacob and some others in the company have been taking turns with yoking the oxen and driving the wagon. I think everything's okay. I hope we did right."

"Did right?" Molly said. "You're a bunch of angels." She hugged Beth.

"Now you come on and have some supper with us," said Beth. "I want to hear all about it. Nothing's happened here since you've been gone, at least nothing beyond the usual routine, and you know all about that. But you've been doing something out of the ordinary, so everybody for miles around is going to want to know about it, including the kids here."

Rob and Olin and Jessie all nodded. "Yeah," Rob said.

"Well, we're pretty tired," Molly said, "and I'm going to put off telling our story till tomorrow and—"

"Aw, Mama," Rob said.

"I would probably go to sleep right in the middle of talking, honey. I need to get a good night's sleep, and I'll tell everything tomorrow. Promise. Will that be okay?"

"Yeah, okay." Molly leaned over and kissed the top of his head.

During supper, Molly assured Rebecca and Jacob and Beth that she was well and would tell all tomorrow, and they were satisfied. After supper, the Manlys withdrew to the tent they had been using since Rob had joined them, and the children were settled in their pallets inside the wagon.

Molly sighed, relieved that she was no longer the center of attention. She poured more coffee in Micah's cup and then her own. She set the pot at the edge of the embers, looked long at Micah. She leaned against him momentarily, then straightened and looked into the fire.

"How did you find me so quickly?" she said.

"When I saw the horses, I knew what happened. I went to the fort, learned the name of the Lakota from the trader, Jules, and he said he would take me to his village." He did not tell her that the conversation with Jules about slow-witted Tashunka had led him to fear the worst.

"How did he take you without me hearing?" he said.

"He came up behind me when I was peeing. He grabbed me and held his hand over my mouth so hard, I thought I was going to choke. He pulled me outside camp a long way off. How he got me up on his horse is beyond me. I pulled his hand off once and tried to yell, but he got his hand back on my mouth, and we rode off really fast.

"When we got to the village, he took me to his tepee, me yelling and kicking all the way. It was just daylight, and women were making fires, and men were tending to horses. They just looked at us. They talked with each other, some with long faces, but they didn't do anything, just like this was something they saw every day."

"Stealing women is not uncommon, but I'll wager some thought stealing a white woman meant big trouble."

"When we got inside the tepee, he hit me and said something, probably told me to shut up. But then the strangest thing happened. He got a look on his face that, so help me, said 'I'm sorry.' He gave me a gourd of water and some dried meat. And some fresh berries.

"I thought about trying to run, but he sat right in front of the tepee opening. Some people walking by looked through the opening at his back and said something. He mumbled something, and they went on.

"He just stared at me. I was afraid at first, but soon I was feeling sorry for him. He didn't know what to do. We just sat there like that, hardly moving. I started to get up once to see if he would let me go outside, but he wouldn't have any of that. He got a hard look on his face and put up a hand, motioning me to sit down. He just stared at me the longest time.

"Then he must have made a decision. He picked up a knife and showed it to me without a word. He stood and motioned me to get up, waving the knife. Strange.

"He walked me down the lane, holding my arm really tight. Every time we passed women working or walking, he tried to hide the knife. I thought about shouting to the women, but I was afraid it would set him off. When nobody was watching, he showed me the knife, I think to remind me he had it. He even touched my arm with the point, just a little prick, but it hurt. I knew he was crazy at that point, and I got pretty scared.

"He got his horse and made me ride behind him. He smelled pretty bad. I don't think he knew where he was going. We'd go in one direction, stop while he looked around, then ride in another direction. We kept doing this till it got so dark, we couldn't see where we were going.

"We stopped, and he collected some wood. It took him forever to make a fire. He muttered the whole time in what must have been cussing in Indian. I was pretty hungry by then, but I guess he had not thought about food. So we just sat by the fire. I thought we would start at daylight, but he just sat there. He didn't know what to do. That's where we were when you found us. That's where we spent the night."

They sipped their coffee. "I knew you would come," she said. She leaned over and kissed him on the cheek.

"How could I not?" he said. She put her arms around his shoulders and leaned against him. "He shorted me five dollars."

She jerked back and swatted him on his arm as he recoiled. "You . . ." She grabbed the arm and pulled him to her, resting her head on the arm. "What am I going to do about you, Micah McQueen?"

He took her cheeks with both hands, looked into her eyes, spoke softly. "Just love me half as much as I love you."

Chapter 11

"What's going on, Micah?"

Molly had finished cleaning up after breakfast and now stood beside Micah as he worked on yoking the oxen. They watched a couple of men nearby who were in the process of sawing their wagon in half just behind the front wheels.

"Well, now that we're done with Fort Laramie, it seems a lot of folks think the trip is just about over, and they want to lighten their load. They want to get to Oregon or California as fast as they can. Some are turning their wagons into carts, thinking they'll be able to move lots faster.

"People been lightening their load ever since a few days out of Independence, you know, throwing away things that they thought they really needed at the start. We've seen it all along the trail. Beds, clothes, tools, stoves, mattresses, anything. Remember even stacks of food near the start, everything from bacon, bread and beans to barrels of flour and rice. Not much food discarded lately. Everybody's light on food, with nothing to spare."

Emigrants tried to buy food supplies at the fort in exchange for anything they could do without, from cooking gear to tools and axes. Some supplicants were able to wheedle some little stocks, but the fort's storerooms could hardly satisfy the need of the stressed emigrants.

"See those wagons over there?" Micah pointed to a score of empty wagons outside the campground. "Those wagons have been abandoned. The owners have turned their horses and mules into pack animals and riding animals, and they've already headed out. Too bad. They're going to find out real fast that the hardest part of this journey is not behind, but ahead. That's not all. There's lots more abandoned wagons just beyond that bunch of pines there." He pointed. "Soldiers had to move them. They were cluttering up the meadow here.

"I heard at the company campfire a couple of nights ago about one fella who was getting so anxious about the slow pace of the train that he said he could walk to Oregon faster. Everybody there said that if he tried that, they would see his bones along the trail to Oregon. He laughed and took off the next morning, carrying a big backpack. I wager we'll see that pack beside his carcass before we go much further."

They turned back to the yoking. Molly had become

just about as proficient as he and required no instruction. "We've been more fortunate, or smarter, than most other people," he said. "We still have your original team and our three horses. Switching oxen about and shoeing 'em all with buffalo hide booties has kept their feet sound. I feel sorry for the people who didn't take care of their oxen's feet, and their hooves just wore right down to the quick. When that happens, those beasts are no good for anything but supper."

The yoking was finished, and Molly patted the lead ox. "On the road!" she said. Micah walked to the loose stock, removed the hobbles from the horses and led them to the wagon where he tied their reins to the tailgate. Meanwhile, Molly walked to Beth's wagon to retrieve Rob.

Micah picked up a short quirt from the floor beneath the wagon seat and walked to the lead yoke. "Giddyap," he said as Molly and Rob walked up. The team pulled into the serpentine line of wagons that were already in motion, and the new day morphed into every day.

With one exception. Leaving Fort Laramie behind, they left the prairie and began the long upgrade in the foothills of the Rocky Mountains. Emigrants realized that the uphill pull was going to be more demanding on their animals, so they continued to lighten their loads. More possessions were left beside the trail as anything not absolutely essential was discarded. The loss of earthly possessions was countered by the realization that they had largely left cholera on the plains.

Walking on the other side of the lead yoke from Micah, Molly stared silently at him across the backs of the team. *How can I be so blessed?*

Micah must have felt her eyes on him for he turned and saw her blank stare. After a moment, he cocked his head, smiled. She smiled, faced back to the front. Closing her eyes, she raised her chin, inhaled deeply, exhaled and looked aside.

In the grassy verge, she saw a field of white bachelor buttons with a sprinkling of blue-petaled buttons. Marigolds and asters swayed in the gentle breeze. Beyond, closer to the pinewoods, chokecherries and black currants beckoned.

Oh, wouldn't they be wonderful in a pie! She considered pausing to gather some, but decided against it. They had talked so much lately about the need to continue moving, even to pick up the pace when the terrain permitted.

THE UPWARD TILT in the trail this day was hardly noticeable to the eye, but a glance at the straining oxen proved that the drive was entering a new phase. Molly's company stopped for noon earlier than usual at a good patch of grass watered by a small spring to let the teams blow and rest.

After unyoking the oxen, Molly and Rob walked to Beth's wagon. They said hello to Beth and Olin and Jessie, and all sat in the shade of a tall spreading cottonwood. The cooling breeze rustled the large leaves, just beginning to show a faint hint of autumn yellow. Captain Bonney said they would extend the nooning to give time for mending wagons and greasing wheels. Most emigrants had long since exhausted their supply of commercial grease and now relied on buffalo fat. Many wheels, desiccated lately in hot days without rain, were particularly melodious. Emigrants had learned that buffalo fat also would give relief to parched lips.

Molly stood. "I need to get back to see if I can help Micah."

"Can I stay here?" Rob said. "I'll stay right here." Molly looked at Beth, and she nodded her approval.

"I'll come back for you," said Molly. "It won't be long." She walked to her wagon where Micah stood beside the oxen in lush grass. He saw her coming, walked to the wagon and took a small pail from the side.

"I saw a chokecherry bush up there near the spring. Looks like a plum tree up there too. Let's see if we can find some fruit." They walked up a slight incline past the grazing animals. "It may be a little early for the chokecherry, but we'll see. If we do find fruit, be careful. The stems and leaves and pit are poison. Eat only the soft flesh around the pit. The plum ripens earlier, so we might find some. If the plum is green, it's not ripe. The ripe ones are a sort of orange-pink-reddish."

She looked at him, cocked her head. "You haven't forgotten, have you?"

He looked aside. "You don't forget the good times."

She half-smiled, unsure whether she should respond. She touched his arm. "You stay here. I'll just be a minute." She walked ahead and around a thick snowberry bush.

He waited, looked up the hillside at a solitary pronghorn. The buck nibbled on a tuft of dry grass. Suddenly his head jerked up. He whirled and bounded up the slope.

"M . . . M . . . Micah," softly, from behind the snowberry.

Micah walked slowly around the bush. There stood Molly, upright but bent forward, hands holding the tops of the bloomers that circled her thighs. He followed her gaze and saw the grizzly. The huge bear pawed the ground in the runoff from the spring, snuffling softly, absorbed in his search for something edible in the soft soil.

Micah touched the grip of his pistol, drew it slowly from the holster.

"What—" she whispered.

"Shh," softly.

The grizzly's head came up, looked directly at Molly and Micah. His head swung side to side.

Micah and Molly did not move, frozen.

The bear took a step toward them, stopped, head swinging side to side. He took another step.

Micah aimed, fired. The water at the bear's feet burst, showering his face, and he jerked sideways. He shook his head, droplets of water spraying from his head and neck. He looked back at his assailants, lowered his head, stepped slowly toward them.

Micah aimed at a small boulder that lay beside the grizzly's path. He fired. The stone exploded, sending sharp slivers into the bear's face. The grizzly stopped, shook his head wildly. He stepped forward, stopped, waved his hanging head side-to-side, eyes fixed on Molly and Micah. Then he whirled and ran up the hill toward a dark stand of pine.

Micah exhaled, slowly pushed the pistol into its holster, turned toward Molly. She watched the grizzly until it disappeared in the sage, turned to face Micah. She started, turned around abruptly, pulling up her bloomers. She turned back to see him watching her, smiling.

"C'mon," he said, "we need to get yoked and on the road. Some wagons have already moved out." She stepped off, bumping him playfully as she passed.

THE UPSLOPE INCREASED on the afternoon drive, and the teams strained. Some emigrants added an extra yoke to their team at nooning, easing the labor of the others. Molly and Micah wished aloud they still had a third yoke.

All were happy when the captain called an early stop for the evening camp. Grass was sparse at the site, but there was some welcome shade from a mixed stand of pine and spruce. A seep in the stand provided some little water for the animals and barrels.

Spirits had lifted since leaving the plains. The heat had given way to a bracing coolness. Game was more plentiful, and fish were taken from the occasional streams.

Beth and the children had walked over after supper. Now Molly and Beth sat beside the fire, watching the sun lowering into a saddle of the mountain range. Above the orb, the wispy layers of cloud were tinted shades of pink, yellow and orange.

"Look at the kids," said Molly. Micah stood with Rob, Jessie and Olin off the trail near the loose stock. He held Rob's and Olin's hands. Some of the animals grazed; others were bedded down. Micah bent occasionally, talking to the children.

"He's a good man," said Beth. "He would be a good father."

Molly glanced sideways at her, looked back at the fire. She picked up a couple of chips and tossed them on the embers. They sat silent, staring into the low flames, glowing orange and yellow.

"What are your plans, Beth?"

Beth did not answer immediately. She shifted, pulled her legs up and rested her chin on her knees. "My plans. Ever since my husband died, ever since we have been with the Manlys, I've tried not to even think about the future, about Oregon, what we're going to do there. I don't know how I would cope, Molly. I don't think I could set up a farm by myself, and I don't know how to do anything else. What would I do? It's at night when everything is still and quiet that I've been terrified to the point of shivering."

Molly touched Beth's hand. "Why not come with us, Beth? We'll have Micah—at least, I think we'll have Micah—and you and I can work together. Rob loves Olin and Jessie and would really like to have them with us."

"That's very kind of you, Molly, but I'm not terrified anymore." She took Molly's hand in both of hers, paused. Molly frowned, waiting. Beth leaned back, looked aside, back to Molly. "I planned to tell you eventually, but I'll tell you now. I'm not going to Oregon. I'm going with the Manlys. Jacob asked me to marry him."

Molly recoiled, grimacing. "Marry? He's got a wife."

"Molly, the Manlys are Mormons! We talked about it, Jacob and Rebecca and me. Rebecca thinks it's a good idea. There will be a lot of work setting up at Salt Lake, and she said I would be a big help. They seem to like the children, and Olin and Jessie seem to like them."

"I don't know what to say," said Molly. "It seems so strange, two wives. The children in a Mormon family must be confused."

"Yes, well. It's still a little strange to me too. Remember when they first took us in, they both had been poorly. That's why they agreed to take us, so I could help. Since then, Jacob has got better, but Rebecca has not. She's seems worse. I wouldn't wish anything bad for her, but . . ." She looked abruptly at Molly. "Don't think bad of me, Molly."

Molly took Beth's hands in hers. "I couldn't think bad of you, Beth. You're a good person, and you'll be fine, no matter how this turns out. I'm happy for you. . . . Have you told the children?"

"Not yet. I still have a few more days before we turn south for Salt Lake. Jacob said we turn off at a place called Fort Bridger. I'll think of something before we get there.

"Molly, don't say anything about this to anybody, except Micah maybe. A lot of people in this train don't like Mormons, even some in our own company. Captain Bonney said some unkind things about Mormons. He's from Illinois where there was lots of troubles between Mormons and people who didn't like Mormons. I was with the Manlys when the captain said it, and Jacob told me later about the Illinois troubles. It's terrible what these people have gone through."

"I don't know anything about Mormon belief," said Molly, "and I don't judge, especially when I'm ignorant. It does seem strange for a man to have two wives, but if you're okay with it, that's all that counts."

"Thank you, Molly, I had to do it. I saw no other way. It'll work out." She stood. "We better get back and let you get to bed." Jessie and Olin came to her call, followed by Micah and Rob. Beth and her two walked toward their wagon, hand in hand. Olin turned to say goodbye over his shoulder to Rob.

"Say goodnight to Micah, Rob, time for bed," Molly said.

"But, Mama, Micah was telling me how to tell when a ox has sore feet. He didn't finish."

"There will be plenty of time for that tomorrow, and the day after that, and the day after that."

"Aw, Mama." He reached up and hugged Micah who returned the hug. Molly cocked her head at Micah who smiled ever so slightly, just a bit embarrassed. She took Rob's hand, and they walked to the back of the wagon. After a moment, she returned to the fire and sat close beside Micah.

They stared into the fire, glanced occasionally at the horizon that glowed with the memory of the day. He leaned over and kissed her cheek. She turned, and they kissed, a soft, sweet kiss. She leaned back, looked at the fire.

"Beth is going to marry Jacob Manly," she said.

Micah turned abruptly toward Molly. "What?"

She told him about her conversation with Beth. "I was shocked. It's all so strange, but I guess it will be good for her. I hope it will be good for her."

"If she's okay with it, it should work out."

Molly added some chips to the fire. "I've heard that some Indian men have more than one wife. Do you know anything about that?"

He glanced at her, then back to the fire. "I was approached by a man in our village who had become a good friend. He said he wanted to express his devotion to me. He said that he would marry Makawee's sister, and we would exchange wives occasionally. I thanked him for his friendship and the offer and declined. He was surprised. It was not an unusual arrangement among the Lakota.

"Makawee was surprised too. She said if I didn't want to do that, then would I marry her sister? She said she loved her sister, and they worked well together. She said her sister would be good in bed. She was puzzled when I said I was satisfied with just her. She was okay with that, but she made me promise that if something happened to her, I would marry her sister. I broke that promise because I could not stay after she was . . . taken."

"I'm sorry, honey," Molly said, "I didn't mean to—"

"Molly, we need to stop apologizing for saying what we need to say. Who else can we talk to, you and me, about what's important to us? I'll hold nothing back, and you should do the same."

She nodded, kissed him lightly on his cheek.

THE MORNING'S DRIVE WAS, as usual, without any notable event, boring. Molly alternately walked beside Micah at the lead yoke and with Rob in the wagon's shade. Rob chattered about almost any subject at hand while Molly listened, responded and hugged him, deliriously happy that she was so blessed to listen to his bubbling enthusiasm, knowing that her joy inevitably would be muted by the memory of Kath. When that happened, not even Rob's happy chatter could alter her dark mood.

At the noon stop, as Micah and Rob moved the oxen to a patch of grass, Beth walked up, almost running.

"Molly! Can you come with me, just for a few minutes? I want you to meet some people. Can you come?"

Molly looked toward Micah and Rob. She called. "Micah! I'm going with Beth a few minutes. You've got Rob." Micah waved. Beth hurried off, almost running, and Molly followed. They walked past three wagons, then between wagons to the other side of the caravan.

They stopped beside two wagons facing the wrong direction, eastward. Molly frowned. These did not look like the usual turnarounds. The wagons were in good condition, the fittings and accessories new or well-maintained. Wagon covers were clean and taut. Eight sleek, muscled horses grazed in a patch of grass just off the trail. Two men rubbed them with clean cloths. A small group of curious emigrants crowded around the wagon, talking. Molly saw the Manlys.

"What's all this, Beth?" Molly said.

"They're Mormons!" Beth said excitedly. "They're from Salt Lake, eight of them. They're missionaries on their way to England."

Molly drew back, frowned. "Mormon missionaries to England?" She frowned again. "Why?"

"All I know is that they say they were called to go."

"Called? Who called them?"

"Well . . ." Beth said, turning aside, then looking at

the crowd, "they said they prayed, asking what they should do to best serve God, and God said they should go to England and preach the word."

"Hmm, guess you can't question those instructions if you're a true believer."

"I don't know about all this, Molly. You know I'm not a Mormon. Not yet anyway. I'll join after I marry Jacob. It was Jacob told me about the missionaries. He thinks what they're doing is wonderful. He told them he wished he could help them. They thanked him and said that God would provide."

"Hmm." Molly stared at the Mormon horses. "If the missionaries don't have a spare horse, I hope God does something about that lame animal there." She nodded toward one of the grazing horses that was favoring a front leg, repeatedly lifting the leg and touching the ground lightly.

"Oh, oh," said Beth, her hand going to her cheek. "I'll tell Jacob." She went to Jacob who stood in a circle talking with the missionaries and whispered in his ear. Jacob turned toward Molly, waved. Molly responded with a smile. Jacob spoke to one of the Mormons, and they walked to the horses.

She watched as the missionary rubbed the horse's lame leg. *God be with you in your journey across this godforsaken land and aboard your ship, and good luck with a three-horse team unless one of your devout gives you a replacement. I can't spare one for you.*

That afternoon, as they walked beside the team, Molly told Micah about the missionaries.

"Does seem sorta strange," he said, "going all the way from Salt Lake to England to preach. Guess they ran out of sinners in this country." He turned to Molly. "They missed us, didn't they?" He reached around her shoulders and under her arm and squeezed a breast.

She pushed his hand away, twisted around to see Rob walking with Olin, chatting and tapping the ground with a switch. She looked back to the front. "Better watch out for Beth. She's converting." Leaning over, she bumped him with a shoulder.

"ARE YOU SURE ABOUT THAT?" Micah said. "I don't believe in coincidence."

"That's from the captain," said Molly. "I haven't been keeping track."

Captain Bonney indeed had passed the word up and down the line to company members that they would arrive at Independence Rock on July 4, two days hence. Furthermore, the company would lay over on the day to celebrate the glorious fourth. He had urged hunters to bring in game and women to scour their food bins and produce as festive a meal as they could come up with. Many women had looked at each other, wondering what festive supplies they might find in their depleted food bins.

The next morning after breakfast, Micah helped Molly yoke the oxen, then rode north with three others from the company to hunt. Micah and one of the others led packhorses. As Molly watched, the hunters disappeared over a rising a mile from the caravan.

Molly turned back to the oxen and looked southward toward the loose stock. Four young riders rode around the herd, hallooing and quirting lazy beasts to get them up and ready to get underway.

Suddenly she tensed. Beyond the herd, riders appeared in the distance, flowing over the rim above a shallow stream. Dozens, and they kept coming, and the dozens became hundreds. They rode five abreast, then ten abreast, bunched and single file. Then the women and young men appeared, some riding and some walking. Then dogs skittering about among the throng, and horses dragging laden travois. It was the first time she had seen the primitive sled, two poles joined by a platform and pulled by a horse or dog, the Indian's answer to the white man's cart.

Molly looked up and down the train. The caravan had been on the verge of departure, but now men and women stood silently, watching. Then men went to their wagons and pulled out their guns. They strapped on belts and checked rifles and pistols to verify they were loaded. Now they stood by wagons, cradling rifles in their arms, waiting.

Captain Bonney walked rapidly along the line of stationary wagons. "Ease up, folks. They've got their women with 'em, so there're not looking for trouble."

"Then why are they painted, cap'n?" It was the emigrant standing by the wagon behind Molly's.

Bonney stopped beside the speaker, eyes still on the Indians. "Now you got me there, Sam."

"What are they?"

"Pawnees, I'm pretty sure," Bonney said. "They can be a bad lot when they've had a run-in with somebody. If that's so, I hope they know it wasn't us."

The captain stepped away from the caravan, turned and shouted. "You five wagons!" He pointed. "Pull out of line and into a double file! Let's give them a wide open space to get through!" He looked back at the Indians, spoke softly to no one in particular. "If that's what they're of a mind to do."

The three leaders of the column stopped twenty paces from the caravan. Their faces were painted red from mid-cheek and nose to the hairline. Each wore a single feather in his hair. They looked up and down the line of wagons, frowning. Followers bunched up behind them. A dozen women continued coming and stopped beside the leaders.

Emigrants watched silently, fidgeting, hands on pistol grips, holding rifles in readiness. Some warriors held bows while others gripped rifle stocks in their fringed scabbards. Warriors and emigrants alike were quiet, waiting.

The three Pawnee leaders walked their horses slowly to the train, reined left, looking at the wagons and the people, then turning around and riding in the other direction. Emigrants watched, glancing at each other, shifting their feet nervously.

What a bunch of showoffs.

The warriors stopped before Molly, looked down at her. She glared at them, then looked at the knot of Indian women who had not moved since walking to the front.

Molly bent and spoke to Rob, who had watched the display, eyes wide and jaw hanging. "Rob, you stay right here. Hear me?"

"I hear you, Mama."

Molly walked by the lead warrior who pulled his horse back in surprise. He watched her walk to the knot of Indian women at the front. The women stepped backward at this white woman advancing on them. She stopped before them, smiled.

"Hello," Molly said. "You don't understand a word I'm saying, but I hope you'll see that I'm friendly, and neither of us has anything to be afraid of. I hope you agree." She smiled.

The women looked at each other, puzzled. One woman stepped forward. She touched the scarf that Molly wore. It was an old red cotton scarf that she often draped on her shoulders in the morning so she could put it over her head to ward off the blazing sun at mid-morning.

Molly pulled the scarf from her shoulders and stepped toward the woman. The woman stepped backward, frowning. She stopped when Molly draped the scarf around her neck. The woman felt the scarf, looked down at it, looked up at Molly and smiled. At this, the other women crowded around the woman and fingered the scarf, chattering, smiling and laughing.

Immediately, emigrant women hurried to their wagons, pulled out bits of clothing and goods they had packed for this very circumstance. The Indian women ran back to travois and pulled out goods for trading. Soon women were mingling, Indian and emigrant, exchanging trinkets and personal possessions.

Watching this interchange, emigrant men hurried to wagons and came back to offer packets of tobacco to the warriors who dismounted. Some accepted with a dour, haughty countenance while others accepted with a smile.

Molly walked back to Bonney, stood by him as she watched. "Cap'n, two of the women in the group I talked to hung at the back. When they saw me looking at them, they moved behind others, I think so I couldn't see them. Their faces were pock-marked, like . . . like . . . could it be the pox?"

"I saw them, and two others among the warriors. Smallpox. The biggest enemy of the Plains Indians is not emigrants, or even the army. It's white man's disease, especially smallpox. Sad. It has destroyed whole villages."

Trading concluded, the Indians, now definitely identified as Pawnees, resumed their northward migration, flowing through the gap between the double line of wagons. Emigrants watched as the Indians moved slowly away from the caravan, across the arid flat and into a shallow ravine. Emigrants appeared riveted by the spectacle, and they watched quietly until the last of the entourage, the dogs and loose horses followed by a few mounted boys, disappeared.

Molly stared at the empty prairie, still touched by the experience with the women, still wondering about these people whose life was so different from hers.

But inside, aren't we all the same?

Captain Bonney declared the show over and shouted for all to get moving. "We'll stop early today to get ready for tomorrow's celebration!" Men responded with shouts and laughter and hurrahs for the captain and the good ol' USA.

Chapter 12

THE COMPANY STOPPED early afternoon in clear view of Independence Rock. The huge mass was imposing to some, a magnificent stony monolith visible for miles in the flat country. To others, it was just a big rock. One emigrant declared that it looked like a huge loaf of stale brown bread. Another said it had the look of a collapsed elephant. All agreed that it was a remarkable sight in an otherwise flat terrain and a marvelous backdrop for a celebration.

The captain picked a most welcome site for the company's campground that afternoon, a grassy flat beside a narrow tumbling stream that flowed into the aptly-named Sweetwater River. Three men caught up in the festive spirit volunteered to unload their wagons and take up the floorboards to use as tables for the banquet.

There was an air of anticipation and energy at the evening camp. The women took inventory of their food stocks and came up with plans for a meal of some appeal and variety, though hardly festive at this point in the migration. They knew that the banquet would reduce supplies, but figured it was okay since they were almost done with this journey. A conclusion that none believed.

Indeed, Captain Bonney, while encouraging all to make their contribution to the joyous celebration, reminded them that their destinations, Oregon or California, still lay many days ahead. But he urged all to take heart since the mountains would add abundant fish and game and fresh, sweet water to their larder.

The hunters returned just as women were building fires and bustling around preparing supper. The men brought antelope, rabbits, sage hens and two fat elk. One hunter complained that he had wanted to bring in a grizzly, but the bear decided he wanted the hunter's horse for his own meal. It required a volley of shots from three hunters to convince the grizzly otherwise.

Micah and the others tied antelope and elk to the lower limbs of a stunted lodgepole pine to finish the dressing out. The hunters carved the carcasses into pieces and carried the chunks to the large community fires where they left them with those who had volunteered to manage the slow grilling all evening.

The company agreed that the display of a flag was essential. Two men went into a streamside stand of willow to find a liberty pole while others scoured the company to find a suitable flag. When they failed to find a flag of any sort, a woman declared that, by damn, you men are useless. My lady friends and I will *make* a flag!

The women scurried about the camp, collecting bits

of colored cloth and pulling scissors, needles and thread from their wagons. When they failed to find enough blue scraps, a woman brought out the long blue dress she had given up to bloomers after only two weeks on the trail. But for the soiled hem, the color was still vibrant.

Micah had ridden out shortly after delivering the wild meat to the campsite chefs. He told Molly that he would be back soon and kicked his horse into a lope before she could question him. She watched him until he disappeared into a pine wood. She would not worry, she told herself, and set to worrying.

She looked up at the sound of a violin, soon joined by a banjo, then a guitar. She glanced around the camp at groups working on dishes for the feast, others roasting meat on beds of glowing embers, still others scurrying about, no longer fatigued and worn, now energized and preparing for the patriotic celebration. Molly had just given a short red coat to the flag-makers, but she had no interest in helping make it.

She was suddenly beset by a gloom that she could not shake. She walked slowly toward Beth's wagon to visit and collect Rob.

She remembered Independence Day celebrations at home. She remembered the gatherings with friends in the front yard, toasting the glorious fourth with cheap whiskey, eating homegrown pork and buttered sweet potatoes and crusty mince pies. She remembered Johnny, silly after more whiskey than he usually drank in a month, holding his glass high, hugging her around the neck with the other arm, kissing her on the cheek and nibbling on her ear, whispering why don't we go in the house just for a little while. Then releasing her and staggering toward a knot of good friends. She had smiled, wondering what he would say next morning when she reminded him of the fleeting tryst. Then Rob and Kath rushing over to ask if they could go with friends to play in the barn. Yes, be careful, she said, stay off the loft ladder, and the children running and skipping toward the barn.

Molly leaned against the wagon she was passing and sobbed into her hands. A woman passing put a hand on her shoulder and asked if she was all right. Molly nodded without turning. The woman walked on. Molly leaned back, eyes closed, wiped her face with a sleeve, inhaled deeply and exhaled. She opened her eyes.

Okay, got that out of your system. Get on with today.

The rest of the camp did not share Molly's dark mood. For a moment, emigrants forgot the trail and the journey, as if one festive evening of music and food, whiskey and patriotic speeches, would erase suffering and loss.

Molly waved to Beth and Jacob Manly who stood beside their wagon with the children. After the adults exchanged pleasantries, Rob asked if he could stay with Olin and Jessie and come to the big camp supper with them.

"Is that okay, Beth, Jacob?" said Molly. Jacob smiled and nodded, turned to Beth.

"Sure," said Beth. "We'll meet you there. I guess I

should still be there working on the supper, but I think I did my part. Rebecca's still there."

"Rob, you're lucky to have two families. You mind Miz Anderson, hear? I can still take a switch to you if you misbehave." She smiled.

"Molly! You know this boy doesn't misbehave. We'll see you at the big fire. I'm sure we'll know it's starting when we hear the music and the singing."

"Or the shots," said Jacob. "I heard there will be some patriotic salutes. Waste of powder and lead, if you ask me."

"WHY DIDN'T you tell me that's what you were doing? I wouldn't have worried." Molly had grabbed Micah as soon as he dismounted and hit the ground. He told her that he had ridden over to Independence Rock to have a look and decide whether they should climb it.

He kissed her, frowned. "Why would you worry?"

She leaned against the side of the wagon as he tied the reins to a hook on the side. "Well, you have done a good bit of wandering in your lifetime. How do I know when you'll be off wandering again?"

"Molly. I'm not wandering anywhere. There's too much right in this camp to hold me."

She smiled, put a hand to his cheek and kissed him.

He turned to his horse, threw the stirrup up over the saddle and concentrated on loosening the cinch. "I wouldn't miss this dinner for anything." He ducked and jumped aside, grinning, as she swung at him. Her fist caught only air, and she grabbed him around his middle and held him tightly, her head resting on his arm.

"Michael Micah McQueen," she said softly, "one of these days . . ."

"One of these days what?"

"One of these days, I'll get over you."

He took her face in his hands, kissed her softly on her lips, stayed nose-to-nose. "No, I don't think so. I've got you, and you're not going anywhere without me. Hear?"

She leaned back, looked into his eyes. "That so? We'll see about that." She released him. "Finish that horse, and we'll go help the others get ready to celebrate the glorious fourth tomorrow."

EMIGRANTS BURST from tents and wagons at a thunderous barrage of pistol and rifle shots that shattered the morning calm. Rubbing sleep from eyes and shivering from the cold snap during the night, they retreated to wagons and tents just long enough to dress.

Precisely at the appearance of the top rim of the sun disc, a group of eager men and boys raised the forty-foot almost-straight wooden flagstaff with the homemade Old Glory affixed at the top. The pole had hardly been secured when every man, woman and child in the camp jumped at the explosive volley from five men aligned near the flagpole. The men slowly lowered their rifles, grinning at the response to their shots.

Fires were kindled and tables set up. Aside from

some little nibbling, no one appeared to be interested in breakfast. Preparations for the noon festivities were underway. Partially cooked chunks of meat were again skewered and suspended over fires. Women brought food supplies and cooking utensils from wagons and set to work.

Micah walked across the campground to a fire circle where Molly squatted, plucking a sage hen. She looked up at him, returned to her work and pulled the last of the feathers from the bare body. She placed it with three other plucked hens, picked up another limp carcass and began pulling feathers.

"The corrals, such as they are, seem to be intact," he said. "The beasts did a bit of jumping and jerking at the shots and bumping at the corral poles, but nobody got out. Good thing we put it together, though. Without the corrals, mules and oxen and cows and horses would be halfway to Oregon by now."

He looked around at the hive of activity, listening to the buzz of conversation. "I don't see any breakfast."

"Nope. It's all about dinner." She motioned toward the roasting fires. "See if you can find a bit of cooked meat. And see if you can avoid being knifed by one of the cooks."

He smiled, bent down and kissed her cheek. "Okay, little mama." He walked toward the nearest roasting fire. She paused, flicked some wet feathers from a hand as she looked at his back, then turned back to her task.

*****

HIGH NOON, and dinner was ready. Tables were covered with dishes of roast elk, antelope, sage hen and rabbits, fried sage hen and rabbits, antelope and sage hen stew. There were bowls of baked beans and rice, still warm biscuits and fresh-baked bread. When some women marveled at the large bowl of steaming roasted potatoes, the donor said that she had hoarded them for a special occasion, and today filled the bill. Another surprise was the assortment of desserts, including pound cake, fruitcake and, wonder of wonders, apple pie. For drinks, there were coffee and hot tea and cold, mountain water, fresh from the brook just outside camp. Sprigs of cedar and pine and bowls of wildflowers decorated the tables.

Captain Bonney, standing at the flagpole, called for attention. The entire company, glancing anxiously at the food tables, crowded around the flagpole, chatting, waiting.

"On this day in our history," said Bonney, "our forefathers declared that we are a free people who chart our own destiny. All of us in this camp, around this pole, declare the same. We are free to do what we wish, well, almost, and go where we wish. And here we are, on the threshold of building a new society, maybe a new state, on the broad Pacific Ocean. So let us all join in saluting Old Glory and singing The Star Spangled Banner."

A cheer rose from the throng, and someone took the lead with a rousing "Oh, say can you see," and all joined in. When the song ended, all cheered loudly, and some shouted patriotic slogans. A few shots sounded from the fringes of the crowd.

Someone shouted from the back: "Let's eat!" The crowd roared in response, and all laughed and swept toward the loaded tables. Men and women filled plates for themselves and their children and wandered about the camp, looking for a place to sit or lean.

At the same time, other men, who had walked to their wagons and tents instead of to tables, now came with bottles in hand.

Whiskey bottles were opened and offered to any who held an empty glass. The toasting began, slowly at first, then in earnest and vigorously. Toasts to the nation and its leaders, to good friends and good times, to the good people who began this march across the country and left us too soon, to those we loved in life and now in memory. Several women and some men who had consumed more whiskey than food wiped their tears, then acknowledged to themselves and others that they would remember, but would carry on. Smiles and laughter returned.

Molly and Micah sat on a fallen log, apart from the festive throng. They ate from loaded plates. Molly pointed at Rob, sitting on the ground with Olin and Jessie at a fire circle, all with full plates in laps. They chatted happily, laughing, Rob throwing back his head, waving a fork at Olin. Rob saw Molly and waved.

Molly smiled and returned the wave. She sobered. "Kath would . . ." She turned away.

"Don't," said Micah.

She looked up at him, then returned to her plate.

"Soon as we finish here," he said, "how about riding over to the rock? I thought we might want to climb it. I hear there's quite a view from the top."

"I would like that."

"Course, that means that we will miss the oration by Jeremiah P. Bartholomew. Bonney appointed him to give a speech to remind us that we are all still Americans. He makes no secret of wanting to get into politics in Oregon. He'll love it."

"Oh, my, do you think we can bear to miss that?" She looked up at him, chuckled. "I think I've already heard that speech. He gave forth a few nights ago at the company fire circle that by moving to Oregon, we're not leaving the United States. 'We are transporting the United States to Oregon in our knapsacks and in our hearts.' That's what he said. Yeah, I think I can bear to miss it."

"Some of the boys who climbed the rock yesterday said it can be a tough climb in places, but I figure we can manage. Better leave Rob here, if that's okay with you."

"I'll check with Beth."

He handed her his plate and stood. "I'll saddle up and be back here in 'bout a half hour. You gonna be right here when I get back?"

She nodded. He stood and walked toward the corral. She set the empty plates on the ground, pulled her knees up and tightened the long skirt around her ankles. She had donned the long dress against the morning cold. She felt a bit conspicuous at first until she saw a few other women coming from tents and wagons in skirts. They had exchanged bloomers for the long skirts; now they exchanged smug smiles. One woman commented that they were the only smart females in the caravan.

Molly stood and carried the plates to the table where women washed dishes in tubs, chatting and laughing. She said she would come back later and help with the cleanup.

"Don't hurry, honey, we got nothing else to do," said one woman who smiled and nudged a co-worker with an elbow, "and I thank you got something else to do. If I had rights to that good-lookin' cowboy, I sure would have somethin' else to do." She and the women at the table laughed out loud.

"Yeah," said another woman, more than twice Molly's age, grinning. "Me, too." More snickers and laughter.

Molly smiled, blushing. She walked toward the wagon, frowning. *You don't blush, dammit, you're a grown woman with lots of experience. You don't blush!*

She stopped beside her wagon. The reins of the two saddled horses were tied to wheels. Micah tightened the cinch on Molly's mare. He looked up at her. "Your face is red. You okay?"

"My face is not red!" She glared at him. "Are we going or not?"

He straightened, still holding the cinch. "Maybe we are, and maybe we're not. Not if you've got a burr in your britches. What's going on?"

She drooped. "Nothing. The ladies were just making light of you and me. The whole company knows about our arrangement."

"Yeah? And? Are we in trouble?" He smiled.

She dropped her head, slowly put her arms around his waist and held him. He released the cinch and encircled her shoulders. "No, it's just . . . far from it, actually." She pulled back, looked up at him. "Did you know that you could probably jump in the bed of every single woman in the company? And probably half the married women if they could shuck the old man for a night."

"No, I didn't know that, but thanks for telling me. I'll sure keep that in mind, especially if you kick me out of your bed some night."

She looked at him sternly. "You do that, Michael Micah McQueen, and I'll take the Colt to you."

"I'll keep that in mind, too." He finished with the cinch, frowned. "Well. Now, I probably shouldn't tell you this, but since you've mentioned some interesting prospects for me, I will. One of the old boys who was tasting the whiskey last evening with a few others, just to be sure it was good for today's festivities, he said, commented on your qualities and told me if I ever wanted to change places for a night, he sure would be interested. Two others said I should count them in, too. They had a good laugh, but I know for a fact they meant what they said. I've seen those old boys and lots of others watching the backside of your bloomers."

Molly cocked her head, pursed her lips. "Maybe you

and I should open some sort of enterprise to take advantage of these sentiments."

"That sure would be a money-maker, but let's not let that thought get passed around. There would be so many takers that it could cause some tensions in the company."

"Yeah, we'll have to mull this over," she said. "In the meantime, are we going to climb the rock sometime today? Rob is staying with Beth, and we need to get back before sundown."

They untied reins, mounted and kicked their horses into a lope along the banks of the Sweetwater toward Independence Rock.

After riding across a bare flat, they reined in at the base of the huge monolith. Tying reins to a sage, Micah watched as Molly pulled the long dress over her head and stuffed it into a saddlebag, smoothed the bloomers over her hips. He watched her, smiling. She ignored him.

Walking along the base, they searched for a way up the almost-vertical stone face. They stopped when they saw names painted some six or seven feet high on the wall. Molly strained, stood on tiptoes. She turned, wide-eyed, to Micah. "There are hundreds!"

"There's more on the top, I'm told." Micah said. "We can get a closer look up there." He walked along the wall, stopped where a thin ledge at a forty-five degree angle protruded from the face of the wall. He put a hand to his cheek.

"How do we want to do this? I could go up first and

find footholds, or you can go first, and I'll catch you when you fall." He smiled.

Molly elbowed him aside and brushed past. She stepped up on the narrow ledge, gripped a protruding stone, and pulled up another step. She looked upward. "Try to keep up. If you get in trouble, call and I'll come back for you." She pulled up another step. He moved up behind her, following her path.

They inched upward, following stony ledges and crevices, Molly ahead, Micah falling behind, looking anxiously below.

"Molly, do you see the top? See anybody up there?"

She stopped, turned and looked down. Now twenty feet ahead of him, she heard the nervousness in his voice. "Pretty close, I think. . . . You okay?"

"Sure, I . . ." He turned and looked down.

"Quit looking down. Look up. We're almost there."

She resumed the climb, testing each foothold gently with a boot before putting weight on it. She moved upward, each step slow and deliberate. Finally, she saw the flat top, crawled over the edge and sat down hard, puffing and legs sprawled.

Looking down, she leaned forward. She gaped. Micah was not there. "Micah?" she shouted. Four emigrants, standing nearby, glanced at her.

One of the emigrants walked to her. "Trouble?"

She ignored him. "Micah!"

"On my way," faintly, from below. She still didn't see him. Then his head appeared around a rocky ledge. He looked up, spoke softly, his voice wavering. "Be there in a minute." He reached for a protruding rock, gripped it and pulled up. His hand shook when he withdrew it and searched for the next handhold.

Finally, he neared the top and reached for Molly. She gripped his arm and pulled him to the top where he crawled away from the edge and collapsed on his belly, panting. Pulling his knees up under him, he stood unsteadily. He stomped, trying to get his balance. He looked down the path he had just climbed.

"Okay, old man?" said the emigrant who had walked over earlier.

Micah nodded, and the man rejoined his companions. Micah took Molly's arm and moved away from the edge. "Let's get away from this drop-off. You might fall." He lowered his head, looked sideways at her with a nervous hint of a smile.

Molly took his arm, steered him towards the emigrants who looked at the ground at their feet. Two men kneeled, peering at the ground. "Let's see what they're looking at," she said. "I'll bet it's the names."

He stopped, and she turned, frowning at the serious look on his face. "Molly, I wouldn't tell anyone else, but I'll tell you. I've never been so scared in my life. I thought I was going to die for sure. I'll tell you something else. I'm going to *live* up here. I'm not going down. I can't do it."

"We'll see about that." She started to smile, but thought better of it and remained solemn.

They came up to the men who indeed were

examining a stone surface on which dozens of names were visible.

"Lots more over there," said an emigrant, pointing to a granite wall nearby. She didn't recognize him.

Micah and Molly walked to the wall covered with inscriptions. Many names in red or white chalk were faint and in danger of disappearing altogether. More distinct were names written with a mixture of what appeared to be tar and some sort of fat. One of the men pointed to a collection of names in black paint. It looked like a substance that a Fort Laramie trader told him was made by combining gunpowder and bacon grease. The clearest names, sure to endure longer than any of the others, were carved into the granite with a knife or chisel.

Molly looked in all directions on the plateau. "Micah, there must be *thousands* of names. All kinds of names. Look," she said, pointing, "here's a name with an anchor beside it. Must be a story there."

She stared at the western horizon. "I wonder where they are now. I wonder if anyone knows, if anyone remembers them. . . . I wonder if anyone will remember me when I'm gone."

He put an arm around her shoulders, and they walked toward the edge of the mound. They stopped there, and Micah looked down, wavered. Molly clutched his arm, and they backed up a few steps. He looked aside at her, smiled sheepishly.

They stared into the distance. South and east, the arid rolling flats stretched to the horizons miles away.

To the west and north, high mountains loomed, snowy peaks rising above cascading ranges of dark purple forest.

Molly held Micah's arm, leaning on him. "Pretty," she said.

"Terrifying. We have to cross that," he said, gesturing toward the mountain range on the western horizon. "Yeah, still pretty."

Molly looked at the emigrants, now walking away from the wall of names. The one who had spoken to Micah earlier turned back. "Say, that way you came up is a killer. This way's easier." He pointed toward his group that were fast disappearing over the edge.

Micah waved his thanks, turned to Molly. "Maybe I won't stay here after all. I don't think it would grow beans anyway. Ready? We'll get back before the sun disappears, in time for supper."

"Let's write our names. So there will be some evidence that we passed here. That we lived. Maybe that's the only way anyone will know." She looked aside.

"Molly, Molly." He took her cheeks in his hands, looked into her eyes. "We're going to be remembered. We're going to be famous. Authors are going to write books about us. Storytellers are going to tell stories about us. People in Oregon years from now are going to beg you to write the story of your life."

"Stop it." She smiled. "Just write the names."

He leaned down and kissed her lips. Pulling a short knife from a boot scabbard, he studied the wall face, selected a spot and brushed it with a glove. Laboriously, he carved her name on the wall. "There."

"Now yours. And Rob. And Kath. And the date."

"Do we have time?"

"Time to remember? Memory written in stone? We have time. Please."

He set to work, scraping and gouging with tiny strokes of the short blade, left hand pressing on the right to increase pressure on the blade. Molly watched as the sun descended and shadows lengthened, as the sun kissed a saddle in the dark range, and day became dusk.

Micah stood, wiped the blade on his trousers, pushed it into the scabbard. Molly touched the wall, traced the letters of the names. Molly Holmes, Rob, Kath, Micah McQueen, July 4, 1850. She opened her palm over Kath's name. Closing her eyes, she leaned forward until her forehead rested on the name and sobbed.

He took her shoulders, turned her around and held her. Raising her chin, he wiped her eyes with his hand and kissed her softly.

"Now we've got to get down off this rock," he said, "or we might need to plant beans after all."

She nodded, and they walked toward the trail pointed out by the emigrant, Molly in the lead. "Stay close. This way looks easy enough, even for an old man like you."

MOLLY AND MICAH sat on a log at a fire circle, Rob on

the ground, leaning against Molly's legs, her hand around his head and cupping his chin. Their empty supper plates lay on the ground at her feet.

Accompanied by a violin, an older woman sang a plaintive Irish air to the gathering, mellowed by the meal, the whiskey and the hour.

Most of the company had already drifted off to their beds before the music began. Those remaining listened silently, some of the men smoking pipes, staring at the memory of the sunset behind faint layers of wispy cloud, slightly tinted with soft pastel shades. More than one listener wiped a tear, remembering a place or a person or a time.

Rob hummed along with the singer when she continued with a second and third verse.

Molly stood, stretched, looked down at Micah. "I'm going to bed. If I stay any longer, I'll start blubbering." She touched Rob's head. "C'mon, sweetheart, let's get to bed. The captain said we won't start till noon tomorrow, so we'll sleep late."

Micah got up, and the three of them walked slowly toward the wagon, heads down, silent, each caught up in their own private thoughts. Rob began humming the tune, and Molly rested a hand on his shoulder.

The start the next day indeed was late. It was high noon when the company wagons got underway and joined the already moving caravan. Micah and Molly walked beside the lead yoke. Rob followed closely, humming a tune Molly recognized from the Independence Day celebration.

Micah looked up at the sun, squinted, pulled his hat brim down and wiped his face with a sleeve. He patted the lead ox on the back, looked aside at Molly. "Already hot. And that's okay. I just about froze this morning." He looked over his shoulder at Rob, who waved at him. Micah returned the wave and looked back at Molly.

"You know why Bonney said we wouldn't start till noon, don't you?" said Micah, rubbing the ox's back. Molly shook her head. "Because he got a snoot full. He carries himself pretty good, but every time I saw him at the shindig, he and somebody else was toasting each other or Old Glory or the glorious fourth or the U.S. of A., or something else patriotic. He knew he wasn't going to be up to the usual early start. Okay by me. I got no schedule I need to follow. All I need to do is get over that mountain yonder before the snows hit." He nodded toward the distant range on the western horizon.

By mid-afternoon, the wagons of the company had crossed the Sweetwater twice and were approaching it again. The river twisted and coiled, but it would have required a detour of many miles to avoid the frequent crossings. The first two transits had been easy over shallow fords. The third crossing appeared more formidable. The stream here was not as wide, but the current was faster, and the dark blue flow appeared deeper.

Drivers were having difficulty convincing their teams that they should enter the water. The trail sloped from the bank to water's edge like the other crossings, but on entering the water, instead of finding depths of a couple of feet, the bottom sloped sharply, and oxen were soon in water that reached their bellies. Teams balked, and drivers applied equal measures of whips and curses. The oxen eventually pulled again, pushing against the current, and climbed the embankment on the far side.

But the balky teams slowed the crossing, and wagons piled up on the bank and the back trail. Before reaching the pileup, Micah turned the team off the track and halted.

"I'm going to saddle up and ride ahead of the lead yoke," Micah said. "I think they'll be more likely to follow that way. You and Rob get up on the wagon seat. It looks like the water is only about three feet on the ford, but you don't want Rob in water that deep."

He went to his horse that was tied to the tailgate. Pulling the saddle from the back of the wagon, he saddled up, mounted and rode to the front of the team. Molly and Rob sat on the wagon seat.

"Okay?" she said.

"Okay, let's get back in line," said Micah.

"Giddyup! Gee!" she shouted. The team leaned into the yoke and pulled to the right. The driver of the wagon beside her glared, but he gave way to let her enter the train.

As the caravan reached the embankment that led down to the ford, the single line of wagons broke into three segments as the oxen slowed and tested the water. Following Micah's signal, Molly guided the team into the line on the far left. Molly's oxen had crossed dozens of streams by now, and they entered the water without hesitation. But when the depth increased and lapped against their bellies, then their sides, they slowed, then stopped.

"Move on! Move on!" shouted the driver of the team behind Molly.

"Giddyup! Dammit, Giddyup!" Molly said. She touched the backs of the two front oxen with the whip, then the two in the rear. She tapped them again. She and Micah rarely used the whip, but the beasts needed encouragement now. She tapped them harder, accompanied by "Giddyup, dammit!" The team moved ahead slowly, the current running just under the wagon bed.

They were in midstream now, and the water had risen to midway up the sides of the team. The current pushed against them, moving them slightly leftward, downstream. Molly looked nervously at the oxen, then aside at Rob, who watched her, solemn.

Then Molly saw the wagon on her right lift gently. She held her breath.

"Watch out!" shouted the driver. His wagon bumped hers lightly before the driver recovered control of his team and pulled the wagon to the right, upstream.

Molly looked down at Rob, wide-eyed and jaw hanging. He grinned. She looked back to the front. She reached out and tapped on the left side of the right front ox with the whip, signaling movement to the right. The team edged gradually in that direction.

Whew. She glanced aside at Rob, faced front again. At mid-stream now, the current quickened and lapped against the side of Micah's horse. Suddenly, the horse jerked its head to the right, thrust its head high, and appeared to slide leftward, dropping in the water. Then the horse almost disappeared. Only the animal's head was above water, and Micah was floating.

"Micah!" shouted Molly.

The horse was swimming, and the current swept Micah from the saddle. He lunged for the horn, but missed. The terrified horse flailed, its head held high, eyes bulging, as it pointed upstream and swam into the current. Micah disappeared below the surface as his hat floated away.

"Micah! Micah!" Molly jumped up. "Somebody help him!"

The horse, well off the ford now, swam against the current. Behind the horse, Micah's head surfaced, then his extended arm holding the horse's tail. The horse followed the course of the wagons and stock toward the far bank, Micah gripping the tail and floating behind, the water lapping at his chin.

Holding her breath, Molly watched as the horse found footing in the shallows, then the embankment, and lunged up the slope. Micah lost the tail at the water's edge and collapsed on his back to the bank, gasping.

Molly exhaled. Her team struggled up the slippery embankment ten feet from Micah, who now sat up, shoulders hunched, watching the wagon pass.

"Stay there!" said Molly. She drove the oxen up the embankment and off the trail. "Whoa! Whoa!" The team stopped, and she jumped down, set the brake and ran back to Micah.

He struggled to sit up, watching her as she came and knelt beside him.

"Stay there?" he said in a small voice.

She smiled, touched his cheek. "I didn't know what to say. I was so scared." She fought back tears. "I thought you were gone."

"Molly, my sweet Molly. I told you I wouldn't go anywhere without you."

"I almost jumped in the water to help you."

He frowned. "You can swim?"

"No."

"Then I would have had to try to save you, and you know I can't swim."

She winced. "Scary."

"C'mon, help me up, and we'll go to Oregon." She helped him stand, and they walked, Micah dripping and stumbling, toward the wagon.

Chapter 13

MOLLY, Micah and Rob sat around a blazing fire. Rob added chips and dry sticks from the stack he gathered as soon as they stopped. Micah's wet clothes hung on sage bushes within reach of the fire's warmth. He wore his only change of clothes.

"You're getting in a habit of disappearing lately," Molly said. Micah looked up, smiled. "Where'd you learn the horse tail trick?"

"As a matter of fact, I did learn it. Almost drowned crossing the Red on a cattle drive from Texas. I was in pretty deep water when my horse got spooked by a water moccasin and bucked me off. I didn't know whether I was going to drown or die from snakebite. Since I couldn't outswim the snake—I can't swim, remember—I decided to ignore the snake and grabbed the horse's tail. Lucky for me, the snake was satisfied to bite the horse and ignored me. We both survived. The horse was a little gimpy for a while, but he made it."

"How did you know to grab for the tail? Just by chance?"

"No, actually I saw it done a few times. Sometimes cowboys will do it on purpose, figuring the horse will have an easier time crossing with somebody hanging on behind than on their back. They strip down to underwear and walk into the water behind the horse, hanging on from the outset.

"One cowboy I saw doing it didn't come out so well. When he was about half way across this big creek, hanging onto his horse's tail, a whole raft of water moccasins came swimming out from both banks. Must have been a few dozen snakes. They got the cowboy and the horse. Not a pretty sight."

Micah stared at a willow thicket down the bank behind Molly. She turned to look, saw nothing but willows. She turned back to see Micah drop a large chip on the fire.

"I'm glad we don't have any water moccasins here," Molly said. "We've had too many water crossings already, and I expect we'll have more."

"Yeah . . . I'm happy about that too . . ." As he spoke, Micah stared at the clumped grass at the base of the willow thicket behind Molly. She noticed and turned around to follow his gaze.

"Just stay still, Molly, Rob," said Micah, softly. Without taking his eyes off the grass, he felt for the holster on the ground beside him, pulled the pistol slowly.

"Wha—"

"Be quiet, Rob," softly.

Micah brought the pistol up slowly, aimed, fired. Molly and Rob jumped, and the oxen rattled the yokes.

"What in hell you doing, Micah McQueen, scaring us!" said Molly.

Micah stood slowly and walked to the thicket. He nudged something with a boot, reached down and picked up a limp rattlesnake. He held it by the tail at eye level, the head touching the ground.

"Wow!" said Rob.

Micah carried the snake to the fire circle and dropped it beside Molly. She jumped up and backed away. Rob stood and bent over the snake.

"I've been watching this old boy ever since we built the fire. As long as he was stretched out, I was content to leave him be. But when he started to coil up, I figured he was up to no good. Too bad. I hate to kill anything without some good reason."

Rob and Molly stared at the snake.

"Hate to let good meat go to waste. How about fixing up some fried rattlesnake, Molly?"

She shuddered. "Not me, cowboy. If you want fried rattlesnake, give it to somebody and have supper with them."

"I was joking, but that's a good idea." He picked up the snake by the rattles and walked to the flat where wagons congregated after the river crossing before pulling back on the trail. He walked from wagon to wagon until he found a taker. The grizzled oldster who accepted the snake grinned, dropped the carcass into a canvas sack and tied it to a peg on the side of his wagon. Micah walked back to Molly's fire circle where she and Rob waited. They had watched his peddling the snake to the drivers.

"That old boy was glad to get it," said Micah. "Said he hadn't had fried snake in years."

"I woulda had snake with you, Micah," said Rob.

Micah squatted beside Rob. "Then we'll have to get us another snake."

"You will not!" said Molly. "C'mon, get your clothes, and let's be off. We've had a nice rest here, so we'll drive this evening till we come up to our company. Late supper. And no snake!" she said, shaking a finger in Micah's face.

Micah smiled; Rob pouted.

Leaving the flats and rolling hills where streams twisted and turned, requiring frequent crossings, the trail entered a land of canyons and steep ascents. The caravan slowed, and some drivers investigated alternate routes to escape the slow progress of the wagons ahead on the main trail. They repeated the every-day slogans: I need to get to the campground before all the good grass is occupied; I need to get to California before the gold is gone; I need to get to Oregon before the best land is taken.

On these exploratory routes, and even on the main trail, the incline often became so steep that drivers who attempted the climb had to turn and come back down.

This required a reversal on the slope that almost overturned more than one wagon until wagons stopped and bunched up at the bottom of the main trail.

The solution was double-teaming. Approaching a particularly steep incline, Micah pulled off the trail beside a wagon without a team. Captain Bonney stood behind the stationary wagon. He waved to Micah, then motioned the driver of the next wagon to pull in behind Molly's. That done, he beckoned the driver of that wagon to join him with Molly and Micah.

"Okay, here's where we are," Bonney said. "Nobody's going to make it up this hill without double-teaming. Eddie, hitch your team in front of Molly's. Micah, Eddie, drive Molly's wagon to the top. Unhitch there, and bring both teams down. Do the same with Eddie's wagon. That okay with everybody?" All nodded.

Micah and Molly walked to their wagon and stopped beside the team. Rob jumped down from the wagon seat. Molly patted him on the head.

"This is going to slow us down a bit, but it's the only way we'll get to the top," said Micah. He rubbed the top of Rob's head vigorously, and Rob jerked away, smiling. "Watch your mother, little buddy, and don't let her get into any trouble." Rob looked up at Molly, smiling.

Micah went to Eddie's wagon. He waved to Marion, Eddy's wife, who looked up from rummaging in the back of the wagon, then walked to the team where Eddie was already removing the wagon tongue. Micah helped him with the tongue, and they walked the team to

Molly's wagon. Marion followed, wringing her hands at her chest.

After attaching Eddie's team in front of Molly's, Micah and Eddie stepped back and surveyed the result. The team of eight oxen stood still, as if the arrangement were normal.

"Honey," said Eddie to his wife, "you're in charge of everything we own. Guard it from all the desperadoes around here." He smiled.

Marion appeared on the verge of tears. "Be careful, you old codger. You're all I got left of family."

He smiled, pecked her on the cheek. "We're not going all the way to Oregon, dear. We're just going to the top of that hill." He pointed. "You can watch us all the way."

Micah and Eddie took their positions, Micah on the left side of the lead ox and Eddie on the right side. "Giddyup!" said Micah. "Giddup there! Gee! Gee!" The team leaned into the yoke, pulled to the right into the main trail and began the ascent. Molly and Rob walked slowly behind the wagon.

Micah looked back. He motioned with an arm. "Molly, Rob, stay away from the wagon. We don't expect any problems, but things have happened, so you should be well clear of the wagon, just in case."

"You're right, there, my friend," said Eddie, "things can happen and *do* happen, really bad stuff. I remember one time—"

"Eddie, what do you say we skip the tales of bad things that are not going to happen on this haul?"

Eddie frowned. "Okay, you say so." He looked to the front, glanced back at Micah.

Micah looked again at Molly and Rob. "Not behind the wagon. Well off to the side." He motioned to them to move to the left, away from the wagon. Molly nodded, and they walked off to the side.

The pull up the slope was slow but steady. Micah occasionally touched the back of the near oxen with a hand or lightly with the whip handle. He muttered softly, "okay, doing fine, good job, not long now, almost there."

Eddie looked aside at him, frowning, shaking his head.

Finally reaching the flat at the top, Micah stopped the team and flexed his back, hands on hips, puffing. He looked over at Molly and Rob, standing in the shade of a tall cedar. Rob waved, and Micah returned the wave. He walked to them.

"Molly, I can tell you the same thing Eddie said to Marion. Your future is tied pretty closely to that wagon. I hate to leave you alone here, but we have no other choice. Get the Colt, and have it handy. You know how to use it."

Rob looked from Micah to Molly. "Wow," he said softly, grinning.

IT WAS MID-AFTERNOON when Micah and Eddie returned to the bottom of the hill with the eight-oxen team and pulled up before Eddie's wagon.

Marion rushed to Eddie and hugged him tightly. Eddie looked aside at Micah. It was obvious that Eddie was not generally welcomed so warmly.

Marion pulled back, lips pursed, embarrassed. Glancing aside at Micah, she smoothed her dress. She fetched buckets from her wagon, and helped the two men water the oxen from the spring just off the trail.

"Let's just set a bit and let the beasts blow," Micah said. "Coming down was easier than going up, but I'll bet the team remembers the uphill pull."

Eddie walked about, pacing back and forth, looking nervously at the wagons moving slowly up the hill. "We need to get on our way, Micah. We're wasting time. We're falling behind."

"Tell that to the beasts, Eddie," said Micah. "They're doing all the hard work. Just a few minutes more."

After about fifteen minutes, they hitched the double team to Eddie's wagon. Micah repeated the admonition to Marion about walking beside the wagon rather than behind. Then they pulled out.

The drive up the hill was a repeat of the previous pull. Steady, but slower as the oxen labored on this second climb. Micah, Marion and Eddie silently plodded ahead, heads down.

Finally reaching the top, Micah stopped the team and set the brake. Molly and Rob came to Micah as Eddie and Marion watched. Rob took Micah's hand as Micah spoke to them, wiping his face with a sleeve, tousling Rob's hair.

Eddie fidgeted. "Ready, Micah?" Micah looked at Eddie, nodded, said something to Molly.

The two men went to Eddie's wagon. They unhitched the double team, got the two teams sorted out and each four-ox team attached to its own wagon. The two men stepped back and surveyed the wagons, ready for travel.

"Okay, that's that," said Eddie. "Now, we've wasted too much time today with this goldarned double-teaming on that goldarned hill. We're gonna make up some time. All the good grass is going to be gone by the time we reach camp." He walked to his wagon, Marion following, looking back at Molly.

"You're going to tie on a drag, aren't you?" said Micah. He looked down the descent. "This downslope is steeper that the climb."

Eddie shook his head vigorously. "Nope, wasted too much time. I'm riding on the seat, and I have a good brake, and I got a skid pole." He climbed up to the seat beside his wife, waved to Micah. "See you in camp. If you can keep up." He laughed, turned to the front.

"Giddyap!" he shouted. The oxen leaned into the yokes, and the wagon rolled slowly off the flat to the steep descent. Immediately, gradually, the wagon rolled faster. The back wheels began to slide right and left, back and forth, as Eddie applied the brake. The wagon hardly slowed.

"Whoa! Whoa!" The wagon was a hundred yards downhill from the top now, and the shout was faint at the top of the hill, but the oxen heard and stopped, struggling and stumbling to keep the wagon stationary. Eddie jumped down from the seat, ran to the back of the wagon. Reaching inside, he pulled out a stout pole about six feet long. He shoved the pole through the spokes of both rear wheels. Walking to the front, he climbed up to the wagon seat.

"Giddyup!" faintly heard in the breezy updraft. The wagon moved off, slowly at first. The rear wheels locked and skidded when the pole through the wheel spokes jammed against the wagon bottom. But the wagon did not slow. It increased in speed as the rear whipped rapidly left and right on the frozen wheels.

"Oh, my," said Micah. "He's in real trouble."

They watched the wagon pick up speed, the rear wheels sliding, jerking to the right, then to the left, increasing in speed, bouncing on the rough trail, the wagon tongue thrusting forward, pulling the stumbling oxen, running now to stay on their feet.

Then the wagon disappeared over a rising in the trail.

Micah watched a moment longer, then shook his head. "We've got work to do." He walked to the side of the wagon, removed an ax and hatchet from a box, and Molly walked with him into the woods off the trail. Rob followed.

It required two hours of hard labor to fashion the drags. Micah found two downed tree trunks about a foot in diameter. He cut the trunks to lengths of six feet with the ax, and he and Molly hacked off branches, leaving stubs of a few inches. They rolled and dragged the logs to the trail behind the wagon where they attached them to the rear axle with chains. Micah pulled hard on both chains, testing the connection.

Without a word, they both sat down heavily, leaning against wheels, legs outstretched, exhausted. Rob sat in Molly's lap, and she pressed her cheek against his back.

"Whew," said Molly. "That was hard work." She squeezed Rob. "You're getting to be a big boy. We'll put *you* to work on the drags next time."

"Yeah!" Rob said. "Can I do that, Micah?"

"Course. We'll put you in charge." Rob beamed.

"Are we ready?" Molly said.

"We are. I'll walk beside the lead yoke, you and Rob beside the wagon, well off to the side." He inhaled deeply, exhaled. "Rob, give me a hand up, and we'll be on our way."

Rob grinned, jumped up, and extended a hand to Micah. He pulled as Micah pushed up with his other hand. Rob extended a hand to Molly. "Now you, mama." She took his hand and let him pull her as she stood. Rob walked to the team and patted the side of the lead ox.

They watched him at the team. "He's grown these months, Molly. He's the future of Oregon. You and me, we'll be placeholders. He's the future." She put an arm around his waist, leaned on his arm.

Rob turned around and saw them watching him. "C'mon!"

Micah waved, turned to Molly. He took her cheeks in his hands and kissed her. "Okay, missy, the boss is calling. I guess I'm rested now, but that hard work made me hungry."

"Hmm. We'll see what we can come up with this evening for you."

"Good. I'll think on that. Maybe I can suggest something or other."

"I'll bet you can." She pulled his head down and kissed him.

They looked at the scattering of wagons on each side of the level space at the top, the drivers fashioning drags, attaching them to their wagons with chains. Other wagons were ahead on the downslope, most pulling drags. A couple of light wagons had no drags, and occasional skidding rear wheels suggested that brakes were effective in slowing the speed on the downslope.

Molly and Rob walked away from the side of the wagon and waited.

"Stay away from the wagon," Micah said, "but ahead of the drags in case one comes loose." Molly nodded.

Micah released the brake. He walked to the front and stopped beside the lead yoke on the left side. He touched the near ox with a hand. "Giddyup." The oxen leaned into the yokes, and the wagon moved onto the trail and the downslope.

There was a slight jerk when the chains went taut, and the logs began to drag. The wagon moved at a normal pace, then began to increase in speed until the snags on the trunks dug into the ground, slowing the wagon until the oxen had to lean lightly against the yokes.

The wagon ahead, pulling a single drag, rolled faster than Micah's, and it disappeared over the rising in the trail. He turned and looked anxiously at the wagon behind him, but relaxed when he saw that it was not closing the gap between wagons. He looked back to the front, concerned that the speed of his wagon might increase when it dropped over the rising ahead in the trail.

"Micah!" He turned aside to see Rob waving, returned the wave. He looked back to the front as the wagon passed over the rising in the trail.

He froze.

Not fifty yards ahead, near the bottom of the slope, a shattered wagon lay in pieces in a shallow gully beside the trail. Goods and clothing and bedding, everything carried in an emigrant's wagon, were strewn about the wreckage. The two oxen in the front yoke lay on their sides, bellowing, one trying to raise its head. One of the oxen in the rear yoke lay on its back, legs extended upward, the other ox buried under the broken wagon.

Two wagons were stationary on the trail near the wrecked wagon. The two drivers walked about the debris. Near the shattered wagon, two women stood with a third woman who held her cheeks with both hands as she rocked back and forth. The stricken woman stared at the ground, then dropped to her knees as the other women supported her.

Micah pulled up behind the stationary wagons. He

ran back to his wagon, reached up and set the brake, and saw Molly and Rob coming at a run.

Molly stopped and grabbed Rob by an arm. "Rob, stay here. Right here by the wagon. Hear?"

"But—"

"Right here! Hear? Guard the wagon."

He nodded. Molly and Micah ran toward the wreckage. They went to the women and saw Marion kneeling beside Eddie's body.

Marion looked up at Molly. Tears rolled down her cheeks. "I told him to be careful." She rocked back and forth. "I told him he was all I had." She collapsed on the body, sobbing. One of the women touched Marion's shoulder, patted her gently. The two helped her stand, and one supported her as they walked toward a stationary wagon on the trail.

"She'll go with us," said the second woman. "We're friends. We'll pick up as much of her stuff as we can carry in our wagons. We'll bring Eddie's body and bury it in the trail this evening." She joined the other woman at the wagon.

Molly watched as the two women stood with Marion beside the wagon, trying to comfort her. Molly recognized the women. They were in the same company, but since she did not socialize much with other members, she knew few beyond a casual greeting or borrowing and lending. She ducked her head in shame when she admitted to being glad that she did not have to deal with Eddie's body or Marion's survival.

What kind of person have I become? Am I losing all

human feeling? Am I declining to an animal state, feeling only hunger and pain, no longer able to care?

She shook her head, saw Micah coming. He had helped the two men place Eddie's broken body in the back of a wagon. She beckoned Rob to come, and the three helped the others gather salvageable food stocks, clothing, bedding and personal items. The others said they had no room in their wagons for Marion's cooking gear, utensils or tools, so they left these things beside the trail. They assumed that following emigrants would search the debris for anything useful.

Micah, Molly and Rob walked toward their wagon. Molly held Rob's hand.

Rob looked up at Micah. "What happened? What—"

"We'll talk about it at camp," Molly said. "It's sad, but you should know about it. We'll talk. But not now."

"WHY AM I SO TIRED TODAY?" Molly walked beside Micah at the lead yoke. "I had enough sleep, I ate breakfast, it's no hotter than usual."

"Yeah, me too," said Rob, striking the ground at intervals with a long switch. He touched an ox's back with the switch. Molly pulled the switch from him and tossed it aside.

"Don't touch the animals, Rob. They won't understand. Unless you're the driver, of course." She tapped him on the head with a hand.

"When are you going to let me be the driver?"

"Let's ask the head driver. Micah, when are we going to let Rob do some driving?"

"Hmm. I think we should start right away. Then I can ride in the wagon and take naps. Are you ready to take charge, little buddy?"

Rob frowned, "Well . . . maybe tomorrow." He looked up at Micah. "So why are we so tired?"

Micah smiled. "Because you've been walking uphill ever since breakfast."

Molly frowned. "We're not walking uphill. We've been in this flat prairie all day."

"Nope," Micah said. "Look at the top of that line of cedars over there." He pointed to a stand of cedar that ran parallel to the trail a mile or so away. "Looks pretty flat on the top, right?" Molly nodded.

"Now look beyond the cedars to the horizon in the distance. What do you see?"

"Well, I'll be," Molly said. "Since the horizon is flat, I suppose that means that the tops of the cedars are slanted. So the cedars are on a slant, and we are walking on a slant."

"Meaning we're walking uphill, but it's so gradual it's hard to notice."

"Where'd you learn this?" she said. "I don't suppose you figured it out by yourself."

He smiled. "Talked with an old trapper at Laramie. He's been over this trail about a hundred times. He said the trail to the pass is so gradual, people don't realize they're climbing till they see the flag.

"Speaking of the flag, look up at that break in the

timber straight ahead. That's the pass. South Pass. Now look just on the right side of the that open spot."

"I see it!" said Rob. "The flag!"

"This is like no pass I ever saw," said Micah. He stood with Molly and Rob on the flat that seemed an extension of the gentle slope they had climbed to reach the summit. Their wagon was one of the dozens of wagons scattered about on both sides of the trail.

Not all of the wagons stopped. Some continued to roll straight over the summit without even a pause and began the gradual descent on the western side, as if there was nothing unusual or notable at South pass.

"Those are the impatient ones, the fearful ones," said Micah. "We've seen plenty of them. I'll bet those people don't take time off in springtime to smell the flowers." They stood silent, watching the exodus.

Rob broke the spell. "There sure are lots of wagons here," he said, looking around. "Are we stopping here?"

"Not for long," said Molly. "See that cabin over there by the flag? That's like a post office. I want to write a letter to Doris back home. You remember her? She's Billy and Harriet's mom."

"I remember. I hadn't thought about them in a long time." He looked aside, kicked a stone and walked off the trail, hands in pockets. He sat on a log, stared blankly at a pine copse.

"It's sad," she said to Micah, watching Rob. "By the time we get settled in Oregon, he will have only vague memories of childhood friends and the farm and Missouri." She looked up at a cloudless pale blue sky. "It's too bad. It was a good life. We . . ." She turned and pressed her face on his chest, her arms hanging. He encircled her shoulders and held her.

"You're going to have a good life again, Molly. It's going to be different, but it'll be as good as you thought it was going to be when you and your husband were planning this trip." He lifted her chin. "Just know that you're going to be happy at the end of this.

"Think about your life next summer when you'll be settled on a going farm. You'll have a house and growing crops. Rob will have new friends, and he'll be going to school. It'll all be new, the sun will shine, and everybody will be happy."

She leaned back and wiped her eyes, looked up at him. "And where will you be all this time?"

"I'll be out in the garden, chopping weeds."

She cocked her head. "And what are you going to do when it's too dark to chop weeds?"

"I'm going to come in the house, clean up, eat supper and jump in your bed."

She frowned, tensed, looked grimly at him. She relaxed and leaned into his face, hands on hips.

"Micah McQueen, are we going to get married or not?"

He took her face in his hands and kissed her forehead, the tip of her nose and her lips, looked into her eyes. "Yes, Molly Holmes. We're going to get married, if you'll have me."

She put her arms around his neck, raised her chin and kissed him softly, leaned against his chest.

"You might want to tell Rob," Micah said. "He asked me that question a long time ago, if you'll remember. I don't think he's going to be surprised. I hope he'll tell me that it's okay with him."

They looked at Rob, still sitting on the log, bending and picking up pebbles, throwing them aimlessly. The last one sent a black-crested jay skittering and squawking. Rob stood, turned around and saw them looking at him. He walked toward them.

Micah looked sideways at Molly. "Uh, I . . . uh, need to check the team."

"You stay right where you are," she said sternly, watching Rob coming. Rob looked from Molly to Micah.

"Honey," said Molly. "We have something to tell you." Rob looked quickly from Molly to Micah and back to Molly.

"We're getting married," she said, smiling.

Rob frowned. "Aren't you married?" Molly and Micah looked at each other.

"I mean *married*, like in a church," she said.

"Oh. Okay."

Micah knelt in front of Rob. He took Rob's hand. "Is that all right, little buddy, me marrying your mom?"

"Yeah." Rob looked from Micah to Molly, still a little perplexed.

Micah stood, "Now I need to have a look at the

beasts." He touched Molly's cheek and walked toward the wagon.

Rob watched him go a moment, then turned to Molly. "Do I have to call him 'Daddy?' I'd rather call him 'Micah.' Is that okay?"

"Yes, that's fine, honey. He likes you to call him 'Micah.'"

"Okay!" He ran after Micah, called over his shoulder to Molly, "I'm going to help Micah with the beasts!"

Well, that's done.

Chapter 14

"YEP, it's downhill to Oregon now, little buddy," Micah said. Since leaving the summit, they indeed had an easy drive, mostly downhill. Micah and Rob walked side-by-side, Rob holding Micah's hand, then sidetracking to investigate a patch of snow or a pile of pine cones, then back to grab Micah's hand.

Molly walked behind, watching, smiling to herself. *My two boys. Maybe it's going to be good.*

She raised her coat collar and tightened the scarf over her head as an icy breeze whipped up from below. Bonney had already passed the word that they would make camp early this evening to prepare for an expected hard freeze and maybe some snow during the night. Though they were on the western slopes of the range, there was still some worry about getting through the mountains before the onset of winter. Early heavy snows could be disastrous for the emigrants.

Micah drove the team off the trail to a broad grassy

flat where company wagons were forming a wide circle, enclosing a large open space in the center. Early arrivals had already begun laying out chains that would run between circled wagons to form a large enclosure for the animals.

Molly and Micah unyoked the oxen, and Rob touched hindquarters gently with a switch, driving them to grass. Micah untied the two horses from the tailgate and released them with the oxen. The animals moved slowly away from the wagon, dropping their heads to graze.

"We've been lucky," Molly said. "They've had it hard, but they're in pretty good shape, don't you think?"

Micah looked around the enclosure where emigrants released more animals that scattered on the grass. Other men lifted chains and tied them between wagons.

"Yeah, they're okay," he said. "At least compared to some other people's beasts. Some people just don't understand how much they depend on their animals. They'll learn when they lose one or two. We're a long way from the coast."

"Yeah, did you hear that the Adamses—the Adamses in our company—lost an ox a couple of days ago? He's put his riding horse into the team."

"Heard about that. Not good. We could put our horses in harness if we have to, but I sure don't want to do that. If I do, old Buck might not be fit for hunting. And then where would we be?"

A strong gust whipped the wagon covers. He

shivered. "Whoo, that's cold. I'll get a fire going while you get some supper, something hot, I hope."

"I can do that, hot supper and hot coffee as soon as that fire is going. While supper's cooking, I'll pull out all the covers I can find. The three of us will bundle up in the wagon tonight."

"Sounds good. C'mon, Rob. Let's get us some firewood, enough for tonight and for the morning fire. It's gonna be cold, boy." He tousled Rob's hair. "And you need to get something warm on that head." They walked toward the pinewoods outside the campground, Micah's hand resting on Rob's head.

Later they sat around a crackling fire and ate a hot supper of rice and beans and coffee. After collecting dishes, Molly told Rob to say goodnight, and she would tuck him in. Rob went to Micah, put his arms around his neck. Micah straightened, put his arms slowly around Rob, looked over Rob's shoulder at a smiling, approving Molly.

She helped Rob over the tailgate and into the blankets. "We'll come to bed soon," she said.

She went back to the fire, sat down and refilled their cups. They stared into the flames, sipping the hot coffee. She looked up at stars twinkling in the cold, cloudless sky.

MOLLY WRIGGLED UNDER THE BLANKETS, pulling them up around her neck. She reached over and pulled the blanket to Rob's chin, and he snuggled against her. She lay back, staring at the dim luminescence of the wagon cover above and listening to the canvas rustling and flapping in the gusts. Without looking, she was reassured by the soft sounds of Micah's regular breathing.

She tried to empty her mind, to sleep. But little by little, images began to appear, enlarging, flickering. Her mind raced as she relived the past few months, the beginning and course of this journey across the plains. Every detail, every triumph, every tragedy, finding Micah, losing Kath and Walter, and almost losing Rob. Her head filled, and her eyes. She rolled her head vigorously, side to side.

And then she was at peace. She relaxed, wiped her eyes with both hands, felt that she was melting into her bed. She was here, with the two people she loved most in the world. They were at the cusp of a new life, a future that was only a dream until this moment. She closed her eyes, and she slept.

MOLLY AWAKENED to the sounds of a morning camp, staring at the canvas peak. The thunk of an axe in dry wood, a sharp admonition to a child, a mule braying, a melding of a shriek, a giggle and a grunt at the end. Molly pushed the blankets down, looked over and pulled them back to cover Rob. She sat up, pulled on her coat and wrapped the scarf around her neck and head. Pulling boots on, she crawled over the tailgate, and stepped into new snow.

She shivered, looked around the camp. The snowfall during the night had turned the campground into a landscape of white shapes and clumps. Wet snow clung to the boughs of pine trees that bordered the camp. She hunched her shoulders, turned up her coat collar, inhaled deeply, smiled at the silvery fog when she exhaled.

Walking around the wagon, she tapped on the ice in a bucket hanging on the side of the wagon. She looked up and saw Micah at the fire circle, dropping short dry boughs onto the leaping flames of a new fire. He dusted his gloved hands together.

He turned to her and kissed her cheek. "Snowed a bit last night."

She encircled his waist with both arms and pulled him close. "I can see the snow, Micah McQueen, and I don't want a peck on the cheek." She buried her face in the folds of his shirt. "Hold me."

He dropped the stick he held and wrapped his arms around her shoulders. He lifted her chin, kissed her lips, leaned back. "I feel good today. How do you feel?"

She inhaled heavily, exhaled. "Good." She released him and stepped back "Now let's get busy. Time to get moving." She walked briskly to the back of the wagon, pushed the blanket back where she had lain, and rustled in boxes for breakfast makings.

Rob stirred, sat up.

"Morning, sweetheart, get dressed. We'll have some breakfast in a few minutes, and you can help Micah get the oxen yoked. Lots to do today. We're going to Oregon for sure!"

*****

Molly and Micah stood with Beth beside Molly's wagon. Rob, Olin and Jessie sat in a circle nearby on the grass beside the trail. The Manlys leaned against the side of their wagon, talking softly, glancing occasionally at the others.

"Beth, you've been a good friend," said Molly. "You helped me over the hard places."

"Molly, it's you that helped me. What would I have done without you?" She looked aside, wiped her eyes. "Look at those three over there," gesturing toward the children. "Olin and Jessie will miss Rob. He's such a sweet boy."

"Well, you're on your way," said Micah, "and you'll see the end of your journey before we will. Jacob, how do you go from here?"

"Soon's I get the team yoked, we're on our way. We're forming up with a dozen or so wagons, people I've talked with from other companies. They're Mormons, though they didn't talk about it, just like us. We'll all be glad to be with our own from here on. Most of the people in this caravan aren't like you two." Wistful, he looked past Micah toward the trail where four wagons rolled southward from the main Oregon trail.

"Shouldn't be but a few days to Salt Lake," Jacob said. "The promised land for us." He ducked his head as his eyes watered. "It's been so long. So hard, so many lost years." He wiped his eyes and turned to his wife.

Rebecca took his hand.

"You've been through a lot," Micah said, "and I wish you the best, Jacob, Rebecca." She smiled, looked aside.

"I'll get the team," said Jacob.

"I'll help," Micah said. Jacob nodded.

Beth took Micah's hand in both of hers, smiled through her tears. She turned and hugged Molly, held her tightly, her head on Molly's shoulder. She spoke softly in Molly's ear. "We've been through a lot, we have. To the very depths of hell and back. We'll make it, you and me."

She released Molly, smiled, turned to the children. "Jessie, Olin, say goodbye. We're going now."

The three children jumped up, turned to each other, the finality of leaving suddenly taking hold. Jessie began to sob as she and Olin walked toward their mother. Rob ran to Molly, pressed his face against her and cried. Olin sniffled and burst into tears as Beth and the children walked toward Rebecca. Beth and Rebecca tried to comfort the two children as they walked to their wagon. Beth turned to wave, tears rolling down her cheeks.

Molly cupped the back of Rob's head as he leaned against her. "Tell you what, honey. As soon as we get settled in Oregon, I'll help you write a letter to Olin and Jessie. You can tell them about your new home, and they will write and tell you about theirs. How's that?"

He leaned back, wiped his eyes. "Okay." He walked

to the grazing oxen, stopped and watched them silently. Molly wiped a tear from her cheek.

"Let's have a look at the fort," Micah said to Molly. "Some of the company's gone on, but most are still here. The captain said we'll gather on this side of a river crossing a few miles on."

"Rob, let's walk up to the fort." Molly said. Rob shuffled over, kicking a pebble. She rested a hand on his head.

Fort Bridger was a disappointment after Laramie. Originally established in the early 1840s both to engage in the fur trade and service emigrants, the fort was an assortment of rudely-constructed log buildings. This year, emigrants found few supplies available. The fort's only attraction to emigrants was its blacksmith shop, which some sorely needed. Micah didn't even need this service since he had taken care to protect the hooves of their animals with the leather booties.

Micah, Molly and Rob and other emigrants strolled about the fort, found little to hold them and returned to their wagons.

DAY FOLLOWED DAY, and the trail routine was now so engrained that the emigrants hardly had to think about it. But change was coming. The weather turned colder, with an occasional dusting of snow. Game was not plentiful as temperatures dropped steadily, but hunters found enough. The sparse game was augmented by trout from the frequent streams.

Indian encounters along the trail were curious and peaceful. Indians were eager to trade for virtually anything the emigrants were willing to exchange. Clothing seemed to be their chief interest, especially shirts, though occasionally an Indian man offered a woman for a horse. One raised his bid to three women for a riding horse.

Indian women often joined in the trading. They offered moccasins, sorely needed by many emigrants who had long since worn out their boots, in exchange for jewelry and trinkets. One old Snake woman wanted to trade Micah a pretty young woman, perhaps her daughter, for his horse. Another offered Molly her baby for the bloomers she wore under her coat. Micah was amused while Molly was horrified.

FORT HALL on the Snake River was the last semblance of American civilization before reaching California or the Oregon coast. Originally a fur trading post, the fort was claimed by both the British and Americans until the settlement of the border between Canada and the United States in 1846 officially placed it in American territory. A military garrison located near the fort was supposed to protect emigrants, but the cost of supplying the garrison from the Oregon coast proved too costly, and the camp was in the process of closing down in 1850.

Most in the company did not question Captain Bonney's judgment when he declared it not worth a visit, especially since it was a mile north of the trail.

Some nevertheless figured they would not likely come this way again and decided to have a look. Molly and Micah were among the visitors. They saddled up and rode to the fort, Rob riding behind Micah.

A look was all they needed. After ten minutes at the fort, Molly looked at Micah, and he nodded. They went to their horses tied outside the entrance, mounted and walked their horses back to the campground.

It wasn't only the lack of interest in the fort that kept some in the camp and impelled the visitors to return quickly to the campground. All emigrants were eager to reach an important milestone in their journey.

Everyone in the company was a bit tense, and some were excited, at the upcoming parting of the ways when the trail would split, those bound for California turning off to the left, southward, and the Oregon-bound taking the right fork, north and west. Most emigrants knew exactly where they were going, but some still pondered, knowing that the course of their lives would be set by what happened at that junction.

As if preordained, the anxiety of the undecided suddenly heightened.

The company had hardly pulled off the trail for the noon stop when two eastward bound wagons rolled into the encampment. Two men sat on the seat of each wagon behind four-mule teams, and five more men rode horseback beside the wagons. All waved to emigrants and called out their greetings. The men on the wagon seats hopped down, and the riders dismounted. They greeted the emigrants cheerfully, shook hands with any who responded.

"Who are those people?" Molly said to Micah. They had stopped what they were doing, Micah unyoking the team and Molly working on lunch, and watched the newcomers. "They don't look like the usual turnarounds. They sure don't look like Mormons on a mission." The mules were sleek, the riding horses stout and muscled. Their clothing, though a bit trail-soiled, appeared new.

Micah returned to the unyoking. "I'm sure they're going to tell us." He led the four oxen to a patch of grass already crowded with oxen and a few mules and riding horses.

Molly and Micah, with Rob in tow, drifted over to the gathering where emigrants crowded around the nine newcomers.

"Yep, we're from California," said the one that appeared to be the leader.

"Didn't you leave a little late in the season?" said an emigrant.

"Yeah, maybe, but we wanted to finish the placer we were working on. I tell yah," he said, bending toward the questioner, "it was the richest stretch of that stream. People watched us taking dust, and we almost had to shoot a few anxious fellas to get 'em to stay away. They soon got the point and left us alone. That's why there's nine of us 'stead of the usual three or four that works a placer."

"So . . . so you were successful?" said another

emigrant.

The spokesman of the group turned to his companions, and all grinned. He looked back at the emigrants' eager faces. "See that wagon just there?" He pointed to one of their wagons that was just a few steps away. "You'll notice that we don't stray far from it. There are a few containers of various sorts in there that are filled with the results of our labor. Those results are going to provide each of the nine of us a comfortable life. I don't mind telling you that each of us is a rich man." He leaned back, smiling, glancing around the circle of eager faces.

Molly took Micah's arm and walked him toward their wagon. Rob followed, looking back over his shoulder at the men. He pulled on Molly's sleeve. "Are we going to California now?" he said.

She put a hand over his head, cupped a cheek. "No, honey, we're not going to California." She stopped, looked down at Rob. "At least, I'm not. You might ask Micah where he's going." She looked at Micah, wrinkling her brow.

"I don't know. Where do you want to go, buddy?"

"I'm going where Mama's going."

"Okay, that settles that. I'm going where you and your Mama's going." He smiled at Rob who took Molly's hand and stepped off toward the wagon. She turned to Micah and cocked her head, smiled. Micah put his arm around her waist, slid it down and squeezed her butt. She jumped aside and swatted him.

Rob turned and saw the swat. "Mama!" he said.

Molly smiled. "Just playing, honey."

"That's what you say every time you hit him. I hope you never get mad at him."

Micah laughed. "Hah! Me too, pard."

Rob ran ahead to the wagon and climbed up over the tailgate. Molly and Micah stopped beside the wagon where Molly had begun making lunch when they went to investigate the newcomers.

"It's not very smart of those boys to be bragging about carrying a large stash of gold," Micah said. "Some of the people in this train are still on the point of despair. I don't think any in our company are desperate enough to steal somebody's gold, but we don't know these people very well. And these boys have such loose tongues the word is going to spread down the line faster than they can travel. People moving west are going to know that two wagons coming their way carrying four men with five outriders are carrying a fortune."

NEXT MORNING, the company's wagons rolled along the formidable Snake River that ran between high walls of black, volcanic rock. They nooned near the base of American Falls, a tumbling torrent with a drop of fifty feet. They had hardly finished putting the unyoked oxen on grass when five Crow Indians walked confidently into camp. The Crow surprised them by offering an abundance of fat trout, which they happily exchanged for two old shirts. The Indians walked away, chattering and laughing.

Micah had taken no part in the trading. He recognized the Indians as Crow at first sight and instinctively touched the Colt at his waist. His hand closed on the grip, and he almost hoped for a confrontation with members of the tribe that had killed Makawee. But he knew that a clash with these five would mean retaliation by their band on the emigrants. He released the grip, but watched them until they walked from the camp.

The noon repast, augmented by delicious trout, was finished quicker than usual. The company collected and yoked their oxen and traveled on to the much-anticipated camp at Raft River, which flowed into the Snake from the south. Molly's company shared the encampment with two other companies at this parting of the ways. At daybreak the next day, those bound for California would leave the Snake and head up the Raft whose headwaters were in the mountains that loomed in the south.

As the sun set, painting the sky a luminous gold, emigrants strolled about the scattered collection of wagons, saying their goodbyes to those they had befriended and with whom they had endured the same hardships. There was much hearty backslapping, and some tears and hugs between old friends.

Molly and Micah knew a few California-bound emigrants, but not well. They had kept to their own company for the most part, and all of Bonney's members would stay on the Oregon road, but for two families who had listened intently around campfires to the fevered conversation of those committed to California and lately to the nine successful Argonauts and were bitten badly by the gold bug. Molly and Micah wished them well, but agreed privately that the families had made a bad choice.

Suddenly all conversation ceased as emigrants stared at three bedraggled men who stumbled into the encampment from the south trail. The men had no animals, no visible weapons and no packs. They stopped and looked blankly around.

"Sorry to startle you folks," said one of the three men, "we know what we look like." He glanced back at his companions who looked side to side. "Okay if we sit by your fire? We've not seen a fire in three days. It's mighty cold out there."

Molly had watched all this open-mouthed. Now she rushed to the three men. "Come to our fire." She took a man by the arm and walked him to their fire. The other two men followed, and all three sat down heavily at the fire circle, reaching their hands toward he flames.

"My, that feels good," said one of the other men. By this time, a circle of emigrants stood a respectable distance behind the men, watching, bewildered, listening silently.

"Are you hungry?" Molly said.

He looked up. "Yes, ma'am, we sure are. It's been three days since we had a bite. I don't want to trouble you, but do you have some water you can spare?"

"I'll get it," said a woman who stood with the other onlookers. She rushed off to her wagon.

"Three days?" said Molly.

"That's when the Indians got us. We left the main trail where there was lots of people to take what a man said was a shortcut. The Indians caught us all by ourselves on the shortcut. They took everything we had, horses, packs, guns, all the food. Left us with nothing. They loaded all our stuff on our horses and rode off, laughing their heads off. At least, they didn't kill us just for the fun of it."

The woman returned with three cups of water and gave one to each man. They emptied the cups. "Thank 'ee, missus, you saved us." She lowered her head, smiled, embarrassed. She collected the cups and hurried away.

"Here, take this." Micah handed each man a plate holding some berries, hard biscuit Molly had baked that morning, and cold elk meat left over from supper that they had put aside for breakfast.

"You're a godsend, all of you," the man said as they cleaned their plates. The woman returned with filled cups and handed them to the men. They nodded their thanks and emptied them again.

The crowd of emigrants encircling the men had grown. All were anxious to hear the story these men had to tell.

"What happened?" Molly said. "Do you come from Salt Lake or California?"

The man leaned back and inhaled, back among the living. "Oh, California. The golden land, you know. I 'spect some of you are headin' there. Good luck to you.

As for us, we seen the elephant, and he stomped hell out of us. We were in th' diggings a year and got nothing to show for it. There was people all around us that found gold, but no matter how hard we tried, no matter where we went, and we followed all the rumors and tales, we just never hit it at the right time.

"So here we are. We're headin' home. I got good memories of home and only bad memories of California." He turned to his companions. "That about right, boys?"

"You said it, Andrew," said one, nodding, solemn, staring into the embers. He stretched, sighed.

"You boys need to rest," Molly said. "I can spare a blanket. I'll get it." She looked around at the spectators. "Anybody spare a blanket for the other two?" A couple of women waved to Molly and withdrew. She turned back to the men. "I have a small tent that I don't need. Use it tonight and on the trail. You'll probably get some snow on your way. We'll try to find a pack or two for you before you get away tomorrow."

Micah, standing beside Molly, spoke to the men. "I doubt you'll find many people on the trail will have much food to spare. You'll find lots of berries. I'll see if anybody in our camp can spare a gun of some sort so you can look for game. Small chance, but I'll try.

"You'll reach Laramie before hard winter hits. Think about wintering there. The army should have something you can do to earn your keep." He turned to go, then turned back.

"Keep the fire going tonight, if you like. Gonna be cold."

The spokesman of the three stood and glanced about the circle. "You're good folks, best I seen since I left Kentucky, seems a lifetime ago. I thought the world had run out of good people."

Molly handed him a blanket. Two more women stepped up and gave blankets to the other men.

Molly and Micah walked to their wagon. They checked Rob who was curled up with only the top of his tousled hair showing. She took Micah's arm, and they went to the other side of the wagon, away from the fire where the dog-tired busted Argonauts were already wrapped in their blankets at the fireside.

"I worry that we might end up something like that," said Molly. "Sometimes when I'm low, I wonder that we'll not find the paradise in Oregon that we expect."

He wrapped his arms around her and held her, leaning his head on hers. "You've got too much time to think." He leaned back, and she looked up at him. "We're going to find everything in Oregon we expect, the end of the rainbow and the pot of gold." He kissed her lips. "We're going to find land with topsoil a mile deep, a farm where there's never any frost, and we're going to have fat cattle that have healthy calves every year and give three gallons of milk a day, and—"

She pushed him away. "Okay, stop it, let's go to bed." She grabbed his arm, pulled him to her. "What would I do without my cowboy?"

Chapter 15

AT DAYBREAK, California-bound emigrants were especially anxious to be on their way. The parting of the trails appeared a milestone that seemed to signal that the end was near.

For the most part, they shrugged off the story told around the fire the previous evening by the three failed miners. They didn't disbelieve the story. They just decided that the three must have lacked the industry or the skill, or they were just plain unlucky. They preferred to remember the story of the successful nine miners.

Nor were they dissuaded by the warnings of old timers that the worst part of the journey from the east was still before them. They told about the waterless deserts and the high Sierra Nevada that must be crossed before heavy snows closed passes.

Never mind. The committed Argonauts were propelled by the fever. They must reach the gold country ahead of those countless other seekers who were arriving daily overland and by ship.

Emigrants continuing on the trail to Oregon were just as anxious to get moving, but they were not so frantic. They must still cross mountains, but they were not so formidable, and the trail generally not so challenging as the road to California. At least, so they had heard and hoped.

While Molly put breakfast dishes away, Micah finished yoking the oxen. Then he walked back to the wagon, reached under the seat and pulled out a rifle. He went to the campfire where the three failed Argonauts were stuffing their blankets and a few necessaries into a couple of packs, all donated last evening and this morning. They also packed some parcels of food they had been given. They looked up at Micah.

"Here's a rifle that a man in our company asked me to give you," said Micah. "He found it in a pile of stuff along the trail a couple of days back. Why anyone would throw away a perfectly good gun is beside me." He handed it to one of the men. "But here it is, and also a few cartridges I was able to scrounge. If you don't waste 'em shooting at shadows, they should get you some meat before you reach Laramie." He reached out and shook hands with the three. "Good luck, boys."

"Thanks. You and the others here saved our lives. We won't forget it. What all these good people did for us makes me almost believe in God again."

Micah smiled, raised an arm in farewell and walked back to the wagon where Molly and Rob waited.

"Are we finally going to Oregon?" she said.

Curling an arm around her neck, Micah kissed her cheek. He rubbed the top of Rob's head vigorously.

Rob laughed and jerked away. "Let's go!" He ran to the lead yoke. "Giddyup!" He touched the side of the near ox with his hand, then jumped aside, wide-eyed, when the team moved off. He looked back at Molly and Micah, grinning.

Molly and Micah looked at each other. Micah cocked his head. "Looks like I'm out of a job. Okay with me. Lead on, pard!"

The team pulled into the line of wagons already heading out on the trail toward the northwest, toward Oregon. Molly and Micah looked back at the wagons of the California contingent moving into line, heading southward.

"Remember the two families in our company that just a few days ago got bit by the gold bug," Molly said, "listening to all the talk about the barrels of gold miners were taking?" Micah nodded. "Well, one of the families thought real hard about that decision after listening to the three men last night. That family is three wagons up there, heading for Oregon." She pointed.

THE CARAVAN MOVED at a steady pace westward as emigrants talked ever more enthusiastically about their plans for the new life they would make in Oregon. Temperatures dropped, but the mountains were soon behind them, and they knew they were approaching the end of the journey.

Now Micah stood at the front of the team, looking out at the broad Columbia. Small birds, blue-headed with an orange neck ring, flitted about the cliff edge, dropping from sight, then reappearing, wings spread and floating in the updraft. A dozen ground squirrels around and under the wagon stood upright beside their burrow holes, watching the birds. An ox stamped a foot, and the squirrels dived into their burrows.

Emigrants had been hearing about the fabled river for months, and most had expressed a determination to see it, both for the spectacle and the proof that the end of their journey was in sight. With the river now accessible, few were willing to interrupt their progress to see it. That river is going to be there a long time, they said; I can see it anytime. What I want to see now is the end of this goldarned journey. What I want to see now is Oregon City.

Molly's wagon rested on a flat a dozen feet or so from the edge of the cliff that dropped off sharply to the river, a hundred feet below. Micah turned around and glanced southward, down the slope to the main trail a mile away where wagons rolled slowly, single file, raising dust that formed a gray tunnel around the caravan.

At the soft sound of hooves, he looked past the back of the wagon and saw Molly and Rob coming, walking their horses. Rob was quite proud of himself now that

Micah allowed him to ride his horse. They dismounted, and Molly tied the reins to a stout manzanita.

"Beautiful," she called to Micah, "sure glad we're not crossing it." She stood with Rob behind the wagon, her hand on his shoulder, looking across the wide river to the far shore, a mile away.

"Yep," said Micah. "Take a last look. We need to get back on the trail. Won't be long now. Just a few days to the end of the rainbow." He looked over the team, checking that all was in order, a chore he performed dozens of times each day, knowing it was not necessary.

Molly went to the side of the wagon and took the cup hanging near the water barrel, dipped the cup into the barrel and drank. She replaced the cup on its peg.

"Mama." She turned to see Rob staring in the direction of the river.

Molly looked toward him. "What?"

"Mama, come 'ere."

She heard something in Rob's voice she didn't recognize. She walked to him. He stared at the cliff edge.

She followed his gaze. "What is it?"

"That." She saw a slight crumbling at the edge, dust lifting in the updraft, heavier particles gently falling away. She watched, frozen. Then, an inch of soil, two feet wide, slowly crumbled and disappeared over the edge.

"Micah," she said softly, trembling, still watching the edge. The crumbling widened. Two inches, three feet wide, slowly crumbled and fell away. "Micah! The cliff is falling."

Micah ran to her, saw the crumbling. "Stand back! It's going!" He ran forward to the team, shouted. "Giddyup! Haw! Haw! Giddyup! Haw!" He slapped the back of the near ox. The team leaned into the yokes, and the wagon began to roll.

Suddenly a large chunk of soil the length of the wagon and team, slowly separated from the flat and crumbled, sliding away. The wagon shuddered, then the right wheels of the wagon slipped over the edge, and the wagon bed dropped to the flat.

"Giddyup! Haw!" shouted Micah, but the wagon did not move.

Molly jumped back, still watching the crumbling edge, and reached aside for Rob. Her hand found only air. He was not there. Then she saw with horror that Rob had jumped up on the tailgate of the wagon, landing on his stomach. He threw a leg up over the tailgate and crawled inside.

"Rob! Rob!" Molly screamed. "What are you doing? Get down! Get down!"

The cliff face beneath the wagon crumbled and fell away slowly, the crumbling moving toward the left wheel. The wagon groaned and tilted lower toward the chasm.

"Giddyup! Haw! Giddup!" Micah shouted.

Molly ran to the tailgate. "Rob! Get out!" The wagon leaned and slid lower on the cliff edge. Rob appeared at the tailgate, bending under the sloping roof, and jumped toward Molly just as the wagon slid out from under him. He collided with her, and she fell backwards to the ground with Rob sprawled on top of her. The box he held fell to the ground beside them.

They jumped up and watched in horror as the wagon and team skidded over the edge and disappeared. Both started to run to the edge.

"Stay back!" shouted Micah. "The whole flat could go. Get the horses, and get back!"

Molly ran to the horses, untied them and backed away from the edge. She grasped Rob's shirt and pulled him along.

Micah walked slowly to them. They looked at the empty flat where the wagon had stood. A small ledge of a few inches separated and fell below. A rising air current along the cliff edge carried the dust away, and it was still again.

Micah put an arm around Molly and the other around Rob's head. He hugged them to him, pulled them with him as he stepped back.

Micah released them, bent down to face Rob. "Rob, what in the world . . ." He frowned, looked up at Molly. "Look at this, Molly." Concerned about Rob, they had taken no notice of the box he held.

Rob looked up at Molly. "You said our farm was in this box, Mama."

Molly bent, wide-eyed, saw the box for the first time, wrapped her arms around him and held him tightly, sobbing. She leaned back, looked him in the face. “Don’t you ever do anything like that again. We could have lost you.”

“But Mama, I had to save the farm.”

“You did that, Rob,” said Micah, “and I’m going to tell everybody in Oregon this story. How my boy risked his life to save our farm. Speakers and book writers for a hundred years will know the story about how Rob saved the farm.” He looked at Molly. “That right, Mama?”

She wiped her eyes, kissed Rob on the cheek and hugged him. She leaned back and took Rob’s cheeks in her hands. “Course it’s right. Now let’s stop wasting time and get on the road.”

She looked at the cliff edge where the wagon and team had disappeared. “I hate to see the team go that way. Brought us all the way from Independence only to die like this. I didn’t hear a sound from them. Poor beasts. I hate it.”

“Yeah, me too. Sad,” said Micah. He looked down the slope at the caravan, then back to Molly. “But we take the hand we’re dealt.” He looked at the river, at the caravan again, back to Molly. “Here’s what we’ve got. We have two riding horses and the clothes on our backs. We’ll beg, buy and borrow till we get to the end of this journey. It’s just a few days. People will help; they’ll understand. Then we’ll use Rob’s treasure to buy a farm and everything we need to run it. How’s that sound?”

“That sounds good!” said Rob. “Let’s go!”

“Okay, sweetheart Mama?” said Micah.

She held her horse’s reins, looked at the empty flat

at the cliff edge. "That wagon held all that I had of my past, Micah, all but memories. . . . I suppose things can be replaced, but . . ." She sighed, wiped her cheek with a sleeve.

She gathered her reins and mounted. "Enough of this. Let's get on with it."

Micah slipped the box into a saddlebag, mounted and pulled Rob up behind him. They kicked their horses into a lope toward the caravan below.

Chapter 16

"THERE IT IS," said Micah, "the end of the rainbow. It all starts right now. This new day."

They sat their horses on a low rising overlooking the settlement called Oregon City. They looked down on a scattering of frame buildings on the banks of the Willamette River that had the appearance of a real town, the first they had seen since leaving the Missouri River.

"Looks like a town with prospects," said Micah, "especially with all these eager souls arriving every day from the States."

"Speaking of prospects, we need to find some place to bed down for a time," Molly said.

"Yep, a snug little place just big enough for three till we decide what comes next. Oh, what a time we're going to have, making plans! We'll talk with everybody in this town. It's all gonna be good, Molly."

They urged their horses to a slow walk toward the settlement. She reined her horse next to his, glanced at

Rob whose attention focused on a boat on the river. She leaned toward Micah, beckoned, and he leaned toward her.

She whispered in his ear. "Better make that a snug little place just big enough for four, cowboy." She smiled, still leaning toward him.

He straightened, frowned. "Four?" His eyes opened wide, and his jaw dropped. "You mean—"

"That's exactly what I mean." She straightened in her saddle.

"Wahoo!" Micah whipped off his hat and sailed it high.

Rob jumped. "What's wrong, Micah?"

"I'll tell you, big brother—"

"Later, you two." She kicked her horse into a lope toward the town, threw back over her shoulder, "let's find that pot of gold."

AFTERWORD AND ACKNOWLEDGEMENTS

If I were to list all of the people who assisted in the writing of this narrative, the dozens who offered snippets of information, suggestions, musings, advice, criticism and glasses of wine, the list would be very long. So I simply thank them and hope they find that I have distilled their data satisfactorily.

Particular thanks to the dozens of colleagues and perfect strangers who graciously responded to my appeals for assistance and information. I am grateful to the scores of unnamed historians and diarists whose works I consulted in order to place my characters in the appropriate places and predicaments.

I am enormously indebted to the Pacific Critique Group for their careful reading of the narrative and for their comments, corrections, useful tirades and inspiration. I could ask for no better editorial support. Special thanks to Mariah Parke and Saeid Banankhah for a final proofing of the entire manuscript.

Special thanks to John Horst for putting the right guns in the hands of my characters and to Chris Enss for helping me dress them appropriately. I am grateful to Anthony Marinelli and Jennifer Hoffman, formatters extraordinaire, and cover designer extraordinaire, Donna Yee.

ABOUT THE AUTHOR

Harlan Hague, Ph.D., is a native Texan who has lived in Japan and England. His travels have taken him to about eighty countries and dependencies and a circum-navigation of the globe.

Hague is a prize-winning historian and award-winning novelist. History specialties are exploration and trails, California's Mexican era, American Indians and the environment. His novels are mostly westerns with romance themes. Two are set largely in Japan. Some titles have been translated into Spanish, Italian, Portuguese and German. In addition to history, biography and fiction, he has written travel articles and a bit of fantasy. His screenplays are making the rounds.

For more about what he has done and what he is doing, see his website at harlanhague.us. Hague lives in California's Great Central Valley.

Made in the
USA
Columbia, SC

81246451R00166